t,

by passion...

D0174617

The Duchess Deal

*I*t wasn't his scars that intimidated her. Quite the reverse. When she stood this close, her gaze couldn't take in both halves of him at the same time. She had to choose a side.

Emma knew with a sinking heart which one would capture her. There were two approaches to successful dressmaking—to find flaws and conceal them, or to bring out the hidden beauty. She'd always believed in the latter method, and oh, it came back to bite her today.

Don't do it, Emma. Don't give your foolish heart an inch of rope, or it will have you tied in knots.

But it was too late. Now, as she looked up at him, all she could see was a man. One with searching blue eyes and a hidden heart beating in a strong, defiant rhythm.

A man with wants, needs. Desires.

A man who'd reached out for her yesterday, and now . . .

And now gave every indication of leaning in for a kiss.

Also by Tessa Dare

Castles Ever After

ROMANCING THE DUKE
SAY YES TO THE MARQUESS
WHEN A SCOT TIES THE KNOT
DO YOU WANT TO START A SCANDAL

Spindle Cove

A NIGHT TO SURRENDER
ONCE UPON A WINTER'S EVE (novella)
A WEEK TO BE WICKED
A LADY BY MIDNIGHT
BEAUTY AND THE BLACKSMITH (novella)
ANY DUCHESS WILL DO
LORD DASHWOOD MISSED OUT (novella)

Stud Club Trilogy

ONE DANCE WITH A DUKE
TWICE TEMPTED BY A ROGUE
THREE NIGHTS WITH A SCOUNDREL

The Wanton Dairymaid Trilogy

GODDESS OF THE HUNT
SURRENDER OF A SIREN
A LADY OF PERSUASION

THE SCANDALOUS, DISSOLUTE, NO-GOOD
MR. WRIGHT (novella)

Tessa Dare

The Duchess Deal

GIRL MEETS DUKE

AVONBOOKS

An Imprint of HarperCollinsPublishers

THE DUCHESS DEAL. Copyright © 2017 by Eve Ortega. All rights reserved. Printed in the United States of America. No part of this book may be used or reproduced in any manner whatsoever without written permission except in the case of brief quotations embodied in critical articles and reviews. For information, address HarperCollins Publishers, 195 Broadway, New York, NY 10007.

First Avon Books mass market printing: September 2017
First Avon Books hardcover printing: August 2017

Print Edition ISBN: 978-0-06-234906-4
Digital Edition ISBN: 978-0-06-234907-1

Cover art © FictionArtist.com

I grew up a PK ("preacher's kid"). Emma, the heroine of this book, is a vicar's daughter. I want to make clear that Emma's father is nothing like my own. My father was—and is—loving, patient, supportive, and understanding.

Thanks, Dad. This book's for you. Please don't read chapters 7, 9, 11, 17, 19, 21, or 28.

Acknowledgments

Writing romance novels is a joy and a privilege. However, sometimes writers suffer for their art. And sometimes writers share that suffering with everyone nearby.

For their patience and support, I am forever indebted to my husband, my children, my family, my friends, my editor, my agent, my editor's assistant, my copy editor, my publicist, my personal assistant, my publisher, my twitter followers, my cats, my pajamas, my coffeemaker . . . and pretty much everyone and everything around me. Except that one neighbor with the drone. You know who you are.

Special shout-outs to Guido, Kirk, Samantha, and Ken for bringing the sexy to this book's cover.

And always, *always*, thanks to my readers. If not for you, I would have to wear pants.

The
Duchess
Deal

Chapter One

*E*mma Gladstone had learned a few hard lessons by the age of two-and-twenty.

Charming princes weren't always what they seemed. Shining armor went out of fashion with the Crusades. And if fairy godmothers existed, hers was running several years late.

Most of the time, a girl needed to rescue herself.

This afternoon was one of those times.

Ashbury House loomed before her, taking up one full side of the fashionable Mayfair square. Elegant. Enormous.

Terrifying.

She swallowed hard. She could do this. Once, she'd walked to London alone in the bitter heart of winter. She'd refused to succumb to despair or starvation. She'd found work and made a new life for herself in Town. Now, six years later, she'd swallow every needle in Madame Bissette's dressmaking shop before she'd go crawling back to her father.

Compared to all that, what was knocking on the door of a duke?

Why, nothing. Nothing at all. All she had to do was square her shoulders, charge through the wrought-iron gates, march up those granite steps—really, there were only a hundred or so— and ring the bell on that immense, richly carved door.

Good afternoon. I'm Miss Emma Gladstone. I'm here to see the mysterious, reclusive Duke of Ashbury. No, we aren't acquainted. No, I don't have a calling card. I don't have anything, really. I may not even have a home tomorrow if you don't let me in.

Oh, good heavens. This would never work.

With a whimper, she turned away from the gate and circled the square for the tenth time, shaking out her bare arms under her cloak.

She had to try.

Emma stopped her pacing, faced the gate, and drew a deep breath. She closed her ears to the frantic pounding of her heart.

The hour was growing late. No one was coming to her aid. There could be no further hesitation, no turning back.

Ready. Steady.

Go.

FROM HIS LIBRARY desk, Ashbury heard an unfamiliar ringing sound. Could it be a doorbell?

There it came again.

It *was* a doorbell.

Worse, it was *his* doorbell.

Damned gossips. He hadn't even been in Town but a few weeks. He'd forgotten how London rumors traveled faster than bullets. He didn't have the time or patience for busybodies. Whoever it was, Khan would send them away.

He dipped his quill and continued the letter to his feckless solicitors.

I don't know what the devil you've been doing for the past year, but the state of my affairs is deplorable. Sack the Yorkshire land steward directly. Tell the architect I wish to see the plans for the new mill, and I wish to see them yesterday. And there's one other thing that requires immediate attention.

Ash hesitated, quill poised in midair. He couldn't believe he was actually going to commit the words to paper. But much as he dreaded it, it must be done. He wrote:

I need a wife.

He supposed he ought to state his requirements: a woman of childbearing age and respectable lineage, in urgent need of money, willing to share a bed with a scarred horror of a man.

In short, someone desperate.

God, how depressing. Better to leave it at that one line.

I need a wife.

Khan appeared in the doorway. "Your Grace, I regret the interruption, but there's a young woman to see you. She's wearing a wedding gown."

Ash looked at the butler. He looked down at the words he'd just written. Then he looked at the butler again.

"Well, that's uncanny." Perhaps his solicitors weren't as useless as he thought. He dropped his pen and propped one boot on the desk, reclining into the shadows. "By all means, show her in."

A young woman in white strode into the room.

His boot slipped from the desk. He reeled backward and collided with the wall, nearly falling off his chair. A folio of papers tumbled from a nearby shelf, drifting to the floor like snowflakes.

He was blinded.

Not by her beauty—though he supposed she might be beautiful. It wasn't possible to judge. Her gown was an eye-stabbing monstrosity of pearls, lace, brilliants, and beads.

Good Lord. He wasn't accustomed to being in the same room with something even more repulsive than his own appearance.

He propped his right elbow on the arm of his chair and raised his fingertips to his brow, concealing the scars on his face. For once, he wasn't protecting a servant's sensibilities or even his own pride. He was shielding himself from . . . from *that*.

"I'm sorry to impose on you this way, Your Grace," the young woman said, keeping her gaze fixed on some chevron of the Persian carpet.

"I should hope you are."

"But you see, I am quite desperate."

"So I gather."

"I need to be paid for my labor, and I need to be paid at once."

Ash paused. "Your . . . your labor."

"I'm a seamstress. I stitched this"—she swept her hands down the silk eyesore—"for Miss Worthing."

For Miss Worthing.

Ah, this began to make sense. The white satin atrocity had been meant for Ash's formerly intended bride. That, he could believe. Annabelle Worthing had always had dreadful taste—both in gowns and in prospective husbands.

"When your engagement ended, she never sent for the gown. She'd purchased the silk and lace and such, but she never paid for the labor. And that meant I went unpaid. I tried calling at her home, with no success. My letters to you both went unanswered. I thought that if I appeared like this"—she spread the skirts of the white gown—"I would be impossible to ignore."

"You were correct on that score." Even the good side of his face twisted. "Good Lord, it's as though a draper's shop exploded and you were the first casualty."

"Miss Worthing wanted something fit for a duchess."

"That gown," he said, "is fit for a bawdy-house chandelier."

"Well, your intended had . . . extravagant preferences."

He leaned forward in his chair. "I can't even take the whole thing in. It looks like unicorn vomit. Or the pelt of some snow beast rumored to menace the Himalayas."

She tilted her gaze to the ceiling and gave a despairing sigh.

"What?" he said. "Don't tell me *you* like it."

"It doesn't matter whether it suits my tastes, Your Grace. I take pride in my handiwork regardless, and this gown occupied months of it."

Now that the shock of her revolting attire had worn off, Ash turned his attention to the young woman who'd been devoured by it.

She was a great improvement on the gown.

Complexion: cream. Lips: rose petals. Lashes: sable.

Backbone: steel.

"This embroidery alone . . . I worked for a week to make it perfect." She skimmed a touch along the gown's neckline.

Ash followed the path her fingertips traced. He couldn't see embroidery. He was a man; he saw breasts. Slight, enticing breasts squeezed by that tortured bodice. He enjoyed them almost as much as he enjoyed the air of determination pushing them high.

He pulled his gaze upward, taking in her slender neck and upswept bounty of chestnut-brown hair. She wore it in the sort of prim, restrained coiffure that made a man's fingers itch to pull the pins loose, one by one.

Take hold of yourself, Ashbury.

She couldn't possibly be as pretty as she seemed. No doubt she benefited by contrast with the revolting gown. And he'd been living in solitude for some time. There was that, as well.

"Your Grace," she said, "my coal bin is empty, the larder's down to a few moldy potatoes, and my quarterly rent comes due today. The landlord has threatened to turn me out if I don't pay the full amount. I need to collect my wages. Most urgently." She held out her hand. "Two pounds, three shillings, if you please."

Ash crossed his arms over his chest and stared at her. "Miss . . . ?"

"Gladstone. Emma Gladstone."

"Miss Gladstone, you don't seem to understand how this whole intruding-on-a-duke's-solitude business works. You should be intimidated, if not terrified. Yet there's an appalling lack of hand-wringing in your demeanor, and no trembling whatsoever. Are you certain you're merely a seamstress?"

She lifted her hands, palms facing out for his view. Healed cuts and calluses showed on her fingertips. Persuasive evidence, Ash had to admit. Yet he remained unconvinced.

"Well, you can't have been born to poverty. You're far too self-possessed, and you appear to have all your teeth. I suppose you were orphaned at a tender age, in some particularly gruesome way."

"No, Your Grace."

"Are you being blackmailed?"

"No." She drew out the word.

"Supporting a passel of abandoned children, *whilst* being blackmailed?"

"No."

He snapped his fingers. "I have it. Your father is a scapegrace. In debtor's prison. Or spending the rent money on gin and whores."

"My father is a vicar. In Hertfordshire."

Ash frowned. That was nonsensical. Vicars were gentlemen. "How does a gentleman's daughter find herself working her fingers to nubs as a seamstress?"

At last, he saw a flash of uncertainty in her demeanor. She touched the spot behind her earlobe. "Sometimes life takes an unexpected turn."

"Now *that* is a grave understatement."

Fortune was a heartless witch in perpetual anticipation of her monthly courses. And didn't Ash know it.

He swiveled in his chair and reached for a lockbox behind the desk.

"I am sorry." Her voice softened. "The broken engagement must have been a blow. Miss Worthing seemed a lovely young woman."

He counted money into his hand. "If you spent any time with her, you know that isn't the case."

"Perhaps it's for the best that you didn't marry her, then."

"Yes, it was excellent foresight that I destroyed my face before the wedding. What bad luck it would have been if I'd waited until afterward."

"Destroyed? If Your Grace will forgive me saying it, it can't be *that* bad."

He snapped the lockbox closed. "Annabelle Worthing was desperate to marry a man with a title and a fortune. I am a duke and ungodly wealthy. She still left me. It's that bad."

He stood and turned his ruined side to her, offering her a full, unobstructed view. His desk was in the most shadowy corner of the room—and purposely so. The room's heavy velvet drapes kept out much of the sunlight. But scars as dramatic as the ones he wore? Nothing but complete darkness could obscure them. What bits of flesh had escaped the flames had only been ravaged further—first, by the surgeon's knife and then, for hellish weeks afterward, by fever and suppuration. From his temple to his hip, the right side of his body was a raging battle of cicatrices and powder burns.

Miss Gladstone went quiet. To her credit, she didn't swoon or vomit or run screaming from the room—a pleasant change from his usual reception.

"How did it happen?" she asked.

"War. Next question."

After a moment, she said quietly, "May I have my money, please?"

He extended a hand, offering her the money.

She reached for it.

He closed his hand around the coins. "Once you give me the gown."

"What?"

"If I pay you for your work, it's only fair that I get the gown."

"For what purpose?"

He shrugged. "I haven't decided. I could donate it to a home for pensioned opera dancers. Sink it to the bottom of the Thames for the eels to enjoy. Hang it over the front door to ward off evil spirits. There are so many choices."

"I . . . Your Grace, I can have it delivered tomorrow. But I must have the money today."

He tsked. "That would be a loan, Miss Gladstone. I'm not in the money-lending business."

"You want the gown *now*?"

"Only if you want the money now."

Her dark eyes fixed on him, accusing him of sheer villainy.

He shrugged. Guilty as charged.

This was the peculiar hell of being disfigured by sheer chance on the battlefield. There was no one to blame, no revenge to be taken. Only a lingering bitterness that tempted him to lash out at anything near. Oh, he wasn't violent—not unless someone really, truly deserved it. With most, he merely took perverse pleasure in being a pain in the arse.

If he was going to *look* like a monster, he might as well enjoy the role.

Unfortunately, this seamstress refused to play the trembling mouse. Nothing he said rattled her in the least, and if she hadn't fled in terror yet, she likely never would.

Good for her.

He prepared to hand over the money, bidding her—and that gown—a grateful *adieu*.

Before he could do so, she exhaled decisively. "Fine."

Her hands went to the side of the gown. She began to release a row of hooks hidden in the bodice seam. One by one by one. As the bodice went slack, her squeezed breasts relaxed to their natural fullness. The sleeve fell off her shoulder, revealing the tissue-thin fabric of her shift.

A wisp of dark hair tumbled free, kissing her collarbone.

Jesu Maria.

"Stop."

She froze and looked up. "Stop?"

He cursed silently. *Don't ask me twice.* "Stop."

Ash could scarcely believe he'd managed the decency to say it once. He'd been on the verge of a private show for the price of two pounds, three. Significantly higher than the going rate, but a bargain when the girl was this pretty.

Not to mention, she was a vicar's daughter. He'd *always* dreamed of debauching a vicar's daughter. Really, what man hadn't? However, he was not quite so diabolical as to accomplish it through extortion.

A thought occurred to him. Maybe—just maybe—he could still manage that fantasy, through different, somewhat less fiendish, means. He regarded Emma Gladstone from a fresh angle, thinking of that list of requirements in his interrupted letter.

She was young and healthy. She was educated. She came from gentry, and she was willing to disrobe in front of him.

Most importantly, she was desperate.

She'd do.

In fact, she'd do very well indeed.

"Here is your choice, Miss Gladstone. I can pay you the two pounds, three shillings."

He placed the stack of coins on the desk. She stared at them hungrily.

"Or," he said, "I can make you a duchess."

Chapter Two

A duchess?

Well. Emma was grateful for one thing. At least now she had an excuse to stare at him.

Ever since the duke had revealed the extent of his scars, she'd been trying *not* to stare at him. Then she'd started worrying that it would be even more rude to *avoid* looking at him. As a result, her gaze had been volleying from his face, to the carpet, to the coins on the desk. It was all a bit dizzying.

Now she had an unassailable excuse to openly gawk.

The contrast was extreme. The injured side of his face drew her attention first, of course. Its appearance was tortured and angry, with webs of scar tissue twisting past his ear and above his natural hairline. What was more cruel—his scarred flesh stood in unavoidable contrast with his untouched profile. There, he was handsome in the brash, uncompromising way of gentlemen who believed themselves invincible.

Emma didn't find his appearance frightful, though she could not deny it was startling. No, she decided, "startling" wasn't the right word.

Striking.

He was striking.

As though a bolt of lightning had split through his body, dividing him in two, and the energy still crackled around him. Emma sensed it from across the room. Gooseflesh rippled up her arms.

"I beg your pardon, Your Grace. I must have misheard."

"I said I will make you a duchess."

"Surely . . . surely you don't mean through marriage."

"No, I intend to use my vast influence in the House of Lords to overturn the laws of primogeniture, then persuade the Prince Regent to create a new title and duchy. That accomplished, I will convince him to name a vicar's daughter from Hertfordshire a duchess in her own right. Of course I mean through marriage, Miss Gladstone."

She gave a strained laugh. Laughter seemed the only possible response. He had to be joking. "You can't be asking me to marry you."

He sighed with annoyance. "I am a duke. I'm not *asking* you to marry *me*. I am *offering* to marry *you*. It's a different thing entirely."

She opened her mouth, only to close it again.

"I need an heir," he said. "That is the thrust of the matter."

Her concentration snagged on that word, and the blunt, forceful way he said it.

Thrust.

"If I died tomorrow, everything would go to my cousin. He is an irredeemable prat. I didn't go to the Continent, fight to preserve England from tyranny, and survive this"—he gestured at his face—"only to come home and watch my tenants' lives crumble to ruins. And that means those laws of primogeniture—since I don't intend to overturn them—require me to marry and sire a son."

He crossed the room, advancing toward her in unhurried strides. She stood in place, unwilling to shrink from him. The more nonchalant his demeanor, the more her pulse pounded.

His face might be striking, but the rest of him . . . ?

Rather splendid.

To distract herself, Emma focused on her own realm of expertise: attire. The tailoring of his coat was immaculate, skimming the breadth of his shoulders and hugging the contours of his arms. The wool was of the finest quality, tightly woven and richly dyed. However, the style was two years behind the current fashion, and the cuffs were a touch frayed at the—

"I know what you're thinking, Miss Gladstone."

She doubted it.

"You're incredulous. How could a woman of your standing possibly ascend to such a rank? I can't deny you'll find yourself outclassed and un-befriended among the ladies of the peerage, but you will no doubt be consoled with the material advantages. A lavish home, generous lines of credit at all the best shops, a large settlement in the event of my death. You may pay calls, go shopping. Engage in some charitable work, if you must. Your days will be yours to do whatever you wish." His voice darkened. "Your nights, however, will belong to me."

Any response to *that* was beyond her. An indignant warmth hummed over every surface of her body, seeping into the spaces between her toes.

"You should expect me to visit your bed every evening, unless you are ill or having your courses, until conception is confirmed."

Emma tried, one more time, to understand this conversation. After running through all the possibilities, one alternative seemed the most likely.

The duke was not merely scarred on his face. He was sick in the head.

"Your Grace, do you feel feverish?"

"Not at all."

"Perhaps you ought to have a lie-down. I could send your butler for a physician."

He gave her a quizzical look. "Do *you* need a doctor?"

"Maybe I do." Emma touched one hand to her brow. Her brain was spinning.

If he wasn't ill . . . Could this be some sort of ploy to make her his mistress? Oh, Lord. Perhaps she'd given him the wrong impression with her willingness to disrobe.

"Are you—" There seemed no way to say it but to say it. "Your Grace, are you trying to get me into your bed?"

"*Yes.* Nightly. I said as much, not a minute ago. Are you listening at all?"

"Listening, yes," she muttered to herself. "Comprehending, no."

"I'll have my solicitor draw up the papers." He returned to his place behind the desk. "We can do it on Monday."

"Your Grace, I don't—"

"Tuesday, then."

"Your Grace, I cannot—"

"Well, I'm afraid my schedule is quite booked for the rest of the week." He flipped through the pages of an agenda. "Brooding, drinking, indoor badminton tournament . . ."

"No."

"No," he echoed.

"Yes."

"Yes, no. Make up your mind, Miss Gladstone."

She turned in a slow circle, looking about the room. What on earth was happening here? She felt like a Bow Street runner trying to solve a mystery: *Emma Gladstone and the Case of the Missing Dignity.*

Her gaze fell on the clock. Already past four. After leaving here, she must return the gown, pay her landlord, and then visit the market.

Having come this far, there was no way she could back down now.

She stiffened her posture. "Your Grace, you called my work 'unicorn vomit.' You asked me to disrobe for money. Then you made the absurd declaration that you would make me a duchess, and that I should visit your bed on Monday. This entire interview is nonsensical and humiliating. I can only conclude that you are making sport of me."

He lifted one shoulder in an unapologetic shrug. "A scarred recluse must have *some* amusement."

"What about your full schedule of drinking and indoor badminton? Isn't that enough?" She had lost all patience now. She enjoyed a bit of teasing, and she could laugh at herself—but she had no desire to be the object of cruel jokes. "I'm beginning to suspect Miss Worthing's reason for jilting you. You are exceedingly—"

"Hideous," he supplied. "Repulsive. Monstrous."

"Exasperating."

He made a sound of bemusement. "So I'm being reviled for my personality? How refreshing."

Emma lifted her hands in a nonthreatening gesture. "Your Grace, I shall impose on you no further. I am going to approach the desk, pick up the coins, and then back away. Slowly."

In a series of cautious steps, she approached the desk and stopped within a yard of where he stood on the opposite side. Without breaking eye contact, she gathered the two pounds, three shillings from the desktop. Then, with the briefest of curtsies, she turned to leave.

He caught her by the wrist. "Don't go."

She turned and looked up at him, astonished.

The contact was electric. Like the jolt one received when grabbing a doorknob on a dry, cold day. Clashing and sparking with a force that belonged to neither of them, but existed only in the space between. The shock buzzed up the bones in her arm. Her breathing and pulse were suspended. She felt stripped down—not to her skin, but to the raw elements that composed her being.

The duke seemed stunned by it, too. His piercing blue eyes interrogated hers. Then he cast a confused look at his hand, as though he weren't certain how it had come to be gripping her arm.

For a moment, Emma's heart invented the wildest fancies. That he was someone other than the cynical, embittered man he seemed. That beneath the Before and After sketched on his face, there was a man—a hurting and lonely man—who remained unchanged in essentials.

Don't believe it, Emma. You know your heart is a fool.

He released her, and the side of his mouth pulled into a wry smile. "You can't leave now, Miss Gladstone. We're just starting to have fun."

"I don't care to play this game."

She gathered as much composure as she could locate. Clutching the coins in one hand, she picked up her skirts with the other and made haste in the direction of the door.

"Don't trouble to bid me farewell," he called.

I won't.

"I shan't bother, either. We both know you'll be back."

She paused—briefly—midstep. The duke believed they would see one another again?

Dear God. Not if Emma could help it.

Not in a thousand years.

"Isn't it silly of me?" Miss Palmer stood in a draped corner of Madame Bissette's shop, holding still as Emma measured her waistline. "More and more plump by the day. I suppose I've been eating too many teacakes."

Emma doubted it. This was the second time in a month Davina Palmer had visited the shop to have a dress let out, and Emma had been stitching her wardrobe since her first Season. She'd never known the young woman to gain weight, and certainly not this rapidly.

Teacakes were not to blame.

Strictly speaking, it wasn't Emma's place to say anything. But she'd taken a liking to Miss Palmer. She was the only daughter of a shipping magnate, and heiress to his fortune. A bit spoiled and sheltered, but she had a sparkle to her. She was a customer who always made Emma's day better rather than worse, and that said something. Most of the ladies who came into the shop looked right through her.

Today, when she met Miss Palmer's gaze, there was no sparkle. Only terror. The poor girl so clearly needed a confidante.

"How many months along?" Emma asked softly.

Miss Palmer dissolved into tears. "Almost four, I think."

"Does the gentleman know?"

"I can't tell him. He's a painter. I met him when he came to paint the portrait of our dogs, and I . . . It doesn't matter. He's gone. Went to Albania in search of 'romantic inspiration,' whatever that means."

It means he's a scoundrel, Emma thought. "What of your family? Do they know?"

"No." She shook her head with vigor. "There's only Papa. He has such high expectations for me. If he knew I'd been so careless, he . . . he'd never look at me the same." She buried her face in her hands and broke into quiet sobs. "I couldn't bear it."

Emma drew the girl into a hug, rubbing her back in a soothing rhythm. "Oh, you poor dear. I'm so sorry."

"I don't know what to do. I'm so frightened." She pulled away from the hug. "I can't raise a child on my own. I've been thinking, if only I could place the babe with a family in the country. Then I could visit from time to time. I know it's done." Miss Palmer placed a hand on her belly and looked down at it. "But I'm growing larger every day. I won't be able to hide it much longer."

Emma offered the girl a handkerchief. "Is there anywhere you can go? A friend or cousin, perhaps. In the country, or on the Continent . . .

Anyone who might take you in until you give birth?"

"There's no one. No one who would keep the secret, at any rate." She clutched the handkerchief in her fist. "Oh, if only I hadn't been so stupid. I knew it was wrong, but he was ever so romantic. He called me his muse. He made me feel . . ."

Treasured. Wanted. Loved.

Miss Palmer didn't have to explain it. Emma knew exactly how the girl felt.

"You mustn't be hard on yourself. You aren't the first young woman to trust the wrong man, and you won't be the last."

And yet somehow, the woman always paid the price.

Emma hadn't landed in Miss Palmer's delicate situation, but she, too, had been punished for the simple crime of following her heart. The memories still pained her—and the thought of watching the same cruel fate befall another young woman? It made her quake with anger at the injustice of it all.

"Emma," Madame Bissette chided from the other side of the curtain. "Lady Edwina's hem won't sew itself."

"One moment, Madame," she called back. To Miss Palmer, she whispered, "Return next week to retrieve your altered frock, and we'll speak further. If there's any way at all I can help you, I will."

"I can't ask that of you."

"You don't need to ask." Emma was determined. Her conscience would allow no less. She took Miss Palmer's hands and squeezed them. "Whatever may happen, you will not be alone. I swear it."

That afternoon, Emma's concentration was so splintered, nothing went right. Twice, she had to rip out uneven stitches in Lady Edwina's hem and rework them.

At last, it was closing hour.

"Are you coming out tonight?" her fellow seamstress asked after Madame had withdrawn to her apartment upstairs. "There's to be dancing at the assembly rooms."

"Not tonight, Fanny. You go on ahead."

Emma didn't have to offer twice. Fanny was out the door as soon as she could blow a kiss.

Another time, she might have enjoyed a rare evening of dancing, but not tonight. Not only was she worried sick for Miss Palmer, she was still reeling from her own encounter at Ashbury House.

The duke was probably laughing at his own cleverness even now. Marry a seamstress? Ha-ha-ha. What a joke.

How *dare* the man? Really.

Emma shook off the memory, telling herself not spare the duke another thought. She had more important things to do.

She took a stub of a candle from Madame Bissette's drawer, placed it on the counter, and struck the flint as quietly as possible. After rummaging for a discarded scrap of brown paper, she ironed it flat with her hands and chewed on a stub of pencil, thinking. Waistlines had started to drop this season, moving away from Empire silhouettes. Concealing an expanding belly would be more difficult, but Emma would do her best.

She placed pencil to paper and began to sketch. Miss Palmer would need a corset with extra give toward the bottom . . . perhaps a frock with small buttons inside the waistline, to gather or let out the skirts. A fetching pelisse was a must—the right embellishments would draw the eye upward.

The task absorbed her attention so fully, she didn't notice how much time had passed until someone knocked at the door.

Thump-thump-thump.

Emma jumped in her skin and crumpled the sketches into her pocket. "We're closed."

The rapping only grew louder. More insistent.

Thump-thump-thump-thump.

With a sigh, Emma went to the front of the shop. She turned the key in the lock and opened the door just an inch.

"I'm sorry, I'm afraid we're shut for the eveni—"

"You're not shut for me."

She found herself pushed aside as a man bulled his way through the door. He wore a dark cape and a tall hat with its brim pulled low, concealing most of his face—but she knew him at once. Only one man would have behaved in such a presumptuous manner.

The Duke of Ashbury.

"Miss Gladstone." He inclined his head in the slightest possible nod. "I told you we'd meet again."

Oh, Lord.

Emma closed the door and turned the key. There was nothing else to do for the moment. She couldn't leave it ajar and risk being seen alone with a gentleman.

"Your Grace, I can't admit visitors after hours."

"I'm not a visitor. I'm a customer." He strolled around the darkened shop, prodding a headless dressmaking form with his walking stick. "I need a new waistcoat."

"It's a dressmaking shop. We don't offer gentlemen's attire."

"Very well, I'm here to order a gown."

"A gown for whom?"

"What does it matter?" He made an annoyed gesture. "For a particularly ugly woman, approximately my size."

Good heavens, what could this man be after? Was his mockery yesterday not enough to satisfy him? He couldn't actually want to retrieve Miss Worthing's gown.

Whatever his aim, Emma meant to exact a price in return. Today, he was welcome to share in the humiliation.

She drew a box to the center of the floor—the one ladies stood upon to have their hems pinned—and waved him toward it. "Up you go, then."

He stared at her.

"If you want a gown—"

"It's not that *I* want a gown."

"If your very ugly, duke-sized friend wants a

gown, I will need measurements. Sleeve, torso, hem." She arched an eyebrow. "Bosom."

There. Surely he would retreat from that.

Instead, the unscarred corner of his mouth tipped with amusement. He set his walking stick aside. He removed his hat. Then his cloak. Next his gloves. And, finally, his topcoat. Without breaking her gaze, he stepped onto the box and lifted his arms to either side, palms up. Like an actor on a stage, expecting applause.

"Well?" he prompted. "I'm waiting."

Emma retrieved her measuring tape. She'd begun this little farce, and she couldn't back down from it.

"How did you know where to find this shop?" she asked, suspicious. "Did you follow me?"

"I am a duke. Of course I didn't follow you. I had you *followed*. It's an entirely different thing."

She shook her head, unfurling the measuring tape. "And yet no less disturbing."

"Disturbing? Yesterday you turned down a lifetime of wealth in favor of two pounds, three shillings in ready coin, and then fled from my house as though it were afire. Has it not occurred to you that I might have pursued you out of some genuine concern for your well-being?"

She gave him a doubtful look.

"I'm not saying I *did*. Only that it should have occurred to you."

Emma moved behind him and stretched her measuring tape from his left shoulder to his wrist, ostensibly taking the length of his sleeve. In actuality, most of her concentration was consumed with ignoring his closeness. Only a single layer of fine, crisp linen separated her touch from his body, and she had no desire to relive that buzzing shock of connection they'd shared in his library.

You can't leave now. We're just starting to have fun.

She took the measurement from one shoulder to the other. When she inhaled, she drew in the masculine scents of shaving soap and rich cologne.

None of this was helping with her focus problem.

"You're not writing these measurements down," he said.

"I don't need to. I'll remember."

Unfortunately. Whether she wished it or not, Emma knew this encounter would be burned into her memory forever. Or if not forever, at least until she was sufficiently old and feebleminded to hold conversations with a squash.

She turned the tape vertically and put one end to the nape of his neck. A mistake. Now, atop all these unwanted memories, she'd added the feel of his shorn hair. It had the texture of expensive velvet, with a dense, luxurious pile.

Velvet, Emma? Really?

"Almost finished. I'll just measure your chest now." She held the end of the tape on one side of his rib cage, and then turned to circle him in the opposite direction, drawing the tape across the satin backing of his waistcoat and all the way around, meeting both ends at his breastbone.

She cinched the tape. He winced.

Good.

There, now. She had the beast on a leash.

So why did she feel like his captive?

It wasn't his scars that intimidated her. Quite the reverse. When she stood this close, her gaze couldn't take in both halves of him at the same time. She had to choose a side.

Emma knew with a sinking heart which one would capture her. There were two approaches to successful dressmaking—to find flaws and conceal them, or to bring out the hidden beauty. She'd always believed in the latter method, and oh, it came back to bite her today.

Don't do it, Emma. Don't give your foolish heart an inch of rope, or it will have you tied in knots.

But it was too late. Now, as she looked up at him, all she could see was a man. One with searching blue eyes and a hidden heart beating in a strong, defiant rhythm.

A man with wants, needs. Desires.

A man who'd reached out for her yesterday, and now . . .

And now gave every indication of leaning in for a kiss.

Chapter Three

$\mathscr{A}$sh had never wanted to kiss a woman more.

He wanted to kiss her so badly, he could taste it. He'd devour the pink sweetness in those lips, stroke all the tart words from the tip of her tongue. Teach her a lesson or two. Leave her breathless. Rattle her to her bones.

He wanted to do far more than kiss her, of course. As he leaned forward, he could peer through the gap of her fichu and catch a glimpse of the valley between her breasts—that dark, fragrant rift that held so many promises of pleasure.

By Venus's hand.

A few years ago, he *would* have kissed her, and more. He would have seduced her with a campaign of little trinkets and witty teasing. She would have come willingly, even eagerly, to his bed, where they would have enjoyed one another. Thoroughly.

But that was in the past. His once-charming wit had been replaced by smoldering anger, and his once-attractive face had been rearranged. No woman would be wooed by the kisses of a bitter, disfigured wretch.

It didn't matter. He didn't need to woo a lover. He needed to secure a wife. Wed her, bed her, and, once she was swelling with his heir, tuck her away in the country. The end.

He straightened, arching a sardonic eyebrow. A fortunate thing, that he still had one eyebrow intact. What was being a duke, if not arching a sardonic eyebrow?

She released the tape. "Choose your fabric at the draper's and have five yards sent over. With your coloring, I suggest a pink brocade."

His tilted his head. "Really? I was thinking of peach."

She gathered his hat, cloak, gloves, and walking stick and pushed them into his arms. "And now I must ask you to leave. I need to be getting home."

"We can accomplish both those things at once. I'll take you home. My carriage is just outside."

"Thank you, I prefer to walk."

"More convenient still. My feet are even closer than the carriage."

She headed for the rear exit of the shop. Ash replaced his topcoat, cloak, gloves, and hat, then followed her out into a dank, reeking alleyway. With his long strides to her short ones, he quickly made up the ground.

Her shoes tapped over the cobblestones at an irritated clip. "I will not be your mistress. My body is not for let."

"That can't be entirely true. You're a seamstress, aren't you? Your fingers are for let."

"If you don't know the difference between a woman's fingers and her womb, I would definitely not share a bed with you."

After a moment's stunned pause, he laughed. It was a rusty, unappealing sound. He supposed he was out of practice.

"I do know the difference." He reached for her ungloved hand and brushed his thumb over each of her fingertips. "You can trust I won't confuse the two."

He stroked a callus on the tip of her second finger. It made him angry. A gentleman's daughter should have soft hands, but life had hardened her in these small ways. He had disturbing fancies of lifting her hand to his lips and kissing all that hurt away.

She sucked in her breath, as if she could read his thoughts. Or maybe her own thoughts had startled her.

She withdrew her hand. "What is your aim? Simply to torment me further?"

"No, that is not my aim. Though I suspect, over time, it will be an unavoidable consequence."

She gave a little growl.

Ash found it wickedly arousing. Not that he would tell her so. He was too distracted by the way she hugged herself and shivered. "Where is your cloak?"

"I left it at your house yesterday."

"Well. I hope that teaches you a lesson about making dramatic exits."

Ash removed his own cape and twirled it about her shoulders, tucking in the ends until she resembled a penguin. "Come along, then." He swiveled her by the shoulders and nudged her into a waddle.

Offering her his cloak was not mere gallantry. It was self-protection. He had gloves, but the leather was too fine, too supple. Without the barrier of the cloak, he could still feel her. He didn't wish to relive the visceral shock that had rocketed through him in his library.

"Now," he said, "perhaps you'll pay attention. I don't recall saying anything about a mistress. I believe I used the word 'duchess.'" He gestured at their bleak surroundings. "I would not trouble to come *here* for any other purpose."

"You can't be serious. Not really, truly, honestly, earnestly, properly."

He allowed a few moments to pass. "Are you quite done listing adverbs? I should hate to interrupt."

His little penguin bounced in agitation.

Ash was agitated, as well. Judging by her insistence that he couldn't possibly want her, he suspected some other man had made her feel unwanted. *That* made him furious.

"Listen to me, Emma."

Look, he was already thinking of her as Emma. A small, stubborn little name, Emma. It suited her.

"The answer is yes," he said. "I am serious. Really, truly, honestly, earnestly, properly. And I mean to have you, completely."

EMMA LOST HER footing and nearly stumbled face-first into an apple seller's cart.

She righted herself, but not before the duke's hand shot out to steady her. He didn't let go, either. Instead, he gripped tighter and guided her around the cart, maneuvering his body between her and a passing carriage.

He moved swiftly, and she struggled to keep pace with him. In truth, she'd been struggling to keep pace with him since the moment she'd entered his library. Wrestling to understand his intentions, sparring with his wit. Chasing after her own body's responses. He was exhausting. Less of a man, more of a gymnasium.

"If it's a wife you want," she said, "surely you could find many women—many well-bred ladies—who would be willing to marry you."

"Yes, but I'd have to *find* them. This saves me so much effort."

She threw him a sidelong glance. "Can you not hear yourself? Do you truly not know how insulting that sounds?"

"I should think it sounds beneficent. I'm offering you a title and fortune. All you have to do is lie back in the dark, then spend nine months swelling up like a tick. What could possibly deter any woman from accepting?"

"What, indeed. Perhaps a disinclination to feeling like a broodmare."

They stepped off the pavement and crossed the street.

"A broodmare. Hm. I'm not certain I mind that

comparison. If you're a broodmare, that would make me the stud."

"And there," she said, "is the injustice of the world in a nutshell."

He ignored her statement. "On reflection, I prefer 'stallion.'"

"Never mind the horses!" She made a strangled noise of frustration. "It's absurd to even suggest we could marry. We scarcely know each other. And what little we do know of each other, we don't like."

"I'm not aware of the courtship customs back in your quaint little inbred village, but at my level of society, wedlock is a matter of two concerns: childbearing and finances. What I'm offering is a marriage of convenience. You're living in poverty, and I"—he laid his hand to his chest—"have a great deal of money. I need an heir, and you"—he waved toward her with a flourish—"have the capacity to bear one. There's no need to like each other. As soon as a child is conceived we'll go separate ways."

"Separate ways?"

"You'd have your own house in the country. I'll have no further need of you then."

When they turned onto a busier lane, he tugged down the brim of his hat and turned up the collar of his coat. Night was falling, but the moon was bright. He obviously didn't want to draw attention. Sympathy breezed into Emma's heart like an unwelcome visitor.

"You're assuming," she continued, "that your

theoretical child would be male. What if you fathered a girl? Or five of them?"

He shrugged. "You're the vicar's daughter. Pray for a boy."

"You are terrible."

"Since we are on the subject of personal failings, you are irrational. You're allowing pride to cloud your common sense. Spare yourself the effort of argument and skip to the inevitable conclusion."

"I conclude that this conversation is madness. I don't understand why you keep speaking as though you'd marry me."

"I don't understand why *you* keep speaking as though I won't."

"You are a duke. I am a seamstress. What else is there to be said?"

He held up one hand and counted off on his fingers. "You are a healthy woman of childbearing age. You are a gentleman's daughter. You are educated. You're passably pretty—not that it's a concern for me, but a child should have at least one nonhideous parent." He was down to his last finger. "And you're here. All my requirements are met. You'll do."

Emma stared at him in disbelief. That was, perhaps, the most unfeeling proposal she could imagine. The man was cynical, insensitive, condescending, rude.

And she was definitely going to marry him.

Against all logic, and contrary to everything she knew of society, he appeared to be making her an earnest proposal of marriage. She would be the greatest ninny in England to refuse.

Seamstresses didn't have many long-term prospects. The years of detailed needlework caused their eyes to fail and fingers to stiffen. Emma knew that her best chance—perhaps her *only* chance—at security was to marry. She would be a fool to refuse any duke, even if he were a bedridden septuagenarian with poor hygiene.

This particular duke was none of those things. Despite his many, *many* faults, Ashbury was strong, in the prime of life, and he smelled divine. He offered her security, at least one child to dote upon . . .

And a house.

A quiet house of her own in the country. Precisely the thing that would allow her to help Miss Palmer, at a time when the poor girl had no one else.

The duke slowed to a halt. "By the Holy Rood. This isn't right."

Drat. That would teach her to dream, even for a second. He'd come to his senses after all. This was the moment where he sent her away, and she ended an old woman on the docks, darning sailors' shirts for ha'pennies and muttering about how she might have been a duchess.

"We're in the middle of St. James Park," he said.

"Are we?" She took in their surroundings. Autumn-browned grass. The half-bare branches of trees. "I suppose we are. What's a Holy Rood?"

"The cross of Christ. And you call yourself a vicar's daughter? You father would be appalled."

"Believe me, that wouldn't be a new development."

"Just where is it you live, anyway?"

"In an attic garret, two doors down from the shop."

"So we're here because . . ."

She bit her lip. "I was hoping to lose you. But I've since changed my mind."

"Damned right you have." With gruff impatience, he drew her to his side, steering her with a hand to the small of her back. "Do you know what kind of scum lurks in St. James Park by night?"

"Not really."

"Pray you do not have occasion find out."

"It's barely nightfall yet. I'm certain we'll be—"

She didn't have a chance to complete the thought. A pair of men emerged from the shadows, almost as though the duke had hired them precisely to prove his point.

And from the looks on their faces, the men were expecting to be paid.

Chapter Four

*A*sh hated always being right.

He positioned himself between the men and Emma, keeping one hand on her back and clutching his walking stick with the other. "Well?" he goaded. "Get to it, already. Tell me what it is you want, so that I can tell *you* to get stuffed, and we can all carry on with our lives. I've a full schedule this evening."

"Toss over the purse, guv. Watches and rings, too."

"Get stuffed. There, now. See how easy that was?" He slid his arm around Emma's shoulders. "We'll be going."

The second man held up a knife. "Hold there. I wouldn't try anything clever."

"I should hope you wouldn't," Ash replied dryly. "You'd no doubt injure yourself in the attempt."

The man with the knife feinted, jabbing it in the direction of Ash's ribs. "Shut it. And give up your coins and baubles, unless you fancy bleedin' to death in front o' your bit of skirt."

His *bit of skirt*?

"Not to worry, miss." The first man chuckled, winding a length of rope around one of his hands and pulling it tight with the other. "We'll be glad to take you off the gentleman's 'ands."

A savage growl rose in Ash's throat. "Like the devil you will." Brandishing his walking stick like a sword, he sliced the air in a wide arc, forcing the footpads back. "Touch her and you will pay with your lives, you diseased, maggoty curs."

He'd gone beyond anger, sailed straight past rage, and crashed into a place of primal fury, where blood ran in colors he hadn't known to exist.

The blade glinted in the gathering dark. Its owner lunged, but Ash stepped to the side, pushing Emma back with his free arm. With a vicious strike, he sent the blackguard to his knees. The knife tumbled into the grass.

Whirling around, he raised his walking stick again, preparing to deal the other cutpurse a backhand blow, hard enough to crush bone.

Before he could swing, a gust of wind dislodged his hat.

In unison, the thieves recoiled.

"Sweet Jesus," one of them whispered.

"Christ 'ave mercy," the other said, scrambling backward on his hands and feet. "'Tis the Devil, to be sure."

Ash stilled, fuming with a wrath that burned his lungs and holding his stick poised for violence. However, violence no longer appeared necessary. After a tense silence, he lowered the stick. "Begone."

Neither of them dared to move.

"Begone!" he roared. "Slink home like the craven whoresons you are, or I swear to you, you will *beg* for the Devil to take your souls."

They scrambled and fled. No victory had ever been so hollow.

On returning to London, Ash had harbored a small hope that he might not look *quite* so monstrous as his few interactions had led him to believe. Maybe Annabelle was just Annabelle—shallow and prizing appearances above all else. Perhaps his former friends truly had been too busy to visit more than once, and the majority of his servants really had needed to visit far-flung relations who'd suddenly taken ill.

Maybe—just maybe—the scars weren't that bad.

He'd been deluding himself. That much was now clear. His appearance was every bit as repulsive as he'd feared, if not worse. Those were hardened criminals he'd sent scurrying like rats into the gutter. And he expected a quick-witted, lovely young woman to rejoice at his offer of marriage?

Everyone would revile him. No woman with any sense would have him. When he turned, Emma would be gone. He was certain of it.

He knew nothing.

She was still there, wielding a tree branch in both hands as she stared after the retreating brigands. His cloak had slipped from her shoulders. Her breaths made angry clouds of vapor in the cold air.

At length, she dropped the branch, then moved to retrieve his hat from where it had landed a few feet distant. "Are you unharmed?"

Ash stared at her in bewilderment. Her question didn't make sense. None of this made any sense.

She'd not only not run, she'd prepared to *defend* him—absurd as that was. He didn't know what to do with her, and he didn't have the faintest notion what to do with himself. He couldn't help but feel . . .

He couldn't help but *feel*. All manner of emotions, and all of them at once.

To begin, he was vaguely insulted by the suggestion that he might *need* help from a wisp of a girl. That led to a growing desire to possess her, to show her just who protected whom in this exchange. And then, beneath everything, there was some quiet, unnameable emotion that made him want to lay down his pride, rest his head in her lap, and weep.

That third was, of course, unthinkable. Never going to happen. Nevertheless, the decision was made. She'd sealed her own fate.

If she meant to escape him, she'd missed her chance.

He'd be damned if he'd let her get away now.

EMMA SENSED THE change in him. The stony set of his jaw. The furious rise and fall of his breath.

No blue remained in his eyes—only a cold, glittering black.

He'd been intense from the first, but now he was . . . so intensely intense, she couldn't find a word to properly describe it. But she felt it. Oh, she felt it to her toes. Each hair on her body lifted at the root; her every nerve jumped to attention.

Her body knew something would happen.

Her mind had no idea what it would be—except that it would involve the unleashing of formidable power.

"Your hat," she said. As if it might need explaining that the hat-shaped object in her hand was indeed a hat and not, say, a joint of mutton.

He took the hat.

He took his cloak from where it had fallen to the spongy turf.

And then he took *her*.

He didn't offer his arm, as gentlemanly custom would dictate. He gripped her by the elbow instead, herding her toward the street. "I'm sorry you had to see that."

"I'm not," she muttered.

Not that Emma was happy they'd been set upon by thieves. That had been terrifying, and she had no desire to ever experience it again. However, now, with the benefit of knowing they'd escaped unscathed, she could revisit the memory and feel a thrill at his instinctive move to guard her and the outraged precision with which he'd dispatched the two men.

No one had ever protected her that way.

Whatever attraction she'd felt toward him beforehand—and she *had* felt an attraction, no matter how unwillingly—was increased a hundredfold.

"I'm the one who should apologize," she said. "It was all my fault. We would not have ended here in the park if—"

"If I'd paid the slightest attention. The fault was mine." He led her out of the park without further conversation. At the nearest crossing, he hailed a hackney cab. "You're going home. My carriage will come for you tomorrow. Have your things ready."

The air vacated her lungs. "Wait. What are you saying?"

"From there, you'll go to a hotel. Mivart's, I think."

Mivart's. The finest, most luxurious hotel in Mayfair. Emma had visited it once, to hem a gown for a visiting Austrian baroness. She had never imagined she would stay in such a place.

"I'll send for you once the solicitors have finished the contracts." The duke opened the hackney's door and stuffed Emma into it. "We'll be married at Ashbury House."

"But . . . but . . ."

He gave directions to the hackney driver, then moved to close the door and shut her inside. "On second thought, *don't* pack your belongings. I'll buy you new. I've no use for moldy potatoes."

She thrust her boot into the door opening before he could close it. "Wait."

He stared at her. "What?"

Excellent question. Emma didn't have the faintest idea what. Only that this was all happening so fast. Too fast. Her life had been set spinning, and she didn't want to make it stop—but she needed some sort of handle to grasp.

"I . . . I insist on bringing a cat."

He made a noise of unmitigated disgust. "A *cat.*"

"Yes, a cat. My cat."

Emma, you idiot. You don't even have a cat.

She would find one, she decided. If she meant to enter a marriage with no promise of affection and inhabit that vast, elegant house, she needed at least one ally. What better than a fuzzy, wide-eyed kitten?

"For a bride of convenience, you are proving to be a great deal of trouble." He tucked her foot into the hackney, then leveled a finger at her before closing the door. "This cat of yours had better be well-behaved."

Chapter Five

The cat was the most foul, filthy, repulsive creature Ashbury had seen in his life, outside of the rare occasions when he regarded himself in a mirror. It was no more than a collection of bones encased in smudge-colored fur, and doubtless crawling with fleas.

His bride clutched the beast with both hands, holding it in front her like some sort of spinster bouquet.

Excellent. What was it they said? Something old, something new, something borrowed, something yowling.

Ash scowled at the thing.

The creature hissed in reply.

The dislike would seem to be mutual.

"Does it have a name?" he asked.

She looked up, as if startled by the question. "What?"

"A name. Does the cat have one?"

"Oh. Yes. Breeches. His name is Breeches."

"Breeches?"

"Isn't that what I said?" She showed no signs of releasing the thing. Instead, she looked about the hall. "Where are we reciting our vows? The library?"

"You can't mean to hold that thing throughout the ceremony."

"But if I put him down, I fear he'll run off. Besides, he wants to be a witness. Don't you, Breeches?" She turned the cat to face her and made a kissy face. "This is the Duke of Ashbury. Aren't you pleased to meet him?" She took the creature's paw and mimicked a wave of greeting in Ash's direction. "He's quite friendly."

The cat's claws made a vicious swipe through the air.

Right. That was it.

Ash reached out, wrested the animal from her grasp, and set it on the floor. The gray beast darted off at once.

"This house is enormous," she objected. "He might be lost for days."

"We can only hope."

He tugged at the front of his waistcoat and turned to have a proper look at his bride. Of all that cat's many offenses, its worst by far was obscuring his view of her. Thus far, he had seen her only two ways: first, wearing a gown made of leprous icicles, and second, wearing a modest shopgirl frock.

The morning dress she wore today was simple, but a welcome respite for his beauty-starved eyes. It was fashioned from wool in a rich, flattering shade of blue. The fit was perfect. He supposed that shouldn't have been a surprise—she'd likely sewn it herself—but the frock embraced her in all the best places. The sleeves were long, and she'd added an edge of slender lace at the wrists. The merest hint of sweetness, like a dusting of confectioner's sugar.

It was charming.

No, no. *Charming?* Had he just thought that word? He wasn't charmed. He was never charmed. Bah.

He was ruttish, that was all. Eager to break an interminable stretch of celibacy. He admired her frock for one reason: because it would make such a satisfying heap on the floor.

What a shame he wouldn't have the opportunity to see it that way. It would be dark when he visited her bed tonight.

Her rose-petal lips moved. Damn it, that meant he'd been staring at them. And now he hadn't heard whatever it was she'd said.

"The curate is in the drawing room," he said.

She hesitated.

He braced himself to hear, *I can't possibly do this,* or *What was I thinking?* or *I'd rather be hungry and homeless, thank you.*

"Which way is the drawing room?"

With a relieved sigh, he turned and offered her his arm. "This way."

Her steps were not precisely light, and he couldn't fault her for it. She no doubt would have wished to marry for love, and he was about to steal that dream from her tiny, work-reddened fingers—replacing the charming, handsome groom of her dreams with an ill-tempered monster.

Guilt jabbed him in the ribs.

He had to ignore it. War had taught him two things. First, life was fleeting. Second, duty wasn't. If he died without an heir, his toad of a cousin would carve up the lands, making every decision for his own expedience and enrichment. Ash would have failed the thousands who depended on him.

And if he failed them, he would not be the man his father raised. No prospect could be more gutting.

The irony of it hit him as they entered the drawing room.

He was the one marrying for love.

Just not hers.

It wasn't precisely the wedding of Emma's youthful imaginings. She'd seen herself having a church wedding, naturally, packed with friends, neighbors, relations. She'd dreamed of wearing pink ribbons and a crown of flowers in her hair. But then, she'd abandoned those girlish fancies years ago.

In the drawing room, there were no guests or flowers—only the curate, the butler, the housekeeper, and a frightful number of papers awaiting her signature. Emma riffled through the pile, intimidated. She supposed there was no better place to begin than the beginning.

She was only halfway through the second page before the duke's patience expired.

"What are you doing?" he asked. "*Reading* them?"

"Of course I'm reading them. I don't sign anything I don't read first. Do you?"

"That's different. I might have something to lose."

And Emma didn't. That was the duke's clear implication. In truth, it would be hard to argue the point. She'd already left the dressmaking shop, her garret, and most of her belongings behind.

He left her to her reading, retreating to pace in circles at the other end of the drawing room. Emma was visited by the strange suspicion he might be as nervous as she was.

No, that couldn't be. More likely, he was eager to have it done.

"May I assist you, Miss Gladstone?" The murmured question came from nearby. "I know how weighty those stacks of paper can be."

She looked up to find the butler standing near. She'd met him the other day. What was his name? Mr. Khan, she thought she recalled.

What she remembered with certainty was that she'd liked him at once. He had bronze skin, an Indian cadence to his speech, and silver hair with a part as arrow-straight as his posture. He'd treated her with kindness, even when she'd appeared on the doorstep with no card and no invitation. In fact, he'd seemed strangely delighted to see her.

"The duke isn't always like this," Khan confided, handing her the next set of papers.

"No?" Emma pounced on the kernel of hope.

"Usually, he's a great deal worse." With a glance over his shoulder, the butler exchanged one set of papers for another. "He's been alone and is determined to remain that way. He doesn't trust anyone, but he respects those who challenge him. I suspect that's why you are here. He's angry, resentful, bored, in more pain than he lets on—and you'll either be the making of him, or he'll be the ruin of you."

She swallowed hard.

"If it helps," he said, "the entire staff is pulling for the former."

"It does help. I think."

Whatever was required to "be the making" of a wounded duke, Emma was positive she lacked it. However, if Khan wanted to be in her corner, she wouldn't complain. She needed to have one friend in the house, and it clearly wasn't going to be her husband.

Nor that cat, wherever it was.

"What's going on over there?" the man in question demanded.

"Nothing," she called. "That is, I'm nearly finished." To the butler, she whispered, "Do you have advice?"

"I suppose it's too late to run."

"Other than that."

"Drink heavily? Someone in the house ought to, and I cannot."

"Khan, stop standing about and make yourself useful. Fetch the family Bible."

The butler straightened. "Yes, Your Grace."

The subtle wink he gave her in parting was one of beleaguered sympathy. *We're in this together now*, it seemed to say.

She reached for the pen.

Once she'd finished signing all the contracts, the curate cleared his throat. "Are we ready to begin, Your Grace?"

"God, yes. Let's get on with it."

As she and the duke took their places side by side, Emma couldn't help but steal a glance at him. His uninjured profile was to her. Decisive and compelling, with no trace of doubt on his features.

Then he suddenly turned his head, displaying his scars. Embarrassed at having been caught staring, she looked away—and instantly knew in her stomach that looking away was the wrong thing to do.

Well done, Emma. Just capital. That won't offend him at all.

As they recited their vows, the duke clasped her hand to slide a plain gold band on her finger. His grip was firm and unsentimental, as if he were asserting a claim. The two servants signed as witnesses, and then they and the curate departed.

They found themselves alone, the three of them. Emma, the duke, and a thick, uncomfortable silence.

He clapped his hands. "Well, that's done."

"I suppose it is."

"I'll have the maid bring some refreshment to your suite. You'll want to rest."

As he turned to leave, Emma put a hand on his arm, stopping him.

He turned back. "What."

The word wasn't a question, but a scolding.

She steadied her nerves. "I want to have dinner."

"Of course you will have dinner. Do you think I mean to starve you? That would hardly suit my purposes of siring a healthy child."

"I didn't mean that I merely wish to be *fed*. I'd like the two of us to dine together. Not only tonight, but every evening. Proper dinners, with multiple courses. And conversation."

From his expression, one would think she'd suggested nightly abdominal surgery. Performed with a knitting needle and a spoon.

"Why would you want *that*?"

"There must be something more than bedding between us. We must come to know one another, at least a little bit. Otherwise, I'll feel too much like a . . ."

"A broodmare. Yes, I recall." He looked to the side, sighed, and then looked back at her. "Very well, we will dine together. However, let's have a few matters settled right now. This is a marriage of convenience."

"That's what we agreed."

"There will be no affection involved. In fact, every precaution will be taken against it."

"I'm surprised you believe we'll need any precautions."

"Only one act is required on your part. You must permit me to visit your bed. I'm well aware of my distasteful appearance. You need not fear any crude or lascivious attentions from my quarter. All encounters will be as dignified as possible. No lights, no kissing. And of course, once you are pregnant with my heir, we will be done."

At this, Emma was stunned. No kissing? No lights? On account of his "distasteful appearance"?

The pain implied in that litany tugged at her emotions. Annabelle Worthing's rejection must have been a cruel blow. Even if he'd formed the idea that his scars were intolerably repulsive . . . Emma was his wife now. She refused to underscore it. She knew how it felt to be an outcast.

He turned to walk away. Once again, she stopped him.

"One more thing. I want you to kiss me."

She was mortified by the way she'd blurted it out, but it was done—and now she must not back down. If she ceded to him on this, she would never regain what little ground she held.

"Have you been paying attention? I only just now stipulated there would be no kissing."

"You said kissing in bed," she pointed out. "This isn't bed. I promise, I'll only ask the once."

He passed a hand over his face. "Dinner. Kisses. This is what I get for wedding a vicar's daughter from the country. Girlish notions about romance."

"Believe me, being a vicar's daughter from the country did *nothing* to fill me with notions of romance."

Strumpet. Harlot. Jezebel.

The cruel words whispered from the shadowy corners of her memory. She tamped them down, as she'd learned to do over the years. Perhaps someday she would learn how to banish them.

"I can do without a jeweled ring, or guests, or a fine gown," she said. "I'm only asking for this one tiny gesture, to make it all feel a bit less . . . cold. More like an actual wedding."

"It *was* an actual wedding. The vows are perfectly legal and binding. A wedding does not require a kiss."

"I think *my* wedding requires one." Her voice gathered strength. "A woman only gets one of these ceremonies, and as hasty and contractual as it's all been thus far, I'd appreciate one small gesture that makes me feel like something other than chattel."

She watched closely for his reaction. His reaction was to refuse to react at all. He was expressionless—both sides of him. The whole, and the scarred. Perhaps he was uncertain of himself. Then again, perhaps he was uninterested in her. Either thought made her throat tighten.

"I could do the kissing, if you prefer," she offered. "It needn't be a long kiss. You only have to stand there."

She stretched up on her toes.

He put his hands on her shoulders and pushed her back down. "The bride does not kiss the duke."

Oh, Lord. This could not possibly be any more humiliating.

"The duke," he continued, "kisses the bride. It's an entirely different thing."

"Is it?"

"Yes. Close your eyes."

Emma closed her eyes. Her heart drummed in her chest as the waiting stretched longer . . .

And longer still.

She was a fool. He was laughing at her. He'd changed his mind. About the kiss. About her. About everything.

She was on the verge of opening her eyes, slinking from the room, and constructing a fortification of pillows, novels, and kittens in which to hide for the remainder of her life, when—

His hands cupped her face. Rough, possessive. And just when she was certain she'd combust from the cruel suspense of it all, his lips touched hers.

Something inside her came apart.

That hidden pocket of yearning that she'd sewn up tight years ago—his kiss ripped it open at the seams. A flood of emotion poured forth, overwhelming her. A surge of passion and desire and . . .

And something else. Something she didn't want to acknowledge, much less name. She'd pore over it later, no doubt. Her mind wouldn't allow her to let it alone. But as long as his lips touched hers, she could delay that dreaded reckoning.

If only this kiss could last forever.

Chapter Six

*G*et it over with, Ash told himself. Touch lips, hold for a count of three—no, two—and be done with the business altogether. Foolish to humor her, perhaps, but a perfunctory kiss seemed the fastest way to end the conversation.

What the kiss ended up being, however, was the fastest way to unravel him completely.

Softness. Warmth. The tastes of sweet and tart and cool. Parts of him went weak, and others were well on the way to rock-hard. She played on so many of his senses, he couldn't sort them out. The kiss unfurled tendrils of madness in his brain, strangling his ability to think, to regain control . . .

To count.

How long had his lips been on hers? It might have been two beats, or three, or a thousand. He didn't care anymore.

Her cheeks flushed beneath his palms, and he thought surely that heat must signal distress or embarrassment. But she didn't pull away. She leaned closer, pressing her hand against his coat.

Not only against his coat, but against the scars beneath it, and straight through to all the pain and bitterness beneath that. The sensation spiraled through him like a whirlwind in a desert, catching bone-dry dust and tossing it up to the sky.

Everything was wrong. Everything was right. Everything was possible.

He lifted his mouth from hers, but he couldn't wrench his gaze from her face. Long seconds passed before she opened her eyes, as though she were savoring the sensations. Stamping a memory. As though she'd *enjoyed* it.

He was a wretched fool for ever indulging her with this kiss. He'd neglected to consider that one kiss made a man want another.

And another.

And yet another still, each more passionate than the last.

He would have her later, in bed and often. But he wouldn't have her like that again. He wouldn't taste the fresh sweetness lingering where her lips had met his. The taste of beginnings, anticipation, and the hope of more.

He released her and stepped back.

She swayed on her feet, finding her balance. "Thank you."

It was entirely my pleasure, he thought. *And I shall never forgive you for it.*

He said, "Dinner's at eight."

WHEN EMMA LEFT the drawing room, she found the assembled servants of Ashbury House waiting in the entrance hall. Khan introduced each servant by position and name. Emma felt certain she would recall none of them. There were simply too many. Housekeeper, cook, upstairs maids, downstairs maids, scullery maids, footmen, coachman, grooms.

"Mary will serve as your lady's maid." He indicated an eager, smiling young woman in a crisp black uniform. "Mary, show the duchess to her suite."

"Yes, Mr. Khan." Mary bounced with enthusiasm. "Please do come this way, Your Grace." Once they were out of others' hearing, she chattered all the way up the stairs. "I'm so glad you've come. We all are."

"Thank you," Emma said, bewildered.

Surely an experienced lady's maid would be insulted to find herself in service to a duchess who had been, until a quarter hour ago, a seamstress. Wouldn't she?

Apparently not.

"Never hesitate to call upon us. We are here to serve you in any way."

"You're very kind."

"Kind?" Mary asked. "Not at all, Your Grace. It's clear at a glance that you're a vast improvement over that horrid Miss Worthing. Once the duke falls in love with you, everything's going to be so much better."

"Wait." Emma halted in the corridor. "Once the duke falls in *love* with me?"

"Yes, of course." Mary clasped her hands at her breast. "What a thrill it would be if it took only a few days. Perhaps it will only take the one night! Though I suppose a few months is the more likely course. We mustn't get too ahead of ourselves."

"I'm afraid you have the wrong idea," Emma said. "This isn't a love match, and I can assure you, it's not going to become one. Not in a few days, nor a few months. Not ever."

"Your Grace, never say it. It *must* happen." Mary looked over both shoulders before continuing. "You don't understand how we suffer here. Ever since his injury, the duke has been miserable—and he's made our lives unbearable as well. He never leaves the house, never has visitors. Never asks Cook for anything but the simplest of dishes. The staff is as lonely and bored as the duke is, and atop it we're in the service of a master whose moods run from black to the darkest gray. We are—all of us—counting on you." She took Emma's hands and squeezed them. "You're our only hope. The duke's only hope, too, I daresay."

Oh, heavens. That was . . . intimidating. Emma had no idea how to reply. She was struggling to retain a few scraps of optimism for her *own* future, plus a thread of hope for Miss Palmer's. Now she had a score of servants depending on her to rescue them, too?

"I have every faith in you, Your Grace." Mary beamed again and opened the door to a lavish suite. "Now this is your private sitting room. The bath is just through that door. To the other side you'll find your bedchamber, and beyond that, the dressing room. Shall I leave you for a bit to settle in? You've only to ring for me when you're ready to dress for dinner. I have so many ideas for your hair." With a little wave and a hop, she disappeared.

Emma wasn't eager to be left alone. This sitting room alone was larger than the garret she'd lived in for the past three years. It must take bushels of coal to heat. If she wouldn't have felt so foolish, she would have cupped her hands around her mouth and shouted her name—just to see if it echoed back.

As she wandered through the other rooms, her gaze skipped from one luxurious furnishing to the next. She didn't know how she'd ever dare to use them.

In the bedchamber, everything was laid out and waiting. The small assortment of belongings she'd brought with her, and many luxuries she hadn't. Fresh flowers, no doubt from a hothouse. On the dressing table, she found a silver hairbrush and hand mirror. The bed was covered with new linens, freshly pressed.

Oh, Lord. The bed.

She couldn't think about that just now.

Her one and only frock remotely fit for a formal dinner had been pressed and hung in readiness. She hoped it wouldn't be obvious that it was merely a years-old bit of rescued silk she'd used to practice new styles. The waistline had been lowered and lifted countless times. The hem had been flounced and unflounced again.

Ribbon trim had been exchanged for lace, then beading. It was hardly a proper gown, but it was what she had.

She took a folded quilt from the edge of the bed and wrapped it around her shoulders before sitting on the hearthrug, drawing her knees to her chest, and curling into herself like a bug.

She wasn't a seamstress any longer. She was a wife, a duchess.

And she was terrified.

AT EIGHT O'CLOCK, Emma found herself seated at one end of a mile-long table. She could scarcely make out the opposite end of it. The white linen surface seemed to disappear into the horizon. A few bits of crystal and silver twinkled like far-off stars.

The duke entered, nodded in her direction, and then began a prolonged, unhurried stroll to the far end of the dining room. It took him a full minute. There, he waited for a footman to draw out his chair, and then he sat.

Emma blinked at the manly dot in the distance. She needed a spyglass. Or a speaking trumpet. Both, preferably. Conversation would be impossible without them.

A servant snapped open a linen napkin with a flourish, laying it across her lap. Wine was poured into her glass. Another footman appeared with a tureen of soup, which he ladled into a shallow bowl before her. Asparagus, she thought.

"The soup smells divine," she said.

In the distance, she saw the duke motion to a footman. "You heard her. Pour Her Grace some more wine."

Emma let her spoon fall into her bowl. This was ridiculous.

She pushed back her chair and rose to her feet, gathering the bowl in one hand and her wineglass in the other. The servants looked to one another, panicked, as she walked the full length of the dining table and set her food at his end. She chose the corner facing his unscarred side, to lessen the awkwardness.

He looked annoyed.

She didn't care.

He broke the silence. "Really?"

"Yes, really. We had a bargain. I admit you to my bed; you appear at the dinner table. And we engage in conversation."

He took a draught of wine. "If you insist. I suppose we can converse as normal English people do. We'll talk about the weather, or the latest horse race, or the weather, or the price of tea, and oh, did we happen to discuss the weather?"

"Shall we talk about life in the country?"

"That will serve. The upper classes always talk about the country when in Town, and the Town when in the country."

"You mentioned that I would have my own house."

"Yes, it's called Swanlea. Situated in Oxfordshire. Not a grand house, but comfortable enough. The village is a few miles distant. No one's been in residence for years, but I'll have it opened for you."

"It sounds enchanting. I'd love to go for a visit. Would it be ready by Christmas?"

Christmas seemed her best chance. It was only some nine weeks away. That would put Miss Palmer at nearly six months pregnant—but with luck and clever dressmaking, she might be able to conceal her condition that long. If Emma could have her settled in Oxfordshire by the new year, this just might work.

"The house will be ready by Christmas," he said. "However, I doubt *you'll* be ready by Christmas."

"What do you mean?"

He waved for the servants to remove the soup. "You won't be going anywhere until you are confirmed to be with child."

What?

Emma choked on her wine.

The servants brought in the fish course, forcing her to hold her tongue.

The moment they had some measure of privacy, she leaned forward. "Do you mean to hold me captive in this house?"

"No. I mean to hold you to our bargain. Considering that the purpose of this marriage is procreation, I cannot allow you to reside elsewhere until that goal is achieved. Or at least well under way."

She searched her brain for a reasonable excuse. "But I've been yearning for Christmases in the country. Roasted chestnuts and sleigh rides and caroling." That much was no falsehood. Passing the holiday alone in a drafty garret had been lowering indeed. "I don't see why I couldn't visit for a week."

He speared a bite of fish. "I know how these things go. A week becomes a fortnight, and then a fortnight becomes a month. Before I know it, you've run off to some seaside hamlet to hide for a year or two."

"If you believe I'd do that, you don't know me very well."

He gave her a sidelong glance. "If you believe you won't be tempted, you don't know me at all."

Emma stared at her plate. This was an unforeseen complication. Helping Miss Palmer was one of the reasons she'd agreed to this marriage. Not the only reason, of course—but an important one. At the least, Emma needed to take the young woman to the country and see her settled, even if the duke insisted she return to London afterward. Now she learned he wouldn't permit any travel whatsoever. Not unless she was pregnant first.

She supposed it was *possible* she could be with child by Christmas, if she conceived soon. Very, very soon. And if she didn't . . . Well, she would just have to change his mind, she decided. He couldn't deny her a brief holiday once she gained his trust.

He doesn't trust anyone, Khan had said.

Wonderful.

"Your Gra—" She broke off mid-syllable, frowning. "What do I call you now? Not Your Grace, surely."

"Ashbury. Or Duke, if you must be more familiar."

Heavens. Being addressed as Duke counted as familiar?

"I'm your wife. Surely that means I've earned the privilege of calling you something more friendly. What did they call you when you were younger, before you inherited? You weren't Ashbury then."

"I was addressed by my courtesy title."

"Which was . . . ?"

"The Marquess of Richmond. A title which will become my heir's. Soon, with any luck. You may as well save it for him."

She supposed he was right. "What about your family name?"

"Pembrooke? Never used it."

Emma wasn't inclined to use it, either. Too stuffy, and it didn't precisely trip off the tongue. "Your Christian name, then."

"George. It was my father's name, and his father's name before that, and the name of every third gentleman in England, it would seem."

"It's my father's name, too." She shuddered. "So that's out. We'll have to find something else."

"There *is* nothing else. There's Ashbury, or Duke. Choose one."

Emma thought on it for a moment. "No, dear husband, I don't believe I shall."

He dropped his fork and glowered at her.

She smiled.

He doesn't trust anyone, Khan had said. *But he respects those who challenge him.*

If respect was what the duke had to offer, respect was what she must earn. Emma could put up a challenge. She hoped her husband was up to the task of meeting it.

She reached for a nearby bowl. "Would you like more sauce, sweeting?"

His fingers strangled the stem of his wineglass. She could practically hear the grapes calling for help. She hoped that was a good sign.

"If you don't cease that nonsense," he said, "you will regret it."

"Is that so, my heart?"

He plunked one forearm on the table and turned to face her. Piercing blue eyes, striking scars, and all. "*Yes.*"

Despite all her intentions to challenge him unabashed, Emma found herself, inconveniently, just a little bit abashed. Perhaps she *should* talk of the weather.

She was saved, however, from starting a discussion about the autumn chill.

A flash of silver fur darted from the side of the room. Breeches leapt onto the table, sank his teeth into the steamed trout, and absconded with it before either of them could say a word.

"That's it." The duke threw his linen napkin on his plate. "Dinner is over."

Chapter Seven

$\mathcal{A}$sh cinched his dressing gown and tied the sash. Then he undid it and tried again. He'd made such a tight knot on his first attempt, he'd impeded his ability to breathe.

He was damnably anxious. Emma wouldn't be the only inexperienced one tonight. He was hardly a virgin himself—but he'd never bedded a virgin before, and he wasn't sure what to expect from her quarter. Would she be merely timid, or outright terrified? How much pain was he likely to cause?

He supposed there was one comfort he could offer her. Considering how long it had been for him, the whole matter ought to be over within minutes. If not seconds.

He padded down the corridor on bare feet. When he arrived at her bedchamber, he gave a knock of warning before opening the door a few inches.

"I assume you're ready," he said.

"Yes."

"Good."

He entered, extinguishing his candle soon after. She had a few tapers of her own burning, and he went about the room snuffing them in turn. When he'd banked the fire to a dim red glow, he turned to join her on the bed.

On his first step forward, he bashed his knee on the edge of . . . something. A table? The leg of a chair?

The bedclothes rustled. "Are you all right?"

"Fine," he said tersely.

"You know, a bit of light might be a good idea."

"No. It would not be a good idea."

"I've seen your scars already."

"Not like this." *And not all of them.* The scars on his face were merely the prologue to an epic tale of deformity.

She might be able to stomach his appearance from across the room or in a darkened carriage, even at the dinner table. But within the intimacy of the marriage bed? Unclothed, in the light? Not a chance. The point been made painfully clear the first—and last—time he'd allowed a woman to view him that way.

The memory remained as sharp and painful as a poison-tipped arrow.

How could I bear to lie with . . . with that?

How, indeed.

Ash had no wish to relive that moment, and not merely to preserve his pride. This was a matter of saving his bloodline. He couldn't afford to frighten Emma off. When it came to bedding, she was already timid about the enterprise. He couldn't risk giving her any further reason to demur. A man was only allowed one wife. If she didn't give him an heir, that would mean the end of his line. At least the end of the decent side of it—the one without irredeemable prats.

"I'm over here," she said. "This way."

He followed the sound of her voice, stumbling a bit over some carpet fringe, but otherwise arriving at the edge of the bed in one piece. After tugging at the sash of his dressing gown, he undid the knot and slipped free of the garment, setting it aside.

He settled his weight toward the foot of the mattress and reached out to grasp—well, whatever part of her he could grasp. This would be a tricky business, deflowering a virgin bride in near-total darkness. Perhaps he ought to have strategized more in advance.

It was too late now. Ash felt around the quilted coverlet until his hand landed on what seemed to be a foot. An encouraging sign. He followed upward, sketching the shape of a leg.

Hm. Her calf was a bit stouter than he'd been expecting. But then, perhaps she was one of those women formed more amply below the waist than above it. It made no difference to him. The female body came in all shapes and sizes, and he'd never seen any reason to complain about the variety.

His hand swept over the familiar knob of a knee, and then up the slope of what must be a thigh. Now he was getting somewhere. A tightness gathered in his loins.

Ash stretched out beside her on the bed, the better to aid his explorations. He tried to murmur something soothing as he skimmed over the prominence of her hip and further upward, until he located the edge of the coverlet. But truthfully, his voice didn't lend itself to calm tones at the moment. Years' worth of pent-up lust coursed through his body. His cock swelled and stiffened against the bedding. By the time he grasped the hem of the coverlet and began to draw it downward, his body was ready. Very, very ready.

He peeled the quilted satin downward and prepared to lay his palm on what he expected would be the linen of her night rail, and some part of her warm body beneath. It was like playing darts blindfolded. There was little way of knowing on which target his touch would land. He would have been satisfied with a shoulder or her belly, he supposed, but by God, he was hoping for a breast. Fate owed him a stroke of luck.

He braced himself for that pleasant jolt of first contact.

No jolt occurred. Instead of her shift and tempting body, his hand connected with . . . a wool blanket? Well, then. It would seem he had another layer to remove.

He drew the blanket downward and made another attempt. This time, his hand connected with a thickly padded quilt. Good God, she was layered like an onion. No wonder her leg had felt thick enough to support a small tree.

"How many of these are there?" he asked, trying to locate the edge of the quilt.

"Only five or so," she answered.

"Five?" He flung back the quilt, not bothering with patience any longer. "Are you attempting to deter me? Exhaust me before I even get to the act?"

"I was cold. And then you banked the fire."

"I think you're playing me a trick. Perhaps I'll keep peeling these away and find there's nothing beneath them but a pair of pincushions and a broomstick."

"You're down to the last one, I swear it. Let me."

Fabric shifted beside him, and beneath it, her body wiggled in a way that was pure torture. He was desperate to be between her legs, inside her. He had a vision of her beneath him, naked. Her legs locked around his waist, and her back arched in pleasure.

Abandon that fantasy, he told himself. It wasn't going to be that way. Not tonight, not ever.

"I'm ready," she whispered.

His cock throbbed at the husky sound of her voice.

Thank God.

When he reached for her this time, he found what he'd been seeking. Her. Emma. His bride. His hand did not land on a breast, he realized with some disappointment, but her waist instead.

That would do.

He made a fist in the fabric of her shift. As he hiked the linen —only daring to raise it as far as her waist—his breath was shaky.

He stroked his hand downward, over her bared hip. He gave a helpless groan. God. He wanted to touch every part of her. The tender skin at her wrist, her lips, her hair. Her *hair*. He wondered if her hair was undone, and whether he dared to reach for the dark, heavy silk of it, twining his fingers round and round.

An imprudent idea, he decided. The way this night was going, he would probably poke her in the eye instead.

He moved his hand in a lateral caress, aiming for the center of her. As his fingertips brushed the tantalizing curls covering her mound, he cursed himself. He'd meant to bring some oil to ease the way.

He couldn't go back to retrieve it. If he stopped now, Lord only knew how many layers she'd be buried under when he returned. Instead, he raised two fingers to his lips and sucked them into his mouth, wetting them.

Then he reached between her thighs.

She gasped.

Clenching his jaw in an attempt at restraint, he focused on the task at hand. He slid his fingers up and down the seam of her cleft. Her breathing quickened—with apprehension, no doubt.

"You do understand what will happen?" he asked belatedly, his voice thick with lust. "What goes where, and all that?"

He felt her nod. "Yes."

"I'll try to be gentle with you. Failing that, I'll be quick."

He parted her folds, and then pressed his second finger inside her heat. Just a fingertip at first, and then a few inches more.

Goddamn. Bloody hell. Jesus Christ.

Fuck.

And every other bit of blasphemy he would have been thrashed as a youth for daring to say.

She was so hot, so tight, and made of the same flawless silk inside as her body was without.

Her breath came faster still, thin at the edges. Damn, he was a monster. She was anxious, even fearful. He was mindless with lust. Lost in the instinctive desire to lick and taste and suck, then take her hips in both hands and thrust deep.

If this didn't happen soon, he was going to spill his seed on all five of her blankets, and the entire exercise would have been in vain.

He pushed another finger inside her, sliding in and out, stretching her body to prepare his way.

Was she ready?

He withdrew his fingers to the tips, then thrust them both inside to the hilt, driving deep.

She cried out in surprise, and her hips bucked. *"Please."*

Her breaking voice pierced through his haze of lust.

Please.

Ash removed his hand at once. Struggling to catch his breath, he pushed himself up on one elbow, then rose to a sitting position. "Sorry."

He fumbled for his dressing gown, and then thrust his arms through the sleeves. By the fact that the thing barely covered his arse when he stood, he deduced that he'd put it on upside-down.

"It's fine," she said. "Truly. We can continue."

"No. I've pressed you too far, too quickly." He thought about attempting to retrieve his candle, then abandoned the idea. His eyes had adjusted enough that he could find his way to the door.

"But—"

"It will wait for tomorrow."

He opened the door, went through it, and closed it behind him. He paused, taking a few deep breaths to steady himself. But when he started to leave, he felt something tugging him back.

Damn it. He'd shut a fold of his dressing gown in the door.

He thunked his head against the doorjamb. Did marriage make utter fools of all men? Or was it just him?

He turned the doorknob again.

"Did you change your mind?" she asked.

"No," he replied, defensive. "I came back to tell you that I hadn't."

"Oh."

"So you needn't worry I'll be returning tonight. Aside from this time, of course."

He shut the door on her reply, but it followed him into the corridor.

"If you say so."

ASH TOOK ALL his unsatisfied lust and carried it out-of-doors, into the night. He'd considered giving himself some manual relief. However, the idea of spending his wedding night with his own hand was too pathetic to contemplate.

Walking it off was the only respectable option.

He stuck to the narrower lanes and the alleyways behind the mews, keeping the collar of his cloak upturned and his hat pulled down over his brow.

Eventually, he out-walked the aching tension in his groin. Yet there was something else he couldn't seem to shake.

Please, she'd whispered.

Please.

The word had shocked him. He'd pulled away at once, uncertain whether she'd uttered it in pleasure or pain. Her breathless voice almost suggested the former—but that was too absurd to contemplate.

First, she was a virgin. Second, she was a vicar's daughter. Third, she was a virgin vicar's daughter. And fourth, he was the scarred, ill-tempered—if fantastically wealthy—wretch who'd strong-armed her into in a marriage of convenience with no courtship whatsoever.

He must have hurt her, or scared her, or—most lowering to contemplate—repulsed her.

At best, he'd merely pressed her beyond her comfort for the first night.

Ash kicked at stones as he walked. Until he kicked something rotted and soft. Ugh. He didn't know what it was, but he was not stopping to investigate. He switched to poking at obstacles with his walking stick.

He would have to revise his plan, he decided. Take the bedding slowly, even if the waiting was torture. If he pushed her too far, too fast, and she shied from him . . . It all would have been for nothing. He would have no legitimate heir, and his father's legacy would die with him.

Unthinkable. He would not allow that to happen. *Please.*

It echoed through his mind again. A fresh shiver of arousal traveled the length of his spine.

He gave himself a mental shake.

She was not *sighing in ecstasy, you clotpole.*

That was only his desperate, lonely, sex-starved imagination, grasping at any phantom resembling affection.

He walked through the shuttered stalls of Shepherd Market, using his walking stick to push refuse out of his way and into the middens.

He prodded at a heap of rags.

The heap of rags stirred.

It unfolded, transforming into the figure of a young girl. No doubt she'd been left there to keep watch on the family stall by night.

"Whassat?" She drew herself up to a sitting position, rubbed her eyes, and turned to blink up at his face.

She blinked again.

And then she shrieked, loud and long enough to wake the dead.

"It's all right," Ash muttered. "I don't wish to—"

She paused for a breath, then unleashed another high-pitched scream. Dogs nearby began to snarl and bark.

"Be still, child. I'm not going to—"

"Get away!" She kicked at his shin, shouting. "Get away! Leave me be!"

"I'm going." He fished for what coins he had in his pocket, placed them beside the boarded-up stall, and made a hasty retreat. His heart was pounding.

See? he chided himself, once he was some distance down the lane.

Children screamed at the sight of him. Dogs howled as they would at a fiend.

No woman would be begging for him now. Not in bed, in the dark.

For that matter, not by day in the park.

Not on land, not at sea. She does not want you, Ashbury.

God, he was a blithering idiot.

Somewhere in the distance, glass shattered. He halted in his paces, turning an ear toward the sound. From the same direction, he heard a wallop, followed by a coarse shout.

Ash frowned. Then he started into motion, following the sounds in brisk strides. Walking stick at the ready.

Whatever the trouble, it wasn't his concern.

But it might prove a welcome distraction.

Chapter Eight

The next morning, Emma took herself to the morning room. It seemed the expected thing. When she entered the sun-washed space, her gaze skipped over the tasseled upholstery and vases of flowers and went straight to the humblest furnishing in the room: an escritoire.

Perfect.

She had letters to write.

She sat at the writing desk, pulled out a sheet of paper, unstoppered the ink, and dipped the quill.

Her first priority was sending a note to reassure Miss Palmer, but Emma wasn't certain how to do so. A message delivered from Ashbury House would raise eyebrows. No one even knew a Duchess of Ashbury existed yet. It wouldn't be wise to call at the Palmer residence, either. Emma was merely a seamstress in their eyes. Once word got about that the duke had married, perhaps, but for now . . .

Fanny. Yes. She would write a note and send it

in care of Fanny, asking her pass it along when Miss Palmer returned to the shop.

That accomplished, Emma turned her attention to another letter.

One that was six years overdue.

Dear Father,

It has been much too long since we've spoken.

But had been too long? Really? Her difficulty in penning this letter suggested it might be too soon.

Dear Father,

I hope this letter finds you in good health.

She stared at the sentence. As many times as she'd wished him to suffer boils, she wasn't certain that was accurate, either.

Emma crumpled the sheet of paper and tried once more. Apparently polite salutations weren't going to serve.

Father,

Do you recall the last time we saw one another? If not, permit me to remind you. You cast me out into a storm, barred me from my home, and told me no respectable man would ever want me. Well, it is my cold pleasure to inform you now, sir—you were gravely mistaken. Someone wanted me after all, and that someone is a duke.

But then . . . once again, she doubted. *Did* the duke truly want her? They'd agreed to a marriage of convenience, no more. For him, bedding her was a means to an end.

Her thoughts returned to their disastrous attempt at consummation the previous night. Perfunctory as the act was intended to be, and all his "rules" notwithstanding, his caresses were tender, patient. His hands told an entirely different story than his gruff, cynical words, and she couldn't help but respond.

She'd been alone so long, isolated and untouched.

Waiting.

He'd awakened her desires. And yet, the moment she'd surrendered to them . . . he'd stopped. As if he'd been shocked by her response, or even displeased with it.

Perhaps he didn't want her, after all. Or more to the point, perhaps he didn't want a freely passionate wife, and that would only affirm her father's judgment.

No decent man will have you.

Devastating.

Yes, their relationship was a convenient agreement. Yes, she'd resolved to keep her reckless, foolish heart uninvolved. Still, she craved a bit of closeness. Though she'd scraped by on her own for years, she was starved for human connection.

And now she'd tethered herself, for the remainder of her life, to a man unwilling to connect with anyone. She felt more alone than ever.

Don't be maudlin, Emma. It was only one night. A bit of awkwardness was to be expected. Surely it would improve with time.

A flurry of odd noises saved her from wallowing in self-pity. Emma rose from the writing desk. The cat had probably found a divan or chaise to claw to shreds. That might be a blessing in disguise if he had. Replacing the upholstery would give her a project to undertake.

As she followed the sounds, however, they sounded less and less likely to be feline. Soft thwacking and muffled grunting emanated from behind a set of imposing double doors.

She approached in soft footsteps and placed her ear to the door.

"Really, Khan." The duke's voice. "Try to muster a bit of effort."

"I am attempting to do so, Your Grace."

"Then muster harder. It's your turn to receive."

Emma pushed the door open a few inches and peered inside. She discovered a grand, open space, floored with inlaid parquet and bordered by walls hung with life-sized portraits. Capping off the opulence, elaborate scrollwork and chandeliers decorated the ceiling.

And across the middle of this majestic ballroom was strung a sort of crude netting. Two men—the duke and his butler—faced off on either side of it.

The duke swung a racquet, sending a plumed cork sailing over the net.

Khan, having caught sight of Emma, paid it no notice—with the result that the shuttlecock bounced directly off his forehead.

"Oh, come *on*." The duke shook his racquet in accusation. "I all but sealed and posted you that one."

Khan ignored his employer, opting to bow in Emma's direction instead. "Good morning, Your Grace."

The duke whipped around, still holding his racquet at a threatening angle. He swept a glance over her. "You."

Be still her heart. What a salutation.

She moved into the room. "I thought you were joking about the badminton."

"I wasn't."

"So I see."

After a pause, he waved her toward the doors. "Well? You must have things to do. Take breakfast. Confer with the housekeeper, now that you're mistress of the place. Do something ridiculous with your hair."

"I've accomplished the first and second, and I will politely decline the third. I'm out of occupations at the moment."

"Wonderful," Khan interjected, striding toward her. "You can take over this one." He pressed his racquet into Emma's hand. Before making for the door, he mouthed two words. *Save. Me.*

"Where do you think you're going?" the duke demanded.

The butler turned in the doorway. "I'm not certain, Your Grace. Perhaps I'll do something ridiculous with my hair."

He bowed, closed the double doors, and was gone.

The duke bellowed after him. "I'll dock your wages for this, you milk-livered cullion."

In the ensuing quiet, Emma regarded the racquet in her hand. "Khan doesn't seem to enjoy badminton."

"He enjoys steady employment. We have sport three times a week. A man needs to keep up his stamina somehow."

Stamina. Yes. Just looking at the duke, it was plain to see that he'd been an active man, long before his injury. Those shoulders and thighs could not have developed overnight. As he bent to retrieve the shuttlecock, she admired the tight contour of his backside. That didn't come from idleness, either.

He stood, and she quickly averted her gaze.

Drat.

Again, she'd been caught staring. Again, he would misinterpret it entirely.

It wasn't her fault, Emma told herself, but simply an occupational habit. Knowing fabric and thread was only part of a seamstress's work. Key to success was understanding the body beneath the garments. How joints fit together; how muscles flexed and stretched. After years of practice, Emma only had to glance at a person to imagine them stripped of all clothing—and when regarding a person so finely formed by God and honed by exertion, the temptation proved difficult to resist.

But how did one say such a thing?

My apologies. I wasn't staring out of horror. I was merely undressing you in my mind.

Oh, that would go brilliantly. Very duchess-like, that.

When the duke finished setting aside the equipment, he reached for his topcoat.

"We . . ." Emma forced herself to say it. "We could play. The two of us. You and I."

He stared at her in disbelief.

He respects those who challenge him, she reminded herself. Although, at the moment, the piercing quality of his gaze didn't strike her as admiration.

But Emma was in for the penny now. She may as well try for the pound.

"I adore badminton." She attempted to twirl the racquet in a casual, sporty fashion. Instead she dropped it, and it bounced off her toe. She bit her lip, holding back a yelp of pain. "Whoops. How careless of me."

She picked up the racquet with as much dignity as she could manage and limped to the other side of the ballroom, ducking under the net.

She gave him a game smile. "Shall we?"

"Very well. Let's wager on it."

"If you like. What is the forfeit?"

Now Emma's interest was piqued. Weren't the forfeits in these wagers typically naughty? A kiss, perhaps, or two minutes locked in the closet.

"When I win, you agree to leave me be. I've already conceded dinners, and further interruptions are unwelcome. I have a dukedom to manage."

Well, and badminton to play, it would seem—which apparently outranked his wife in his leisure-time priorities.

"Fine," she said, feeling testy. "But if I win, you agree to treat me with a modicum of respect."

"Oh, come now. I already give you a *modicum*."

"More than a modicum, then." Emma considered. "How much *is* a modicum, anyway?"

"Somewhere between a soupçon and a whit, I imagine."

"Then I want an ounce."

"An ounce?"

"Two ounces. Actually, no. I should like a full pint of respect."

He shook his head. "Now you're just being greedy."

"*Greedy?* I realize I may not be as captivating as a shuttlecock or a decanter of brandy, but I am your wife. The woman who is to be the mother of your child."

After a pause, he said, "There's no purpose in arguing the point. You're not going to win."

That's what you think.

She might not win this silly game, but she was determined to triumph eventually. The battle began here and now.

He retrieved his racquet and a shuttlecock, took his position on the court, and, with a flick of his wrist, sent the shuttlecock sailing over Emma's head before she could even move.

"Well done," she said. "One point to you."

"That wasn't even a serve. I was merely lobbing you the shuttlecock. First service should be the lady's. There's your modicum."

"But of course. Thank you, darling." With an awkward swipe of the racquet, she managed to send the shuttlecock flying . . . straight into the net.

This time, he was the one to stand still in the center of the court. "What did you call me?"

"I called you 'darling.' We discussed at dinner yesterday that I must call you something. I refuse to address you as Ashbury or Duke, and you didn't like 'dear husband' or 'sweeting' or 'heart.'" She motioned toward the shuttlecock lying on the floor. "I believe it's your turn, darling."

"I am no one's darling." He batted the shuttlecock with a fierce backhand swat.

To her surprise, Emma managed to scramble under the falling missile and return it. "I don't know if you have a say in that."

"I'm a duke. I have a say in everything."

Another effortless return on his part; another ungainly, desperate swipe on hers. This time, she missed.

"Darling is in the eye of the beholder." Emma was already a bit out of breath as she retrieved the dropped shuttlecock. "If I choose to make a darling of you, there is nothing you can do about it."

"Of course there's something I can do about it. I can have you sent to an institution for the feebleminded and insane."

She shrugged. "If you say so, cherub."

He leveled his racquet at her. "Let's set something straight, the two of us. You seem to be plotting a campaign of kindness. No doubt with the aim of soothing my tortured soul. It would be a waste of time. My temperament was not created by injury; it will not be magically healed by sweetness or pet names. Am I making myself clear? Do not harbor any illusions that my scars transformed me into a jaded, ill-tempered wretch. I was always—and shall remain—a jaded, ill-tempered wretch."

"Were you always this long-winded, too?"

He growled.

Emma's next attempt at a serve skittered across the floor. No matter. She was enjoying this game anyway.

"Ashbury is my title. It is what I've been called since my father died. No one calls me anything else. I've told you this."

"And as I told *you*, I am your wife. Being the only one who addresses you differently is rather the point."

Speaking of points, Emma had lost count of how many points she was behind.

He sent a serve back toward her. Emma noticed a hitch in his swing. He winced ever so slightly. Perhaps the reason behind the thrice-weekly sport was not mere boredom, but restoring the use of an injured arm. If so, his wounds must extend beyond his visible scars.

She wondered how severe those wounds were. She wondered how much they still pained him.

Too much wondering. It wouldn't all fit in her brain. Instead, it traveled down to her chest and tightened there.

She smiled. "Shall we continue, poppet?"

His glare in response could have shattered marble.

After a few minutes' practice, Emma's agility had improved. She could hold her side of a respectable volley.

"What about 'precious'?" she suggested.

"No."

"'Angel'?"

"God, no."

"'Muffin'?"

In response to that, he hit the shuttlecock so hard, it sailed all the way to the back wall and thwacked one of his ancestors right in the powdered wig.

She cheered. "Well done, my precious angel muffin."

"This stops," he said. "*Now.*"

Ignoring his outburst, Emma retrieved the shuttlecock. She served, barely managing to scrape it over the net. "I warn you, I don't give up."

"I warn *you*, I am more stubborn by far."

"I left home at sixteen."

"Orphaned at eleven," he replied, sounding bored.

"I walked to London by myself. In the snow."

"I marched a regiment to Waterloo."

"I had to make a new life on my own. Begging for work. Stitching my fingers to nubs." She dashed across the ballroom, rescuing the shuttlecock just before it hit the floor. Her swing sent it rocketing upward, almost to the ceiling.

He stood beneath the bundle of cork and feathers, waiting on it to swirl back to earth. "A rocket exploded in my face. I spent months near death. The scars left me a living monster. I quit opium by sheer force of will. My intended bride turned from me in revulsion. I'm still here." He struck the shuttlecock, driving it into the parquet at her feet. "I win."

She put a hand to her side, struggling to breathe. "Very well. You win."

Emma felt chastened, and a bit ashamed. She'd been brave when she left home. People she held dear had turned from her, too. But the courage she'd been forced to summon couldn't match that of a soldier in battle. As for the duke's wounds, his scars . . . Vain and shallow as Annabelle Worthing might be, her rejection had heaped insult atop injury. The broken engagement must have deeply wounded his pride, if not his heart.

She bent to pick up the shuttlecock.

"Wait." He jogged toward her, ducking under the net. "This will never be a proper match. Your volley is passable, but your serve is a disaster. Give it here, I'll show you."

Casting his own racquet aside, he plucked the shuttlecock from the floor and came to stand behind her, closing his right hand over hers where she gripped the racquet, and reaching around her with the other arm to position the shuttlecock.

She was in his embrace.

However unbelievably, for a couple who'd been engaged for a week, wed a full day and a night, and come within inches of consummating their union . . . this was the first time he'd held her in his arms.

All at once, the ballroom became a glasshouse— one filled with a steamy, intimate heat that amplified every sound, every scent. Sweat beaded at the nape of her neck, and she was deeply conscious of each wisp and strand of her hair that had tumbled free.

Mostly, though, she was aware of him. The wall of his chest against her back, and the strength of his arms around her. The soap and sandalwood scent she was coming to recognize. She stared at his hand. Last night, in the dark, those sure, confident fingers . . . they had been *inside* her.

"Hold it this way." He shifted her grip on the racquet handle. "Better."

A small vibration of joy went through her. Two curt syllables of praise from him, and her heart thrummed like a dragonfly's wings.

Don't, she bid it. *Don't you dare.*

Her heart didn't listen to her—but then, it never did.

Chapter Nine

This was the stupidest thing Ash had done in . . . at least twelve hours.

Between his walk last night and the sport this morning, he'd only just managed to push the thought of Emma from his mind. Now here he was again, right up against her, teetering on the edge of lust.

It wasn't only desire tearing through him, however. There was seething anger, too.

Who was the villain who'd hurt her?

Someone must have hurt her, to send her fleeing her home for London at the age of sixteen, alone and penniless. Ash wanted to hurt that someone back. With something sharp. And deadly. He was hardly an empathetic man, but he was offended indeed when someone dared to threaten anyone in his protection.

And Emma was now in his protection.

Hell, she was in his arms.

Standing this way, with the top of her head tucked under his chin, he felt like a battered, scuffed-up case made to hold something delicate and lovely.

He could also see straight down her frock.

"It's all in the timing," he said. "You can't release it and hit it at the same time. Wait a beat, then swing." He demonstrated, dropping the shuttlecock in front of her racquet, then guiding her arm to give it a sound thwack. "See?"

"I think so."

"Then give it a go."

He stepped back, giving her the space to attempt it for herself. She bit her lip, and her brow pinched with concentration. Then she released, waited, swung—and succeeded in an almost respectable serve. The thing got over the net, at least.

To watch her, though, one would think she'd claimed a ten-guinea prize. Ash wished he could feel as joyful about anything as she felt about hitting a shuttlecock. She bounced in triumph and turned to him with eyes lit up like . . . like a pleasure garden, or an opera house, or a royal ball, or some other place he would never, ever be able to take her. Damn it all.

"Well . . . ?" she prompted, clearly eager for praise.

He tilted his head, making her wait for it. "Not bad."

"Thank you." She gave him an impish smile. "That means a great deal coming from you, lambkin."

"Oh, now that is quite enough." He lunged for her.

She darted away with a shriek of laughter.

By ducking under the net, he headed off her escape. He caught her by the waist and swept her off her feet, tossing her over his good shoulder.

A mistake. The sudden motion sent pain screaming from his neck to hip. He had to pause, breathing through the fiery, wrenching ache.

"Are you well?" She added no absurd endearments to the question, and there was genuine concern in her voice.

"Fine," he said tightly.

He wasn't really fine, but sometimes the pain was worth it.

To distract himself, he entertained lewd fantasies. Ideas of laying her down on the settee, and tossing her petticoats to her ears. Or more depraved still, pressing her against the wall and trapping her there as he disappeared under her skirts. Anything to get her legs around him. Any part of him. Gripping his waist, wrapped over his hips, hooked over his shoulders . . . he wasn't particular.

As the pain dulled, he forced himself to set aside those imaginings. Oh, she would be his. But he must wait until nightfall, unwrap his Egyptian mummy from her ten blankets, and take her in apologetic silence.

He let her slide down his body, her soft curves dragging over him as she descended. The sweetest torture. She was breathing hard from the laughter and the chase, flushed with pink in all the best places.

As she looked at him, her smile faded. "You *are* in pain."

"No, I'm not."

She prodded his bad shoulder. He winced.

"It's nothing. Nothing to concern you, at any rate."

"I am your *wife*. If you're hurting, it concerns me."

Stop, he silently pleaded. *Don't do that. Don't come any closer, don't ask about my wounds, don't prod at them. Don't care.*

A better man would have been grateful for such sweet concern. And a part of him *was* grateful. A part of him wanted to fall at her feet and weep. But that bitter, scarred-over half of his soul couldn't stomach her pity. The devil in him would lash out at her in some unthinking, unforgivable way—until she was so busy licking her own wounds, she couldn't spare a thought for his.

"Is there anything I can do?" she asked.

"Yes," he said sternly. "You can let me be."

See? She looked wounded already. For her own sake, and that of the son she would bear him, he had to push her away.

But he didn't know how.

Just then—miracle of miracles—Khan had a well-timed bout of usefulness.

The butler opened the ballroom doors and cleared his throat. "Your Grace, I hate to interrupt."

Ash stepped away from his wife, relieved. "Liar. You love to interrupt."

"Surprisingly enough for us both, this time I

am being sincere. Your solicitor's secretary has arrived. I've shown him to the library." With a bow, Khan left the way he'd arrived.

Ash gestured toward the door. "I should really—"

"Go manage your dukedom," Emma finished, smoothing her frock. "Yes, I know. Leaving you alone was my forfeit."

With a nod of agreement, he quit the room.

Just as well they'd been interrupted, he told himself. Fortunate, even. This marriage wasn't about games. Pleasure wasn't the goal. And any form of affection would be disastrous.

He would bed her for a few weeks. With luck, that would be sufficient to get her with child. He would have done his duty.

And then it would be over.

THAT EVENING'S DINNER was uneventful, and Emma was thankful for it. In fact, the meal was almost too short. She found herself with a surfeit of time to while away before he would visit her.

Mary came up to brush her hair and help her change out of her one and only evening dress. After she'd gone, Emma paced the bedchamber. She stared at the clock, willing it to tick faster. The idea of reading or stitching didn't appeal— she'd never be able to concentrate. Finally, she decided she might as well prepare the room, and herself. She extinguished the candles and climbed into bed.

As she tucked herself under the quilts and blankets, she admitted the truth.

She wasn't nervous.

She was impatient.

She wanted to feel his touch again, quite desperately. Not only his touch, but his tenderness. He might be snappish and aggravating during the day, but in the darkness last night, he'd seemed an entirely different man. Patient, respectful. Sensual.

This time, Emma resolved, she wouldn't ruin it. The sooner this reproduction effort was under way, the better for all concerned.

At last, a knock at the door.

He entered without waiting for her answer.

"Tonight, this will be all business," he announced. "In. Out. Done."

Possibly the least seductive words imaginable, but Emma was apparently a madwoman, because they excited her all the same.

He did not bank the fire completely, leaving a bit of warmth and a faint amber glow. With less stumbling than last time, he joined her on the bed. He found the edge of the quilts—she'd limited herself to two tonight—and flung them back in one motion before stretching his body alongside hers. She held her breath, waiting for the first brush of exquisite contact.

"Good God," he said. "You're *naked*."

Well, this wasn't off to the most promising start.

"Why would you be naked?"

Had she heard him correctly? Had he truly just asked *why* she would be naked? How could this even be a question?

"I didn't disrobe last night only because I thought you might want to undress me."

He was silent.

"Shall I undress *you*?" she asked.

"No." And then, with a tone of resignation, "Let's just get on with it."

Oh, now that was too much to be borne. She couldn't remain silent any longer.

She pushed up on her elbow. "What am I doing wrong? Surely your previous lovers were active participants in the act."

"Yes, but they were experienced. A few of them professionals. You're a wife. You're not supposed to enjoy this, you're supposed to lie there and endure it."

"So that's what you expect from me. A silent, listless partner."

"Yes."

"Very well," she said, disheartened. "I'll try."

His hand settled on her thigh, and he nudged her legs apart with a brusque motion.

Then he paused, keeping his hand utterly still.

When he resumed touching her, everything was different.

Despite his stated resolve to be quick, and his professed displeasure at finding her naked, he seemed to have changed his mind about making this a hasty, dispassionate encounter. In fact, his entire demeanor transformed. Once again, his brusque touch became a caress. As he explored her body, he made quiet, growly sounds of approval that thrilled her to her toes.

His palm covered her breast. Racked by pleasure, she bit her lip to stifle a soft cry of joy. He kneaded and stroked the soft flesh, switching from one breast to the other and back again. Her nipples puckered, begging for attention. The lazy, teasing back-and-forth of his thumb was the sharpest, sweetest pleasure—but it wasn't enough.

Her breath quickened. She wanted him to hurry, but he took his time. His palms skimmed along her every dip and curve, painting her body hot with desire.

Most arousing of all, he began to speak.

"How is it you're here?" he murmured. Not to her, but seemingly to himself. "How the devil did I manage it?" He wove his fingers into her hair and pulled away gently, letting the locks glide through his fingers. He exhaled on a single, stirring word. "Lovely."

She reached for him, longing to touch and explore in return. She placed her hands flat against his chest, skimming over the thin lawn of his shirt.

He stiffened. "Don't."

She let her hands fall to her sides. "I—I'm sorry, I—"

Emma didn't know what to say. That brief, stolen caress was burned into her palms. In one of her hands, she balanced a memory of strong, sleek muscle beneath ironed-flat linen. On her other palm, however, a different sensation lingered. The firm ridges of scar tissue, stretching and tugging across his chest like a fiendish spider's web.

"I'm sorry," she repeated.

He turned aside, and Emma despaired. Had she discouraged him from continuing? *Again?*

Instead, he reached for a small vial of some kind. She heard the sound of it being uncorked. An exotic scent wafted in her direction, and she glimpsed him pouring a few drops into his hand. Some sort of oil, perhaps?

Her guess about the substance was proven correct. His fingers slicked over her sex without friction, stroking up and down her intimate folds. The sensations were as impossible to catch as running water, and they made her just as wet.

By the time he settled between her thighs, she was desperate for him, awash with a deep, sweet ache that she somehow knew only he could satisfy. She knew what it was to bring about her own pleasure, but she'd never been able to fill that hollowness. Not on her own.

The rigid column of his manhood connected with her belly, sliding downward on the thin sheen of oil. The feeling of his steely hardness against her aroused sex . . . it nearly undid her, there and then. She whimpered with frustrated desire, rolling her hips to seek more contact.

He froze again.

"Don't stop," she begged, breathless. "Please. I'm fine. I promise. I'm very, very, *very* fine."

He hushed her. "Don't make a move."

"Why not?"

"Because we're not alone."

Chapter Ten

*A*sh found himself staring into a pair of fire-lit eyes, glittering at him from the corner of the room. The base of his spine tingled. His heartbeat went from a gallop to a standstill.

An intruder.

How the devil had someone slipped in?

Never mind, he told himself. That question could wait. The more pressing inquiry at hand was this: How was he going to kill the bastard? He mentally ran through the available weapons in the room. The fireplace poker would be most effective, but it was out of reach. The sash of his dressing gown could make a decent garrote, in a pinch.

If needed, he'd fight hand-to-hand. His only concern was keeping Emma safe.

He rolled to the side and came to his knees, putting his body between her and the threat. "You have three seconds to leave the way you came," he ordered. "Or I vow to you, I will snap your knavish neck."

The intruder struck first, leaping forward with a fiendish yowl.

Something that felt like a dozen razor-sharp barbs pierced straight through his nightshirt, digging into his shoulder and arm. He gave a stunned shout of pain.

Emma flung back the bedclothes. "Breeches! Breeches, no!"

The *cat*?

Claws. Teeth. Hissing.

The *cat*.

Ash stumbled from the bed and whirled in a backward circle, whipping his arm to shake off the beast, all while guarding his breeding organs with the other hand. He could afford to lose a lot of bits, but not those.

From the bed, Emma shouted and pleaded with the hellish creature, to no avail. She heaved a pillow, which hit Ash in the face and did nothing to dislodge the demon she'd brought into his house. His next lashing attempt cleared the dressing table of anything that could break into tiny shards, as his bare feet quickly learned. He flung himself against the bedpost repeatedly, trying to startle the thing into letting go. Didn't work. The cat only clung to his shirt—and flesh—like a burr. A yowling burr with teeth.

Ash was ready to plunge his arm, cat and all, into the fire—what were a few more burns, after all—but burning fur was a disgusting scent, and he was just decent enough to balk at the idea of murdering Emma's pet before her very eyes.

No, he would take it out into the garden tomorrow and murder it there.

At the moment, however, he just needed the cursed thing *off*.

Leaving his groin unprotected, he reached around, grabbed the cat by its scruff, and shook both of his arms until he had it free. The little devil hit the ground running and disappeared into the shadows. Never to come back, if it knew what was good for it.

Ash checked the family heirlooms. All still present and apparently unscathed, but both bob and bits had pulled so far up into his body, there would be no coaxing them back out tonight. Not for all the tits in Covent Garden.

That was that. He would be taking another long, frustrated walk tonight.

"Are you bleeding?" Emma asked.

"Only in about twenty places." He touched his shoulder, wincing. His fingers came away wet. "The fly-bitten measle."

She fell back onto the bed with a pitiable sigh. "I'm so sorry. I had no idea he was even in the room."

"Mark my words," Ash said grimly. "Tomorrow night, he will not be."

"DID YOU TRULY marry the Duke of Ashbury?" Davina Palmer laced her arm through Emma's, drawing close enough to whisper as they strolled through the park. "If you don't mind me asking . . . How did that happen?"

Emma laughed a bit. "I don't mind at all. I've been asking myself the same question. Hourly."

She drew Miss Palmer away from the crowded path. Too great a risk of being overheard. As they circled a pond flecked with ducks, Emma related a brief version of the tale. Miss Worthing's gown. The duke's pressing need for a wife. His strange proposal, now merely a week past, and their hasty wedding.

"As shocking as it was, I couldn't refuse him."

"Refuse a duke? Of course not. No woman in England would, I wager."

One woman in England had done so. Social-climbing Miss Worthing, of all ladies, had declined Ashbury's hand. The more Emma ruminated on it, the less sense it made.

But that wasn't the question of the day.

"If only I had your good sense, Emma." Davina's voice quivered. "What an idiot I was to land in such a situation."

"You were *not* an idiot."

"I still don't understand how it could have happened. I took every precaution against conceiving."

Emma lowered her voice. "Do you mean the gentlemen withdrew, before he . . . finished the act?"

"No."

"A sponge, then."

"A sponge? What would I do with a sponge?"

"So he wore a French letter?"

Davina gave her a blank look. "What's that?"

Emma was nonplussed. "Precisely what precautions *did* you take?"

"All the usual ones. After it was done, I jumped up and down for ten minutes. Sniffed pepper to make myself sneeze three times, and drank a full teacup of vinegar. I did *everything* right."

Emma pressed her lips together. If this was Davina's idea of contraception, perhaps the girl was just a *little* bit of an idiot. Nevertheless, she shouldn't pay for one mistake for the rest of her life.

"The important thing is that you have a friend in me. To start, I've drawn up some patterns for your wardrobe, to conceal the fact that you're increasing. I'll have Fanny send word when they're ready. Beyond that . . ." Emma took the girl's arm, drawing her close as they walked. "The duke says I'm to have a house of my own in Oxfordshire. I'll invite you for a nice long visit." Assuming, of course, that Emma could travel there herself. "You can stay with me in the country until you've given birth."

"Are you certain the duke won't object?"

"He won't even know. It's a marriage of convenience. All he needs is an heir. Once I'm with child, he will want nothing to do with me." Emma smiled. "We will be a pair, the two of us. Sitting with our swollen ankles propped on the tea table, gorging ourselves on sweetmeats and knitting tiny caps."

"Oh, it sounds perfect. But what will happen afterward?"

"That will be your decision. But if you're set on finding a family to take the child in, perhaps we might find one nearby. Then you could visit whenever you liked. Our children could play together."

Davina clasped Emma's wrist. "I can't believe you would do this for me."

"It's no imposition. You can't know how happy it makes me to help you this way."

"Oh, but I shall need Papa's permission first. That's the only snag."

"Surely he wouldn't deny you the chance to visit a duchess."

"Well . . ." Davina looked hesitant. "It's merely that—"

"I'm not the usual sort of duchess," Emma finished. And for that matter, her husband wasn't the usual sort of duke. He hadn't been seen publicly in years, and then he'd wed a seamstress.

"There will be a certain amount of curiosity," Davina said.

Curiosity. What a charitable way of saying gossip.

Emma knew the unkind things ladies said about one another. In the dressmaking shop, they'd spoken in front of her as though she didn't exist.

"But surely the duke will expose you to society," Davina said. "He'll *have* to introduce you at court. From there, simply ask him to take you to balls and the opera and dinners."

Hah. To be sure, Emma could simply ask him. And he would simply say no.

This plan of hers was becoming more and more complicated. In order to help Davina she must either get pregnant immediately—which fate and felines were conspiring to prevent—or convince the duke to allow her a holiday despite it. Meanwhile, she must make herself a respectable duchess in the eyes of the *ton*, so that Mr. Palmer would allow his daughter to join her.

It all felt rather hopeless.

"What if your father won't grant you permission?" she asked.

"I suppose I shall be forced to run away," Davina said softly. "I'm the only child, and Papa wants me to marry a well-placed gentleman who can take over his business affairs. If I'm ruined, his plans will be ruined, too. Can you understand?"

"Yes. I can."

Emma understood perfectly. She, too, had adored her father. But when she'd needed him most, he'd chosen to protect appearances rather than protecting her.

She refused to let the poor girl face this alone. Though Emma's own situation had been different, it had felt no less dire. She still carried the cruel reminders: Some were visible, while others lurked deep inside. There was no way to erase the pain in her past, but she had a chance to save this young woman's future.

No matter what it took, she would find a way.

And her best strategy, at the moment, was to go home and entice—or drag, if need be—her husband to her bed.

"YOUR GRACE, WOULD you describe yourself as clumsy?" Mary asked the question as she arranged Emma's hair for dinner.

"No," Emma answered. "Not particularly."

"Oh, that's too bad."

"Why is it too bad?"

"Well, I was thinking . . . what if you tripped, and the duke had to catch you? That would surely encourage his affection. Or spill wine on your dress, and he would whip off his cravat to mop it up." Before Emma could respond, Mary perked with another idea. "Ooh, you might even turn your ankle. Then he would have to carry you. *That* would be romantic."

"I'm not going to turn my ankle."

"You don't think you could try? Even just a little stumble?"

"No."

"Never mind it. We'll think of something else. I was pondering, what if you went up to the attic . . . and then Mr. Khan sent the duke up to the attic . . . and then you and the duke were locked *inside* the attic, together. Accidentally."

"*Mary*. You need to abandon these ideas. The duke is not going to fall in love with me—not even in a locked attic. In fact, he's rather put out with me at the moment."

Or at least he was put out with her cat.

With a sigh, Mary put the last pin in Emma's hair. "There, now. Turn and let me have a look at you."

After looking Emma over, Mary reached forward and grasped the sleeves of her gown, slid them off her shoulders, and tugged the bodice down so far, it barely covered her areolae. "That's something, at least."

When Emma arrived in the dining room, the duke wasn't even there to angle for a glimpse of her areolae. She waited a quarter hour. Nothing.

He must truly be infuriated with her. Perhaps she wouldn't see him later tonight, either. At this rate, they would never accomplish procreation.

She prepared to return to her rooms, planning to ring the maid for a dinner tray and sink into bed with a novel. As she passed down the corridor, however, someone called to her in a low whisper.

"In here."

She turned, curious. The duke was in his library, barefoot and sitting cross-legged on the carpet, staring at the empty, unlit fireplace.

"What are you doing?"

"Shh." He raised an open palm in her direction. "No sudden movements."

"All right." She drew out the words, kicking off her slippers and making her way into the room on stocking feet, sitting next to him on the floor. She folded her legs beneath her skirts and stared into the fireplace, too. "What are we looking at?" she whispered.

"Your cat. The little beast is hiding behind the grate. We've been waiting one another out."

Emma peered into the dark fireplace. Yes, she could just make out a set of green eyes gleaming back at her from the sooty recesses of the hearth.

"How long have you been here?" she whispered.

"What time is it now?"

"Half seven."

"Four hours, then."

"Four hours? And how long do you plan to stay like this?"

He set his jaw and glowered at the fireplace. "As long as it takes."

She noted an open trunk sitting on the opposite side of him. Two thick leather straps with buckles lay at the ready.

She gasped. "You're going to lock Breeches in a *trunk?*"

"For the night, yes. Doors don't seem to contain the beast."

"With no food, no water?"

"I made air holes. And believe me, he's fortunate to get that much."

"But . . . why?"

"Is it not obvious?" For the first time since she'd entered the library, he slid a glance toward her. "Because I intend to impregnate you tonight, or make a valiant attempt at it. And this time, there will be no interruption."

He turned back to regarding the grate.

"Oh." Emma bit her lip, trying to ignore the hot flush creeping from her neck to her hairline.

"Were you terribly hurt last night? Are you furious with me?"

"I don't know that I can ever forgive you," he said in a dry tone. "I'm going to have a scar."

She paused a moment, then laughed.

The corner of his mouth quirked with a smug little smile. He was pleased with himself for having provoked her to laughter. Emma was pleased, as well. When he wasn't using that sharp wit to slice her to ribbons, he had a rather charming sense of humor.

"I'll be back," she said, drawing to her feet.

A quarter hour later, she returned with a tray of sandwiches, two glasses, and an uncorked bottle of wine.

"Here." She offered him a roast beef sandwich. "To keep up your stamina."

He accepted it and took a large, manly bite.

"No progress?" She bit the corner from an egg-and-cress sandwich.

He shook his head. "Where did you acquire this pestilent, mewling jackanapes?"

"Where did *you* acquire the habit of cursing with such imagination?"

He reached for another sandwich. "For that, you can thank my father. The summer I was nine, my mother overheard me utter some foul words I'd learned at school. My father drew me aside and told me, in no uncertain terms, that I was an educated gentleman and he *never* wanted to hear me use such crude language again. He said, 'Blaspheme as you will, but at least use words from Shakespeare.' I'd read all the plays by the summer's end."

"Quite ingenious of him."

"He was a wise man. A good man. I may not be a wise or good man, but I at least possess a sense of duty. His legacy, and everything and everyone he protected, has fallen to me. I won't let that wither and die."

"And you still draw your curses from Shakespeare."

"I try, in speech at least, as a way to honor his memory. I cannot claim my thoughts are always so literary in their inspiration."

Emma let the quiet abide for a moment. "You must miss him a great deal. And to lose him so young. How did it—" She broke off the question. Perhaps she was delving too deep.

"A fever took them both. I was away at school."

"Oh, dear." She inched a bit closer. "That must have been terrible."

"I'm glad I wasn't there to see them ill. They'll always be strong in my memory that way. Likewise, I'm grateful they never had to see me after I was . . . you know. Like this."

She gathered his meaning, but she didn't believe he was sincere. Having a loving family around him would have made all the difference.

He downed a large swallow of wine, then glanced toward her. "What about your parents? You mentioned leaving home for London at a tender age. What was that about?"

She chewed a bite slowly. "The usual. Strict discipline. Youthful rebellion. Words exchanged that couldn't be taken back."

"That," he said, "was not an answer."

"Yes, it was. You asked a question. I replied. With words and everything."

"I gave you details. Ages, events . . . *feelings*. I cracked open my soul."

She gave him a disbelieving look.

"All right, fine. I don't have a soul. But the point remains. You can be more specific than *that*."

"It's a boring story, truly." Before he could object, she withdrew a clipped bit of newsprint from her pocket. "Now *this* is an interesting story. 'Cloaked Monster Menaces Mayfair.'"

He paused. "Sounds ridiculous."

"I thought it sounded exciting." She cleared her throat and read aloud. "'For the second time in as many weeks, a chilling specter has wrought mayhem and terror in the most un-likely of neighborhoods: Mayfair. The ghoul is described as a tall, narrow figure clad all in black, with fine boots and a beaver hat pulled down to meet the upturned collar of his cloak. This reporter interviewed a well-shaken fellow who attested to seeing the caped monster in St. James Park this Thursday past. Only yesternight, witnesses residing near Shepherd Market tell of a demon with hideous face and a twisted snarl roaming the alleyways. The apparition threat-ened no fewer than a dozen souls—among them, three innocent boys—before disappearing into the night. Mothers are advised to clutch their children close, lest the Monster of Mayfair strike again.'" She lowered the paper. "Well?"

"Sensationalist rubbish."

"I thought the writing was evocative." Emma folded the clipping leisurely and tucked it away. "Any ideas who this 'monster' might be?"

He was silent.

"It's quite a coincidence. Because we were in St. James Park last week. And you do happen to have a tall hat and black cloak. But of course you wouldn't go around terrorizing innocent boys."

He gave in with a huff. "Innocent boys, my eye. The brats knocked over a flower seller for her pennies. They deserved whatever they got."

She smiled. "Do you know, I suspected you were a good man, deep down. Even if very, very, very deep down. In a fathomless cavern. Underneath a volcano."

There was more to him than she'd suspected. More than anyone suspected, perhaps. Humor, patience, passion. She found it all distressingly attractive.

Come along then, Breeches.

At last, there was a stirring in the dark corner behind the grate.

"Hush now." He pinched the corner from a salmon sandwich and leaned forward, holding it out until it was close enough to provide an irresistible feline temptation. "Come on then, you odious, mewling bugbear," he crooned. "I have your dinner."

With a steady stream of low, deceptively tender insults, he drew the cat out from the fireplace. Emma remained absolutely still, so as not to startle the creature.

"That's it," he whispered, drawing his hand closer to his lap. Reeling the cat in like a fish on the line. At last, he allowed Breeches to catch the bait. The starving cat attacked the sandwich in ravenous bites. "There you are, then."

He had the little beast eating out of his hand.

Monster of Mayfair, indeed.

While Breeches ate from one hand, he reached out with the other—grabbing the cat by the scruff. He scooped the creature up, placed both cat and sandwich in the trunk, and latched it tight. Breeches didn't even make a complaint.

Then he stood and dusted his hands before offering Emma assistance in rising to her feet.

"Now," he said. "I am going to ring for a footman to clear this tray and place the cat under lock, key, bolt, and guard. Then I'm going to go upstairs, find a fresh shirt, and rinse the soot from my hands. In all, I estimate that will occupy three minutes." His intense eyes caught hers. "That's how much time you have."

"How much time to what?"

"To make ready. Before I come to your room and pin you flat against the bed."

"Oh."

He leisurely strolled over to ring the bell. "Make haste, Emma. You're down to two and a half minutes now."

Emma swallowed hard.

Then she turned and ran.

Chapter Eleven

*E*mma didn't bother to retrieve her slippers. She dashed on stocking feet for the staircase, gathering her skirts in both hands to lift them out of the way.

When she reached her suite, she chased away the maid and went directly to the bedchamber. As she rushed, she tugged at the buttons of her frock with one hand and went about snuffing candles with the licked fingertips of her other, leaving only the dim firelight. She still didn't see any reason for darkness, but she didn't wish to waste time arguing.

Not tonight.

She'd barely succeeded in loosening her bodice when he opened the door.

No knock. No greeting. He was true to his word.

He strode to her, put his hands on her waist, lifted her off her feet, and tossed her onto the bed.

Her breath left her. When the capability returned to her hands, she fumbled to find her buttons and continue disrobing.

"Don't bother," he said, in a gruff, commanding voice.

Very well, then.

She never would have guessed she'd find this curt, brutish treatment arousing . . . but she did. Oh, she did. He *was* capable of patience and tenderness. He'd demonstrated as much downstairs with the cat. The knowledge made her feel safe, even if he overwhelmed her now. Besides, she knew from experience, he'd stop the moment she expressed the slightest discomfort.

She didn't want him to stop.

He stood at the foot of the bed, a dark silhouette, wrestling with the closures of his falls, then shucking his trousers.

She was panting with arousal by the time he joined her on the bed.

He straddled her hips and pulled at her bodice, tugging it down. She heard a seam rip. No matter; she could mend it tomorrow. Before she'd finished deciding if she had the right color of thread, he had her breasts bared and his hands fitted over them, kneading and stroking. Desire shivered over her skin. Her nipples tightened, and he found them with his thumbs. As he rolled and pressed the sensitive peaks, she writhed under his expert teasing.

"You like this." Half smug statement, half question.

She nodded, then realized he might not be able to see the gesture. "Yes."

"And this?"

He pinched her nipple, and she had to chase after her thoughts before she was able to reply. "Yes."

"Just making certain. Before I do this."

"Do what?"

He cupped one of her breasts and lifted it. She felt a cool swipe across her nipple.

He'd *licked* her.

She jolted with the keenness of the sensation. "I thought you had a rule," she gasped. "No kissing."

"This isn't kissing. It's licking." Another gliding caress—warm this time—swirling in terrible, wonderful circles. "And sucking." He pulled her nipple into his mouth, drawing on her with no mercy.

She cried out and bucked. She reached instinctively to grip his shoulders, remembering too late he didn't wish to be touched.

He sat up, caught her hands, and pushed them back against the mattress on either side of her head. "We discussed this."

"I know. I'm sorry, I forgot. I can't think when you touch me that way. Or when you touch me *this* way, for that matter."

The commanding way in which he gripped her arms only pitched her excitement higher. The pulses of her wrists thumped wildly beneath his palms, and her heartbeat was a clamor in her ears.

"Don't forget it again," he said in a low, thrilling voice. "Or I'll be forced to tie you to the bed."

At the suggestion, her intimate muscles fluttered. "Is that meant to be a threat? Because I . . . I don't seem to find the idea entirely objectionable."

"You don't?"

She licked her bottom lip. "Well, you're very good at this, apparently. And what with the dark . . . It's all very shadowy and sensual. Like one of those feverish dreams one has on a hot summer's night."

"This is something you'd dream about. Being pawed by a hulking stranger in the dark."

Emma squeaked out her tentative reply. "Maybe?"

Unbearable moments passed in silence.

"You are incredible."

Whether he meant that as a compliment or censure, she didn't know. She didn't have a chance to ask. He released her wrists and moved between her legs, shoving her skirt and petticoat to her waist.

Rubbing his fingers up and down her sex, he made a sound of approval. "Wet for me already."

The heel of his hand pressed against her mound. Emma tried her best to remain still. It wasn't easy. But if he stopped now, she would expire of frustration. His fingers penetrated her, stroking deep. Oh, God. Perhaps she would expire not of frustration, but of bliss.

Instead of shifting his weight to move atop

her, he lowered himself onto one elbow. She felt his tongue again. Not on her nipple this time.

There.

She couldn't help it now. Her body convulsed with pleasure, arching and twisting beneath his mouth. He licked her over and over, spinning her into new landscapes of arousal with languid strokes of his tongue. All the while, he kept up rhythmic thrusts with his fingers, hitting a place deep inside her that made her clutch the bed linens in her fists.

Emma didn't know how much more she could take. But even if she wished to beg him for mercy, what would she cry out? Duke? Ashbury? No. She refused. Intimate moments called for intimate address, and she feared his wrath if she tried "dear" or "darling" or "precious angel muffin" instead.

No, there would be no begging for mercy. She surrendered to the pleasure, letting him nudge her closer and closer to the brink of madness with each flick of his tongue.

She whispered, "Don't stop."

DON'T STOP.

As if she needed to tell him so.

Ash would not have stopped for anything. Never mind a feral cat. The royal menagerie could crash down the chimney, and he would not have lifted his head from his task.

She was so close. He could feel it. He could

taste it. And as badly as she needed to come, he needed her to come even more.

Bringing a woman to orgasm had always been a particular pleasure for him. With most women he'd known, even if no deep affection was involved, a climax required a bit more than a skilled tongue and fingers. It took closeness, trust. Intimacy. Feeling a woman come beneath his hand, his mouth, his body—well, it made him feel like king of the planet, of course—but it also made him feel connected. Human.

Now he was a monster.

Look, it even said so in the *Prattler.*

Ash had expected—he'd feared, to put a finer point on it—that he'd never know a woman's intimate trust again. Not this way. What woman would allow this scarred, repulsive face between her thighs?

Emma would, apparently. Whether that labeled her a lunatic or a fool, he would decide later. She was likely both. He'd convinced her to marry him, after all.

Then she arched her hips and began to ride his tongue in a halting rhythm, chasing her own bliss. The unbearable sweetness made him moan. His already hard cock pulsed with impatience.

Now. By the gods, let it be now.

She gasped, her full body tensing as the pleasure took her. The wet heat of her sex squeezed his fingers. He savored each shudder, each soft, lovely sigh.

When her body relaxed, he slid his hand free and stroked her silky essence over his cock. She parted her thighs, and he knelt between them, hooking her legs over his hips. Taking himself in hand, he placed the broad crown of his erection where it needed to be, tensed his thighs . . . and pushed.

Then he was in her. And in her. And God, so exquisitely *deep* in her—and still he wanted more.

He couldn't help but groan.

He began to thrust in earnest, working himself further and further into that narrow tunnel of heat. He hoped she'd experienced the worst of her discomfort last night, because gentleness was beyond him now. He thrust with purpose, determined to get at the very heart of her and feel her body sheathing him whole. She made a bridge of her body, lifting her hips to connect his pelvis to hers.

"That's it," he whispered between shaky breaths. "Just like that."

He worked both hands beneath her bottom and lifted it, tilting her hips. Her body yielded to him a fraction more, and he sank home.

Perfect. So perfect.

Still on his knees, he held her by the hips and thrust faster. With the help of the dim firelight, he could just make out the taut globes of her breasts, rolling with his every stroke. God, how he wanted to see those breasts in full daylight. The nipples alone. He'd learn their color; trace their shape with his fingers, then his tongue. Nuzzle and feel the softness against his cheek.

But as much as he wished to *see* them, Ash had

to admit that picturing them . . . It was working, too. Really, really *working*. It threw him back to his youth, when he'd made do with nothing but a hand and his imagination. Except this *wasn't* his callused hand, and his imagination had never been anywhere near this good. This lover wasn't a fantasy, but real. She had shape and heat and scent.

She had a name.

"Emma."

When he called to her, her body tightened deliciously around his cock.

So he did it again.

"Emma." The pleasure was keen, slicing through him like a knife. He gritted his teeth. *"Emma."*

Words were beyond him after that. He squeezed her plump little bottom in both hands and took her hard and fast, relentless in his race to the peak.

And then he came. He came *hard*, spending into her with fierce joy. His hips jerked with each wrenching spasm. The climax seemed to go on and on, approaching forever. And yet it wasn't nearly enough.

He collapsed on the bed beside her, weakened and emptied. If he'd known taking a wife would be like this, he would have married ages ago.

Of course, marrying ages ago would have meant taking a different wife. He wasn't certain wives like this one abounded.

He turned his head to face her in the dark. "Where on earth did you come from?"

She was silent for a long moment. "Hertford-shire."

He laughed, without restraint or apology.

"You really must give me something to call you," she said. "If we go on like this, I'm going to need a name to cry out, and I don't think you want it to be honeybee."

"Just try it, blossom." He sat up in bed. "But if you insist on something else, just use Ash. It's what my friends call me." *Or called me, when I still had friends.*

He reached for his trousers.

"You don't mean to leave me," she said. "After *that*?"

Her obvious satisfaction swelled his pride, but staying the night was out of the question. He was not going to allow her to wake up beside him in the full light of day, mere inches from his mangled face, let alone the wreckage that remained of his neck, chest, shoulder.

Not now, not yet. Perhaps not ever.

She'd think she'd woken from a nightmare. She'd shrink from him. Run from the room. Worse had happened before. Unless she was pregnant with his child, he could not take that risk. And once she *was* pregnant, they were done.

The sooner that happened, the better.

He left her room on wobbly legs, then sank against the door.

Please be fertile, or you'll be the death of me.

Chapter Twelve

$\mathcal{W}$alking through the streets that night was a novel experience.

Forget stalking and prowling down the darkened alleyways. Tonight, Ash was all but skipping. Gamboling.

He didn't encounter any enraging specimens of human refuse.

He was no longer sexually frustrated to the point of irascibility.

He felt almost . . . human again.

He even strolled across an open square.

"Say!" someone called. "You're the Monster of Mayfair!"

And with that, Ash's lightened mood popped like a balloon. So much for feeling human.

A gangly figure jogged across the green to him. Ash pushed back the brim of his hat, revealing his face, and scowled. That always worked on the children.

For it was, in fact, a school-aged boy who'd approached him. One who'd clearly learned to curse this past Michaelmas term at school.

"I'll be damned." The boy whistled low. "You truly are as fearsome and ugly as the papers said."

"Oh, really. And do they say anything about this?" Ash brandished his walking stick. "Now go home. Your nursemaid will be missing you."

He turned and kept walking. The lad followed.

"I saw you over by Marylebone Mews," the boy called out. As if they were two old chums holding a conversation at the club. "You thrashed that gin-soused cur. The one who was beating his wife, remember?"

Yes, of course Ash remembered. It was only two days past.

"That was bloody brilliant." By now the youth was scampering alongside him. "Just capital. And I heard about the footpads in St. James's, too. All of London has."

Ash released a long, slow breath. He refused to be baited. *The more thoroughly you ignore him, the faster he'll go away,* he told himself. *Like a canker sore.*

"So where are we off to tonight?" the boy asked.

We?

Now that was too much.

Ash halted in the center of the empty square. "Just what is it you want?"

The boy scratched his ear and shrugged. "To see you thrash someone new. Give some fellow what's coming to him."

"Well, then." Ash lifted his walking stick and gave the lad a shove with the blunt end, sending him arse-first into the shrubbery. "There you have it."

SEVERAL DAYS LATER, Emma stood before a terraced house faced with white stone and corniced windows, having made the journey across Bloom Square. As short a distance as it was, she seemed to have dropped her bravery somewhere along the way.

She knew she must not indulge her nerves. She needed to start moving in society, and asking the duke to squire her about Town would be a waste of breath. If Davina wanted permission to visit her at Swanlea, Emma must form acquaintances with ladies of impeccable breeding and genteel accomplishment—not as their seamstress, but as their equal. Today was an important first step.

She looked down at the invitation and read it again.

To the new Duchess of Ashbury—

Warmest welcome to Bloom Square! Every Thursday my friends come around for tea. We'd be most delighted if you would join us.

Lady Penelope Campion

P.S. I should warn you: We're different from other ladies.

That last line gave Emma hope—and the courage to knock.

"You came!" A young woman with fair hair and rosy cheeks pulled her into the entrance hall. She'd scarcely closed the door before kissing Emma on the cheek in greeting. "I'm Penny."

"Penny?"

"Oh, yes. I should have said. I'm properly called Penelope, but the name is rather a mouthful, don't you think?"

Emma was amazed. This was Lady Penelope Campion? She opened her own door and greeted perfect strangers with kisses on the cheek? Apparently her note of invitation hadn't been an exaggeration: She truly wasn't like other ladies.

Emma curtsied, probably more deeply than a duchess would—but the habit was ingrained in her. "Delighted to make your acquaintance."

"Likewise. The others are dying to meet you."

Lady Penelope took Emma by the wrist and drew her into a parlor. The room was a jumble of unquestionably fine furnishings that seemed to have seen better days.

"This is Miss Teague," she said, swiveling Emma toward a ginger-haired young woman dusted with freckles . . . and a fine white powder that looked like flour. "Nicola lives on the southern side of the square."

"The unfashionable side," Nicola said.

"The exciting side," Lady Penny corrected. "The one with all the scandalous artists and mad scientists."

"My father was one of the latter, Your Grace."

"Don't listen to her. She's one of the latter, too."

"Thank you, Penny," Nicola said. "I think."

"And this is Miss Alexandra Mountbatten." Emma's hostess turned her to the third occupant of the salon.

Miss Mountbatten was small of stature and dressed in unremarkable gray serge, but her appearance was made stunning by virtue of her hair—an upswept knot of true black, glossy as obsidian.

"Alex sells the time," Lady Penelope stated.

Emma could not have heard that correctly. "Sells the time?"

"I earn my living setting clocks to Greenwich time," she explained, curtsying deeply. "It's an honor to make your acquaintance, Your Grace."

"Do sit down," Penny urged.

Emma obeyed, taking the offered seat—a carved chair that must have been rescued from some French chateau, if not the royal palace. The upholstery, however, had been worn to threads—even slashed in places, with tufts of batting peeking through.

A bleating sound came from somewhere toward the rear of the house.

"Oh, that's Marigold." Penny lifted the teapot. "Never mind her."

"Marigold?"

"The goat," Nicola explained.

"She's sick in love with Angus, and she's most displeased about being quarantined. She has the sniffles, you see."

"You have two goats, then?"

"Oh, no. Angus is a Highland calf. I shouldn't encourage them, but they're herd creatures. They each need a companion. Do you take milk and sugar?"

"Both, please," Emma said, a bit dazed.

Nicola took pity on her. "Penny has a soft spot for wounded animals. She takes them in, ostensibly to heal them, and then never lets them go."

"I do let them go," Penny objected. "Sometimes."

"Once," Alexandra put in. "You let one go, once. But do let's try to hold a normal conversation, just for a few minutes. Otherwise we'll frighten Her Grace away."

"Not at all," Emma assured her. "I'm happy to be here." The elegant, imposing ladies would wait for another day. "How did you know to invite me?"

"Oh, it's a small square. Everyone knows everything. The cook tells the costermonger, who tells the maid down the street . . . so on and so forth." She handed Emma a cup of tea. "They're saying you were a seamstress until only last week."

Oh, dear. Emma deflated. She supposed it was unrealistic to hope she could hide it.

Penny clasped her hands together in her lap. "Tell us everything. How did you meet? Was your courtship terribly romantic?"

"I don't know that one could call it romantic." In fact, one could call it just about anything else.

"Well, for a duke to marry a seamstress is an

extraordinary thing. It's like a fairy tale, isn't it? He must have fallen desperately in love with you."

That wasn't the truth at all, of course. But how could Emma tell them that he'd married her chiefly because hers was the first convenient womb to appear in his library?

She was saved from answering when a pincushion nestled in a nearby darning basket unfurled itself and toddled away. "Was that a hedgehog?"

Penny's voice dropped to a whisper. "Yes, but the poor dear's terribly shy. On account of her traumatic youth, you see. Do have a biscuit. Nicola made them. They're heavenly."

Emma reached for one and took a bite. She'd given up on trying to understand anything in this house. She was a barnacle on the hull of the HMS *Penelope*—she'd no idea of their destination, but she was along for the ride.

Goodness. The biscuit *was* heavenly. Buttery sweetness melted on her tongue.

"Please don't think we're mining you for gossip," Miss Mountbatten—Alexandra, was it?—said. "Penny's only curious. We wouldn't tell anyone else."

"We scarcely *talk* to anyone else," Nicola said. "We've a tight little club, the three of us."

Penny smiled and reached for Emma's hand. "With room for a fourth, of course."

"In that case . . ." Emma thoughtfully chewed her last bite of biscuit, washing it down with a swallow of tea. "May I be so bold as to ask for some advice?"

In a unanimous, unspoken *yes*, Penny, Alexandra, and Nicola leaned forward in their chairs.

"It's about . . ." She lost her nerve for honesty. "It's about my cat. I took him in from the streets, and he hasn't a proper name. Will you help me make a list of possibilities?"

Ash. That's what his friends called him, he'd said. It felt like progress to be admitted to that inner circle, but Emma wasn't certain she liked that name, either. For man who'd survived severe burns, Ash sounded ironic at best. At worst, it felt cruel.

Besides, she was having too much fun with the others.

She needed to draw him out. Gain his respect. If luck was with her, a pregnancy would take root, but could it be assured in time to help Davina? Doubtful. She must convince him to change his mind, if it didn't.

In the days since their first night together— their first *successful* night together, at any rate— he'd made every effort to assure her pleasure. A man who cared for her satisfaction in bed could be convinced to honor her wishes outside it, couldn't he? She had begun to care about *him*, however unwillingly.

"If it's pet names you want, you've certainly come to the right place," Penny said.

Nicola took a tiny pencil from the notebook

hanging about her neck on a silver chain. "I'll keep a list."

"It must be something affectionate," Emma said. "For the cat. He's rather untrusting and prickly, and I can't seem to draw him out."

"Well, if it's a sweet little name you want, there are all the delightful words for new creatures," Penny said. "Puppy, kitten, piglet, foal, fawn, calf, polliwog . . ."

Alexandra reached for her teacup. "Oh, dear. She'll go on forever now."

"That's just the beginning," Penny went on. "There are the birds. Duckling, eaglet, gosling, cygnet, poult . . ."

Nicola looked up from her scribbling. "Poult?"

"A turkey hatchling, fresh from the egg."

Emma laughed. "As tempting as calling him a turkey might be, I think it's polliwog, duckling, and piglet that are my favorites thus far."

"I can contribute a few astronomical ones, I suppose," Alexandra said. "Bright star, twinkles, moonbeam, sunshine . . ."

"Oh, Lord." Emma could just imagine the duke's reaction to "Twinkles." "Those are perfection. What do you think, Nicola?"

"I don't know. I'm surrounded by gears and levers, for the most part. Pet names aren't my forte." Her eye fell on the biscuits. "I suppose there are the sweet things. Sugar, honeycomb, tartlet."

"I'm afraid I've tried most of those already."

"Sweetmeat?" she suggested in perfect innocence.

After a moment's pause, the rest of them dissolved into laughter.

"Oh, dear heavens." Alexandra dashed a tear from her eye.

Nicola looked at the three of them. "What?"

"Nothing," Emma said. "You truly do have a brilliant mind." She nodded at the notebook. "You must most definitely add sweetmeat to the list."

A half hour later, she left Lady Penelope Campion's house with a packet of leftover biscuits and a quiver full of verbal arrows. Hopefully one or two of them would pierce the reserve of laughter in his chest. She knew better than to aim for his heart.

Penny embraced her in farewell. "Do keep trying with your cat. The creatures most difficult to reach make the most loving companions in the end."

Emma felt a sharp twinge of irony. She had no doubt in Penny's ability to tame not only cats, but pups and goats and Highland calves and even traumatized hedgehogs.

But the duke she'd married was a different sort of beast.

Chapter Thirteen

*B*ang.

Ash lifted his head from the accounts ledger.

Don't mind it, he told himself. Mrs. Norton will see to whatever it is. *It's not your concern.*

But when he lowered his head, he found himself unable to focus on the work at hand. He pushed back from the desk and stood, leaving the room in brisk paces.

If he'd ever possessed the ability to ignore explosive noises, he'd left that talent behind at Waterloo.

After tense moments of searching, he discovered the source of the clamor. A brass embellishment had crashed to the morning room floor. That sight, in itself, was nothing particularly remarkable. What took him aback was the other half of the scene: His wife standing on a ladder and clinging to the curtain rod, a good twelve feet above the floor.

She craned her neck to look at him. "Oh, hullo."

"What is this?"

"I'm taking down these draperies."

"Alone?" He crossed the room and put his hands on the ladder. Someone had to be near her in case she tumbled and fell.

"Sorry if I alarmed you with all that noise. I lost my grip on the finial."

She'd lost her grip on the finial. Bully for her. Ash was losing his grip on his sanity.

"Since you seem to need reminding, you are a duchess. Not a circus performer or a squirrel."

She made a dismissive noise. "It's a ladder, not a trapeze. And I engaged the wheel lock. I promise, I do know how these things work."

"Yes, but apparently you don't know how servants work." He braced the ladder under her feet, wheel lock or no. If she insisted on risking her neck, he felt entitled to bark at her. "Come down from there, then."

"I may as well finish what I came up here for. Or else all of this effort will have been for nothing."

"Oh, do go ahead," he said in a bored tone. "It's not as though I have anything else to do. I'm only amusing myself overseeing estates all over the country. Making improvements to the land. Looking out for the welfare of thousands of tenants."

"I won't be but a minute."

"Fine." He tilted his head. "But as a penalty, know that I'll be looking up your skirts the entire time."

He couldn't see all that much, unfortunately—

just a pair of slim legs disappearing into a cloud of petticoats—but the sight stirred him all the same. Her stockings were knitted of plain, pale wool. Demure, innocent. Unspeakably arousing.

"There," she declared.

A waterfall of blue velvet rushed to the floor. The room flooded with sunlight.

Ash caught the ghost of his reflection in the windowpane. What a picture. Emma, descending from the heavens above him on a cloud of muslin, and him, the monster lurking beneath.

When she neared the last rung, he placed a hand on the small of her back to steady her. He extended his fingers as far as they would stretch, claiming as much of her as he could.

All too soon, her slippers met the floor.

He took a few steps in retreat before she turned around. There was too much light, and she was too close. He didn't wish to startle her.

She brushed the dust from her hands. "Oh, that's so much better."

"No, it's not. I can't imagine what you have against draperies."

"To begin, this house is a cave. We can't live in the dark."

"I like the dark."

"It's not good to work and read in dim lighting. You'll go blind."

"Hah. If frigging myself raw in adolescence and having a rocket explode in my face haven't accomplished that . . . Doubtful."

"Well, I'm not doubtful. I've seen it. It's what

happens to seamstresses after too many years of fine stitching by weak light. Even I can't read for more than an hour at a time, and it's only been six years."

What an inconveniently affecting statement. It made him want to roll her into a ball and hold her in both hands forever, so that nothing could wound or frighten her ever again.

"Anyhow, these are lovely fabric." She reached for the edge of the fallen drape. "This velvet could be put to better use."

"No." He put his foot down, literally. With his boot, he pinned the river of blue velvet to the floor. "Absolutely not. I forbid it."

"Forbid what? You can't even know what I have in mind."

"Yes. I do. You have the ridiculous idea that you'll make a gown out of *draperies*. And I forbid it."

She stammered and flushed. "I . . ."

"You," he interjected, "are a duchess. You shop for your gowns. You ask servants to climb ladders. And that is the end of any argument."

This wife he'd acquired was far too enamored of economy. She'd come by the habit out of necessity, he supposed. Ash could understand that—even admire it, to a degree. He didn't like waste, either. However, she was under his care now. There would be no "making do" or scrimping for the mother of his heir.

She certainly wouldn't be caught wearing *draperies*.

"Tomorrow, you'll order a full wardrobe. I'll see that you have lines of credit at all the best shops in Bond Street."

"Madame Bissette's is the best dressmaking shop in Town, and the only one I could fathom entering without crumpling into a ball of fraudulence. But how could I return to the shop as a customer, mere weeks after leaving her employ?"

"That would be the best part. Think of the envy you'll inspire. The vindication after being undervalued."

"No doubt other women might enjoy gloating. But I wouldn't. Madame gave me a post, and she taught me a great deal. And the other girls in the shop were my friends. I don't want to embarrass them. Besides, paying a modiste to make me a wardrobe would be a waste. I have nothing if not time. I know the latest fashions. I've made gowns for many a fine lady."

"Yes," he said tightly. "I'm well aware of that."

She cringed. "Of course you're aware of it. I'm so sorry. I didn't mean to bring up Miss Worthing. I know how it must pain you to—"

"What pains me is the thought of my wife going about clad in draperies. You will not sew your own wardrobe." He tugged on his end of the velvet.

She tugged back. "Aren't ladies encouraged to do needlework?"

"That's different." He yanked with both hands, pulling her off balance. She stumbled toward him a step. "Fine ladies make *useless* things, like wretched pillows, and samplers no one wants, and disturbing seat covers for the commode. They don't use their skills to perform common labor."

"This isn't common labor. I enjoy it, when it isn't a twenty-hour-a-day task. There's a creativity to it. I never had any talent for music or painting, but"—she clutched her end of the velvet and leaned back, putting her full weight into resisting him—"I'm good at this."

With a flick of his wrist, he wrapped the fabric around his left forearm, just as he'd do with the reins when driving a team. And then he braced his legs, flexed his arm, and gave a full-strength pull.

She came reeling toward him. He caught her in his arms.

His brain promptly went to porridge. Their little tug-o'-wills suited her. The exertion made her cheeks pink, and her labored breathing did delicious things for her breasts. Ash had to admit, she would look lovely in a dress of that sapphire velvet.

Nevertheless, it was out of the question. Emma would not sacrifice the pleasure of *reading* in favor of sewing her own gowns. He'd allow her to go about naked before he consented to such a thing.

Damn. Now he was picturing her naked.

"Listen to me. I know very well you can stitch a gown. You could be the best dressmaker in England, and I still wouldn't permit this." He reached for her hand and turned it palm side up, like a fortune-teller. With meaningful intent, he brushed his thumb over the calluses on her fingertips, lingering over each proof of her labor. "There'll be no more of these now."

She was quiet for a moment. "That's shockingly caring of you."

"It's not caring."

"Then how would you describe it?"

"As . . . something else." Anything else. Imagining her naked was only natural. Protecting her was his duty. Caring was much too dangerous. "I don't know. I'm not a dictionary."

She gave him a chastening yet affectionate look. A wifely look. "No, you aren't. You are very much a man."

His heart kicked and thrashed like an unbroken colt in a stable.

A man, she said. Not a title. Not a fortune. Not a twisted monster formed of scars. She couldn't know how those two simple words affected him.

She looked down at her hand, cradled in his. Then she turned it over, so that their palms pressed together and their fingers interlaced in a tight clasp.

Sunlight gilded the wisps of hair framing her face. Her dark eyes were wide, sincere. Unafraid. So lovely. Her gaze met his and held it, never straying to his patchy hair or his twisted cheek.

The moment was glorious.

And wonderful.

And accompanied by soaring orchestral music.

And exceedingly, unforgivably imbecilic of him to allow. This sort of thing could not happen. This kind of closeness was too great of a risk.

Ash cleared his throat. "This, uh . . . This thing we're doing is probably a bad idea."

"Yes. Yes, of course. Precautions." Her hand slipped from his. "I'll order a wardrobe tomorrow."

He stepped away. "You'll order a wardrobe later in the week. Tomorrow we're taking an outing."

"An outing? To where?"

"Swanlea. Your future house." Before she could grow too excited, he held up a hand. "Not to stay. Just for the afternoon, so you can make a list of what needs to be done."

They had an agreement, and for the good of them both, he needed to remember and adhere to it.

"Be ready tomorrow. We'll leave at dawn."

Chapter Fourteen

*O*h."

As she alighted from the carriage, Emma's lungs relaxed with the most silly, sentimental sigh. She even pressed both hands to her chest. "Oh, it's lovely."

Before her stood a perfect dream of a house. It featured a façade of solid brick, studded with enough windows to give the appearance of an open, friendly abode. A shallow pool in front of the house reflected the rows of gracious elms on either side. Unlike Ashbury House—designed to impress at best, and at worst, intimidate—Swanlea was not too grand, not too humble. It looked like a home.

"It's on the small side," the duke said. "Only twelve rooms."

She slid a look at him. *Only?*

The coachman, Jonas, flicked the reins. The team pulled the carriage away.

"Where is he going?" she asked.

"To the market town to change horses. If we're

going to make the journey back this evening, we need a fresh team." He opened the door with the key and waved her over the threshold. "The house has been closed for some time. Twenty years."

"So I see."

In fact, the place was nearly empty. Only a few furnishings remained—scattered chairs here and there, a few chests and cupboards. The wall coverings were peeled in places, and the plaster ceilings were cracked. It charmed her, all the same. Weathered floorboards creaked beneath her feet, telling stories of children chasing one another up and down the stairs, and exuberant hunting dogs jumping to greet their beloved masters. The kitchen worktable had been scored by generations upon generations of knives— some cleaving game birds, others trimming pastry. Sunlight streamed through the uncovered windows.

Emma had the notion that the house was happy to see her.

Delighted to make your acquaintance, too.

"Have a look around," he said. "Make a list of the furnishings you'll need purchased, colors for the decor, any changes or modernizations you'd want. There are a great many repairs to be undertaken. The gardens no doubt need attention. There's an older couple who live on the property as groundskeepers. I'll have them hire maids and laborers to begin the work."

"Surely that's not necessary. I adore the house

as it is, and at most it would need a staff of two or three. Putting you to that needless expense would seem wasteful."

"Think like a duchess, Emma. Cleaning, furnishing, and repairing the home will give employment to dozens of people, many of them in dire need. It's not wasteful. It's patronage."

"Yes, of course." She bit her lip. "I hadn't seen it that way."

Here was the man's single indisputable virtue. He was always thinking of the people who depended on him. He would not have married Emma otherwise. It was for their good that he wanted to quickly produce an heir.

I warned you, she wanted to say. *I warned you I wouldn't make a proper duchess. You should have married a lady, not a seamstress with the thinnest claim to gentility.*

But she *was* the duchess now. She'd undertaken the role, and she must do her best to fulfill it.

"Very well," she said. "If it's work they need, it's work we shall give them." She took out a notebook and licked the tip of her pencil. "I'll start a list."

The next few hours flew by as Emma traveled from room to room. She gave each chamber a purpose. Bedchamber, maid's chamber, morning room. Nursery. She scribbled lists of furnishings, requests for new paint and wall coverings, all the while noting any crack or dent needing repair. Modernizing the baths and kitchen—that would keep more than a few men employed. She walked the grounds next, listing trees in want of pruning and noting patches of brush by the stream that were overgrown. The pond likely required stocking. The kitchen garden was in need of a complete replanting. And while she was dreaming up work . . . why not put in an orchard?

When she was finished, she looked about for her husband. He wasn't in the house. Eventually she found him at the edge of the stream that ran through the property. He'd removed his topcoat and held it by two fingers, slung casually over his shoulder.

"There you are, bunnykins. I've been searching everywhere." She slapped the notebook into his hand. "Enough to employ half of Oxfordshire, I think."

He tucked the notebook into his waistcoat pocket without comment.

She turned her gaze to the arching branches above them. The stream spilled over a rocky patch, chattering and burbling in conversation with the birds. "This is an enchanting little spot, isn't it?"

"Best fishing on any of the ducal properties. Across the way, there's an excellent chestnut tree for climbing. It's a good place to raise a boy."

He clearly spoke from experience. The house had been closed twenty years, had he said? That made sense. It would have been shut up after his parents died. It was difficult to imagine him ever climbing chestnut trees and splashing about in a stream. But even the most imposing of men had once been a boy. With him divested of his coat, clad in only his waistcoat and shirtsleeves, she could almost see it.

They walked the short distance back to the house.

Emma didn't see the carriage. "Evening's coming on. Shouldn't we be starting home?"

"Yes, we should be. Jonas still hasn't returned."

She tucked her skirts under her thighs and had a seat on the front step. "I suppose we'll wait and enjoy the sunset."

They waited. And waited.

The sun set.

Still no Jonas. Still no carriage.

It was full evening now, and fast fading to night.

"Where the devil is he? He could have broken a team of wild horses by now."

A knot of suspicion formed in Emma's stomach. "Oh, dear. I have a bad feeling about this."

"Don't fret. He's an experienced coachman. He won't have encountered any serious difficulty."

"That's not what I mean. I have a bad feeling that Jonas won't return tonight at all. Not because of an accident, but on purpose."

"What possible purpose could that be?"

Emma propped one elbow on her knee and rested her chin in her hand. "It's the servants. All of them. They have formed this silly notion that if they force us together, we'll . . ."

"We'll what?"

"Fall in love."

"FALL IN *LOVE*?" Ash couldn't believe what he was hearing. "That's—"

"Absurd," she finished. "Of course it is. I tried to tell them as much. It's not going to happen, I said."

"The very idea is—"

"Ridiculous. I *know*. But they seem determined to force the matter, one way or another. They've been concocting all manner of schemes. Telling me to trip and turn my ankle. Spill wine on my gown. They even contemplated locking us in the attic of Ashbury House. It seems they've settled on abandoning us here for the night."

How dare they. Ash didn't care about his own comfort, but to leave Emma in an empty house overnight? Insupportable. If not criminal. After a moment of grim silence, he rose to his feet.

"Where are you going?" she asked.

"I am going to walk into the village and find that perfidious runagate."

She leapt to her feet. "Oh, no, you won't. You're not leaving me here. It will be full nighttime before half an hour is out. I'm not staying here alone."

He could hear the quaver of fear in her voice. She was right. It was too late to leave her here by herself.

"Don't worry. I won't leave you." He put his hands on her arms and rubbed briskly. "Let's go inside. I'll make you a fire."

He set aside his irritation. There was nothing more to be done about his traitorous house staff at the moment. Emma must be his concern for now. She was his wife, by Jupiter, and the least he could do was keep her safe and warm.

He walked into the house, draping his topcoat over the staircase banister in the entry. She followed with caution, clinging to his side. When his foot fell on a creaky floorboard, she jumped.

"Sorry," she muttered. "Suddenly this house doesn't seem as friendly as it did this afternoon."

Just wait until night's properly fallen, he thought.

There would be no moon tonight, and Swanlea was too isolated to catch any light from a neighbor's lamps or hearth. They would be two fleas swimming in a bottle of ink.

"With any luck, there'll be a tinderbox in the parlor."

Ash used the last fading glimmer of twilight to search the area near the hearth. Yes, there was the box—and it still held a bit of crumbling moss and a flint. Thank God.

What he lacked, however, was wood.

There was no chance of locating an ax at this hour, let alone finding and hacking down a small tree. He would be just as likely to chop off his own hand. However, he'd promised Emma a fire, and he'd be damned if he'd let her down.

His gaze fell upon a solitary chair. He lifted it by two of its legs, reared back, and bashed it against the stone mantel. At the other end of the room, Emma jumped. The back of the chair dangled loose, but other than that, the thing remained intact. Curse his grandmother's appreciation for fine craftsmanship.

He reared back for another swing. The second crack was enough to splinter one leg from the base. Another few good cracks, and he had a pile of flammable wood and a wicked pain shooting from his arm to his neck.

"How are you able to do that?" she asked.

"Do what?"

"Swing with such force, despite the injured shoulder."

He arranged the chair legs in the fireplace, then stuffed tinder in the cracks. "When I woke from fever, the surgeon told me I must stretch and lift the arm every day if I wanted to keep the use of it. Otherwise the scars will heal too tight and then there's no moving it at all. It's as though the joint rusts over."

"So you play badminton."

"Among other things." He struck the flint.

"And it doesn't pain you any longer?"

Hurts like hell every time.

"No," he said.

Crouching, he blew steadily on the ember until it caught and crackled into a flame. The lacquer helped the bits of chair catch quickly.

"There." He stood back, chest heaving with exertion. "I made you a fire. You may now admire my manliness."

"I do, rather."

Emma moved forward and held her hands out to warm them over the growing blaze. He had precisely three seconds to admire how her skin glowed in the firelight before thick smoke began to billow from the fireplace. They backed away, coughing into their sleeves.

Ash's eyes burned. With a rather unliterary curse, he kicked at the small fire, breaking it apart until a few glowing coals were all that remained. For a minute or two, all they could do was cough. Eventually, the smoke dissipated.

"The flue must be clogged," he said. "Bots on it."

"Bots?"

"Horse worms." To her expression of disgust, he replied, "You asked."

"I suppose I did. The chimneys all need a thorough sweeping, I'd imagine. We'll add it to the list. Tomorrow."

No way to write it down tonight.

He paced the room, his frustration boiling over. "If you knew the servants were scheming, you should have told me. I would have driven any such notions out of their heads."

"I *tried* to do just that. I told them this is only a marriage of convenience."

He wiped soot from his face with his sleeve. "Apparently you weren't convincing."

"Well, maybe they wouldn't be so hopeful about it if *you* weren't such a miserable employer."

"If that's their problem, I can solve it for them. I'll sack them all directly."

"Don't, please. You know we'd never find replacements." She wrapped her arms about herself and shivered. "I don't recall seeing any blankets in the house, did you?"

"None. We'll have to—"

"No," she interrupted. "We can't. That's exactly what they want."

He was baffled. "What's exactly what they want?"

"Huddling."

"Huddling?"

"Yes, huddling. Together. For warmth. The two of us. That's obviously their plan, and we should refuse to play into it."

He bristled. "You don't have to sound quite so disgusted by the idea."

"I'm sorry. It's not you I object to, of course. It's the principle."

"Principles won't keep you warm tonight." Ash made his way to the entry and found his coat, then returned to drape it over her shoulders. "There. That's a start. Now . . . there was a settee around here somewhere."

His shin found it. Ouch.

They settled on opposite ends of the uncomfortable horsehair bench. The thing had so many lumps, Ash expected there'd be divots in his arse tomorrow morning. His stomach rumbled in complaint. "If they were going to strand us here, they might have at least packed us some dinner."

"Please don't mention dinner," she said weakly.

This was going to be a long, miserable night.

She jerked with surprise. "What was that noise?"

"What noise?"

"That scratching noise." She shushed him. "Listen."

He sat in silence, listening.

"There!" She smacked his shoulder. "There, did you hear it just now? And there again."

Yes, he heard it. A light scraping noise that coincided with each slight breeze.

"Oh, that," he said. "That's just the Mad Duchess."

"The Mad Duchess?"

"The resident ghost. Every country house has one." He made his voice mysterious. "The story is that my great-grandfather took a wife. A bride of convenience, for the purposes of siring an heir. She was pretty enough, but he began to regret the match soon after the honeymoon."

"Why?"

"A hundred reasons. She tore down the curtains. She conspired with the servants. She called him ridiculous names. Worst, she had a demon consort that assumed the form of a cat."

"Oh, really."

"Yes, really."

"She sounds terrible."

"Indeed. She was so much trouble, he locked her in a cupboard upstairs and kept her there. For years."

"*Years?* That seems extreme."

"Extreme was what she deserved. She'd driven him mad, and he meant to return the favor. Locked her up. Tossed in a crust or a dampened sponge from time to time. On cold nights, you can still hear her scratching and clawing to get out. Do you hear it?" He paused. "There it is. Scratch. Scratch. Scratch."

She swallowed audibly. "You are a cruel and horrid man, and I hope you get the bots."

"If you doubt me, feel free to go upstairs and see for yourself."

"No, thank you."

All was silent for several minutes, during which Ash felt rather smug.

Then it was Ash's turn to jerk in surprise. "What's *that* noise?"

"What noise?"

"That . . . crinkling noise. It sounds like someone removing a paper wrapping."

"I don't know what you're talking about," she said. "Perhaps it's the Mad Duchess."

The crinkling sounds stopped. But other sounds took its place. Small, wet sounds. Like sucking and chewing.

"Are you eating?" he asked.

"No," she said.

A few minutes of silence.

There it was again. That crinkling, followed by light smacking of lips. "You're eating something, I know it."

"I am not," she said. At least, he thought that was what she intended to say. It came out more like, *Ah mmf nah.*

"You little dissembler. Share."

"No."

"Very well, I'll leave you here." He rose to his feet. "All alone. In the dark. With the noises."

"Wait. All right, I'll share."

He sat down.

She touched his arm, felt his way down his shirtsleeve, and placed a small packet in his hand. "They're just a few boiled sweets. I bought them when we stopped to water the horses."

Ash unwrapped a morsel for himself. "The scratching sound is the branch of an oak tree that grows at the back of the house. It scrapes the windowsill of my old bedchamber. I climbed down that tree many a night to find mischief of one sort or another." He popped the sweet into his mouth. "You'd better not give my heir that room."

"I'll give *you* that room."

"I don't need a room," he said, speaking around his own mouthful of sweetness. "This is your house."

"Well yes, but . . . You'll come for visits, I assume."

"I don't plan on it."

Her silence was astonished. "Will you not wish to see your child?"

God love her. She didn't understand. It didn't matter if Ash wished to see his child. The child would not wish to see him.

His wanderings through the London streets by night proved just how well children took to him. Screaming terror was the most common reaction, with mute horror following close behind.

The Mad Duchess had nothing on the Monster Duke.

He sucked on the sweet. "I will, of course, expect regular assurances of his well-being and education through correspondence."

"Correspondence? You would raise your own son through the *post*?"

"I'll be occupied. In London, and at the other estates. Besides, you've a surfeit of affection and bossiness. I don't expect you'll require my hand in his raising at all. My heir—"

"Your *son*."

"—will be far better off in your keeping."

"What if I don't agree?" she asked. "What if I wish for him to know you? What if *he* wishes to not only know you, but love you, the way you loved your own father?"

Impossible.

Ash's son could never admire him the way Ash had worshipped his own father. His father had been unfailingly wise, good-natured, and patient. Not ill-tempered and bitter, as Ash had become.

His father had been strong. Able to lift his son onto his shoulders without wincing.

His father had possessed a handsome, noble face. A face that had never failed to make Ash feel protected and secure. If Ash couldn't give his own son that bone-deep feeling of safety, it was better that he stay away.

"No more chatter. Go to sleep."

Within a few minutes, however, she did begin to chatter. This time, not with her lips and tongue—but with her teeth. Soon the entire settee began to shake. She was shivering like a struck tuning fork.

"Emma?" He slid toward her side of the settee. She'd drawn her feet up under her skirts, hugging her knees to her chest.

"S-s-sorry. It will stop in a m-minute."

"It's not that cold," he said, as if he could reason her out of it.

"I'm always c-cold. I can't help it."

Yes, he recalled the five blankets.

Ash took her in his arms, holding her tight to share his warmth with her. Good Lord. She was trembling violently from head to toe. This couldn't be a result of the weather. He laid his wrist to her brow. She didn't feel feverish.

Only one explanation remained. She was frightened. His little wife, who didn't fear dukes or footpads, was scared out of her wits.

"Is it the darkness?" he asked.

"N-no. It's . . ." She clung to his waistcoat. "This just h-happens sometimes."

He tightened his arms about her. "I'm here," he murmured. "I'm here."

He didn't ask her any further questions, but he couldn't help but think them. His gut told him this wasn't just a quirk of her character. It had an origin. Something, or someone, had caused it.

Emma, Emma. What is it that happened to you?

And who can I throttle to make it better?

After several minutes, her shivering began to

ease. So did the worry in Ash's stomach. He'd been so concerned, he'd begun to consider attempting to carry her into the village for help.

"Attempting" being the infuriating word in that sentence. With the injuries to his shoulder, he didn't think he could manage to carry her half that distance. Damn it, he despised feeling so useless.

"I'm better now. Thank you."

She attempted to slip out of his embrace, but Ash was having none of it. He cinched his good arm tight. At least he could do that much. "Sleep."

It wasn't long before she obeyed. All that shivering had sapped the last of her energy, no doubt. Ash was left alone in the dark silence with his thoughts.

This excursion had gone all wrong. She was meant to be enthralled with the prospect of an idyllic country life without him, and he was supposed to remind himself of his original intentions. Marry her, impregnate her, tuck her away in the country, and reunite with his heir a dozen or so years down the line.

Instead, now she was tucked securely under his arm, and he didn't want to let her go. To make it worse, he couldn't stop sniffing her hair. It smelled like honeysuckle. He hated that he knew that.

He should have blamed Jonas, or the entirety of his staff. But in truth, this was his fault.

Like everything else in his life, it had backfired in spectacular fashion.

EMMA WOKE WITH a start.

Where was she?

Oh, yes. Tucked under her husband's arm. Bang in the middle of a disaster.

When she thought of her pitiful trembling last night, she cringed. Of all the times for one of those episodes to strike. In the past year, she'd suffered only a few bouts of the violent shivering, and the last one had been several months past. She'd thought perhaps they'd finally gone away.

Apparently not.

She turned her head stealthily and looked up at him. He was still asleep, thank goodness. His spare hand lay neatly on his chest. His legs were outstretched in an arrow-straight line, crossed at the ankles. The pose was very male, very military, and it made Emma acutely aware of her own ungainly sprawl of limbs. It wasn't only his posture that made her self-conscious. Why was it that men woke up looking just as handsome as they had when falling asleep—if not more so? Ruffled hair, an attractive shadow of whiskers. It wasn't fair.

Sliding out from under his arm, she made a few hasty efforts to repair her own appearance. She quickly unpinned her hair, combing it with her fingers, and pinched color back into her cheeks.

When he stirred, she flopped down on the opposite side of the settee, laying her cheek atop her hands and pretending to be asleep. When she was certain he'd awoken enough to notice, she allowed her eyelashes to open with a gentle flutter. She rose to a sitting position, stretching her arms overhead in a gentle salute to the rosy dawn. Then she shook out her hair, letting it tumble about her shoulders in waves.

She cast him a shy smile and tucked a wisp of hair behind her ear. "Good morning."

His gaze roamed her face and body.

Why yes, I do wake up this beautiful every morning. When you leave me at night, you should know this is what you're missing.

He scratched behind his ear like a flea-bitten dog and yawned loudly before reaching for his boot. "I'm dying for a piss."

Emma blew out her breath. Fine. Sleeping Beauty and her prince they were not.

In that case, she would stop pretending. "That was the worst night imaginable."

He shoved one foot into its boot. "If that's the worst you can imagine, your imagination is lacking."

"It's hyperbole," she said. "You know what I mean. It was terrible."

"Perhaps. But we survived it, didn't we."

He rose to his feet and offered her his hand. She took it, and he pulled her to her feet.

"You're right." She tried to smooth the wrinkles from her skirt. "I've been through worse in the past, and I know you have, too. At least we had each other."

His gaze changed, the way it did in rare moments. Their icy blue melted to pools of deep, unspoken emotion. Compelling and dangerous. She was drawn to them. She could drown in them.

"Emma, you—" He broke off and began again. "Just don't get used to it. That's all."

"The thought never crossed my mind," she lied.

"Good."

Emma had no logical reason to feel hurt by his words, but she did.

The rumble of carriage wheels coming down the drive rescued them from the charged silence.

He tugged on his waistcoat. "Now if you'll excuse me, I have some eviscerating to do."

Chapter Fifteen

ome in, come in. I'm so glad you're here."
Emma handed Alexandra's rain-spattered cloak
to the maid. "I can't believe you came in such a
downpour."

"I'm always punctual," Alexandra said, taming the rain-frizzled wisps of her black hair.

"Yes, I suppose you would be."

"I've brought the chronometer." She opened
her valise on a nearby bench, withdrawing a
brass instrument that looked like a giant's pocket
watch. "I can assure you, the time is accurate to
the second. I take it to Greenwich once a fortnight to be synchronized at the meridian, and
once a year it's calibrated by—"

"You don't need to sell me on your services,
Alex. I have every confidence."

Alexandra smiled. "Thank you."

Emma drew her into the sitting room. "First,
tea. You need something to warm you after coming in from that rain. Then we'll make a survey
of the house and take an inventory of the timepieces."

"You needn't do that. The housekeeper can take me around."

"Believe me, it will be a useful exercise. There are wings of this place even I'm not familiar with yet."

"Yes, but in the other fine houses, I only set one or two clocks, and then the butler—"

Emma cut her off. "This is not one of the other fine houses. You alone will set each and every timepiece in the house. Weekly. And you will bill us at three times your usual rate."

"I couldn't do that."

"Very well, then. We'll multiply it by five." The maid brought in a tray with cups and a teapot. Emma waited until she'd left, then lifted the pot to pour. "I know—all too well—what it's like to be an unmarried young woman in London, working for a living at criminally low wages."

Alexandra accepted the teacup and stared into it. "If you'd truly like to do me a favor . . ."

"Anything."

"I need a new walking dress. Something a bit smarter, for when I go calling on potential customers. Perhaps you'd be so good as to advise me on the style, or help me select the fabric?"

"I'll do better than that. I'll sew it for you myself." She held off Alexandra's objection. "I would love nothing more."

"It's too much."

"Not at all. Other ladies have the pianoforte or watercolors. My one accomplishment is dressmaking. Strange as it sounds, I miss the challenge. It's you who'd be doing me a favor."

Many of the ladies who visited Madame's had been elegant and fashionable to begin with—but Emma's favorites were the ones who weren't. The quiet girls, the spinsters, the simply overlooked. Dressmaking wasn't superficial with them. A well-made, flattering gown had the ability to draw forth inner qualities: not only loveliness, but confidence.

Alexandra Mountbatten was a beauty in hiding.

"If you insist," she said shyly.

"I insist. I'll only need to take your measurements, and then I'll draw up a few sketches."

"Goodness. We had better see to the clocks before all that."

They began a survey of the house. It became clear after just a few rooms that this was going to take a bit of time. The drawing room alone had three clocks: one standing, one ormolu, and one a sort of Viennese fancywork with a dancing couple who twirled on the hour.

They worked their way through the morning room, the music room, and the dining room. Alex kept notes of every timepiece, room by room.

When they came to the door of the ballroom, Emma stopped and pressed her ear to the door. Clanging and intermittent grunting could be heard from within.

"We'll come back to that one later," she whispered, steering Alex back down the corridor to the safety of the entrance hall.

They made their way upstairs, where Emma struggled to remember the names of all the guest bedchambers. Some were easy, like the Rose Room and the Green Suite, but they had to resort to making up names for the rest: the Unsettling Portrait Room, the Hideous Wallpaper Annex, and the Suite of Ridiculous Size.

"What's this one?" Alex opened the next door. "Oh, it's the grandest yet."

"These are the duke's rooms."

Emma paused in the corridor. She hadn't been prepared for this. To be honest, she only knew these rooms to be her husband's because they were just down the corridor from hers. She'd never been inside them, and she was embarrassed to admit it. Even to Alex.

She shouldn't be ashamed to enter, should she? She was mistress of the house, after all. It was no intrusion for her to come in and inventory the clocks. It wasn't as though she meant to rifle through his chest of drawers and sniff his laundry.

Besides, she knew him to be downstairs— clanging and grunting with poor Khan. Lord, what suffering he inflicted on the man.

Emma moved into the room, pretending to have the same confidence she'd shown when exploring the others.

Alexandra scribbled in her *carnet*, taking note of the clock on the mantel of the antechamber before proceeding into the bedroom. There, she peered at the small timepiece at his bedside.

"Is there a clock in the dressing room?" Alex asked.

"I don't . . ." Emma cursed her own ignorance. Rather than admit it, she plowed forward in false surety. "I meant to say, no. There isn't."

"Did you want me to set the pocket watch?"

"The pocket watch?"

Alexandra nodded toward the washstand. To the side of the basin and ewer stood a military rank of gentleman's toiletries: tooth powder, shaving soap and razor, cologne, a linen towel . . . and at the end of those, a silver tray holding a stickpin, pocket watch, and an assortment of shillings and pence.

"I'm not certain," Emma said, unwilling to go that far. "I'll ask him about it later."

Her gaze tracked back to that shaving soap and razor. She'd never stopped to consider it before, but it must be astoundingly difficult for him to shave around his scars. Yet he did so anyway, every day. Every evening, too, come to think of it. When he suckled her breasts or settled between her thighs—her skin heated at the memories— she never felt the scrape of whiskers against her skin.

Did he go to all that trouble just for her?

The thought was deeply stirring. She felt her body softening in unconnected places. The corners of her mouth. Her knees. Her heart.

To distract herself, she wandered to a corner of the antechamber, where a Holland cloth had been draped over some tall, narrow furnishing.

Could it be another clock, out of use? If so, Emma hoped it needed repair. She could pay Alex a frightful sum for mending it.

However, when she pulled the cloth aside, she did not discover a clock behind it.

She found a mirror.

A full-length looking glass in a gilt oval frame, cracked to pieces. A spiderweb of splinters radiated from the center. Each shard reflected at a different angle, piecing her image into a patchwork Emma.

She touched her fingertips to the center of the shattered web. It looked as if someone—a strong, tall someone—had driven his fist into the glass.

A lump rose in her throat.

Alexandra tugged at her elbow. "Emma, someone's coming."

Oh, no.

Someone *was* coming. Worse by far, she knew who it must be. Steps that heavy could only belong to one person in this house.

The duke.

"We should move on anyhow," Alexandra said.

Emma whirled in place, desperate. If they left the suite now, they would confront him in the corridor—and he would be suspicious of her intent. Displeased, or even furious.

A door creaked. He'd entered through the antechamber.

Emma grabbed Alexandra by the wrist and tugged her to the other side of the room. Together, they dove behind a settee.

"Why are we hiding?" Alexandra whispered. "It's your house. Your husband."

"I know." Emma fluttered her hands. "But I panicked."

"I suppose we're stuck now. Let's hope he doesn't mean to stay."

Emma put a finger to her lips for silence as the duke's footsteps moved into the bedchamber. The room fell almost silent. When she couldn't bear it anymore, she peeked around the corner of the settee. His back was to her, and he—

God have mercy. He was disrobing.

She slunk back to the other side of the settee and quietly thunked her head against the upholstery.

Why, why, why? Why now, why here?

Well, she supposed "here" was the logical place to disrobe, it being his bedchamber. But that answer did nothing to assuage her rueful, silent bemoaning of the entire situation. She had never felt so stupid.

"What is it?" Alexandra whispered.

Frantic, Emma made every hand signal she knew to indicate the need for absolute silence. She probably invented a few new ones, as well.

Remain calm, she told herself. Most likely he'd only come up to exchange his coat, or retrieve his watch or some other small item. Otherwise, wouldn't he ring for his valet?

After waiting through twenty heartbeats—which likely added up to four seconds on Alexandra's chronometer—she peeked again.

Oh, *Lord*. He'd tossed aside the coat, unbuttoned his waistcoat, and—as she watched—tugged his shirt free of his breeches and pulled it over his head.

Her pulse stopped—and then began again as a low, painful throb.

Dear heavens.

The left side of him was muscled and sculpted and Roman-godlike and all the other descriptors a woman could muster to signal attractiveness and sheer, raw lust. That ridge between his flank and his hip alone . . . the way his trousers rode it, dipping to reveal an enticing glimpse of taut, firm backside.

Emma wished she could claim she was riveted to *that* sight. All the places where he was strong and perfect. She wished her gaze had never wandered to the wounded side of him and stubbornly stuck there.

But it had.

And now she couldn't look away.

The injuries he wore on his face were only the beginning. His torso bore a long, angry swath of scars that snaked from his neck, down the right side of his shoulder and chest, and then blazed around his ribs to end at the small of his back.

As he splashed water over his face and neck, the rivulets followed a tortuous path downward. His flesh was raised and twisting, as gnarled as the bark of ancient tree. Warring scars tugged at each other with aggressive fingers. And then there were a few bits of him that were simply . . .

missing. Depressions that deepened into hollows, where fire had carved him away to sinew and bone.

What a miracle that he'd survived at all. Then again, he was excessively ill-tempered and intractable. No doubt he'd simply refused to follow when death beckoned. That would be so like him.

Oh, you stubborn, brave, impossible man. Curse you for being more attractive than ever.

Conflicting emotions overwhelmed her. She was seized by the urge to run to him, but she didn't know what she'd do when got there. Kiss him, hold him, grope him, weep over him . . . ? She'd probably make a fool of herself doing all four at once. It was for the best, she supposed, that she was forced to remain behind this settee until he left the room.

A clattering noise startled her out of her skin.

Alexandra's *carnet*—and its metal case—had tumbled to the floor. *Sorry*, she mouthed.

"Who's there?" The duke grabbed his razor from the washstand and whirled around.

Emma cringed. There was nothing else to be done.

"It's me." She popped up from behind the settee, giving him a smile and a jolly wave. "Just me. Only me. Definitely no one else."

He stared at her with an expression that blended anger and disbelief. "Emma?"

She gave Alexandra a soft kick before coming out from behind the settee and approaching her husband. "I . . . I thought you were downstairs. In the ballroom."

"I *was* downstairs. Then I came upstairs."

"Yes, of course."

Behind him, Alexandra crawled out from behind the settee and began to scurry across the bedchamber carpet on all fours.

If Emma didn't keep his attention focused on her, he would see Alexandra, and this already uncomfortable scene would enter . . . well, not quite the ninth circle of Hell, but Dante's lesser known invention: the sixth octagon of awkward.

She asked breezily, "More badminton this afternoon?"

"Fencing."

"Oh, yes. Fencing." She touched her ear. That would explain the clanging, wouldn't it.

In her peripheral vision, she saw Alexandra's farewell salute from the other side of the door. She exhaled with relief.

"My turn to ask the questions," he said. "What the devil do you mean, coming in here to spy on me?"

"Before I continue, could you . . . put aside the blade?"

He looked surprised that he was still holding the thing. He folded the razor closed and tossed it on the washstand, where it landed with a bang. "Now explain what you were doing crouched behind my settee."

She set her chin with confidence, having thought of the perfect excuse. "I was looking for the cat."

"The cat."

"Yes. The cat."

"You mean *that* cat?" He nodded at the settee she'd been hiding behind.

She turned. Breeches was curled up on the cushioned seat, asleep.

When had *that* happened?

As if he knew himself to be the subject of conversation, the cat lifted his head, stretched his long legs, and gave her an inquisitive, innocent look.

Not since she'd been sixteen years old had Emma felt so thoroughly betrayed.

You furry little beast. I found you starving in the streets, took you in from the cold, and this is how you repay me?

"Enough," her husband said. "Just admit that you came to gawk at me. To invade my privacy against my wishes and satisfy your curiosity."

"No." She shook her head in vehement denial. "No, I would never."

"Don't lie to me," he thundered.

She swallowed hard.

He spread his arms and turned in a slow circle. "Well, take what you wanted. Have a good, long look. And then get out."

Once he'd finished his display, Emma locked her gaze on his, careful not to let it stray. "I didn't come here to spy on you. I swear it. Though I won't deny that once I was here, I couldn't help but stare."

"Of course you stared. Who wouldn't? There

are freak shows in the Tower of London that you'd have to pay a sixpence to see, and they aren't nearly this grotesque."

"Don't say that," she pleaded. "Do you really have such a low opinion of me?"

"I have an understanding of human nature." He thumped a fist to his chest. "I want you to own the truth. This is hardly the first time I've caught you staring, even if it is the most intimate intrusion yet. Do you dare deny it?"

"No. I can't."

He advanced on her. "You came here—hid behind my settee—to indulge your morbid fascination."

She shook her head.

"Admit it."

"I can't admit it! It isn't true. I . . ." Her voice wavered. "I do stare at you, yes. But it's not because I find you grotesque. It certainly isn't morbid fascination."

"Then what, pray tell, could it be?"

Her heart pounded in her chest. Did she dare admit the truth? "Infatuation."

"Infatu—" He retreated a pace and stared at her. As if she'd sprouted horns. And then sprouted pansies and teacakes *from* the horns.

Emma didn't know what to do or say. She'd already done and said too much.

Without another word, she ran from the room.

Chapter Sixteen

$\mathcal{T}$hat evening's dinner was uncharacteristically free of Emma's usual teasing and relentless chatter. Ash could only suppose his wife was ashamed of herself, and well she should be. He wished he could stop caring—about her intrusion, about her lies.

And about the way she wasn't taking any food or wine whatsoever.

"You're not eating your soup," he finally said. "It's putting me off mine."

"I . . . Never mind." With a dutiful grimness, she took a tiny spoonful of soup.

He rolled his eyes. "Spit it out then."

She froze, spoon poised in midair.

"Not the soup. Whatever it is you mean to say."

She put down her spoon. "We need to talk about this afternoon. About the fact that I'm infatuated with you."

Ash shot a glance at the footmen. *Go. Away.*

They went.

He returned his attention to his addlebrained wife. "Why do you keep saying that?"

"Because you keep asking! Because I must tell someone, and I don't know how to tell anyone else." She studied her soup. "I'm infatuated with you, however unwillingly. It's a problem."

"It *would* be a problem," he said, "if it weren't a product of your imagination."

"I'm not imagining things."

He shrugged. "Maybe you're nearing your monthly courses. I hear women become seething maelstroms of irrational emotion at that time."

"Well, *now* I'm seething." She gave him an irritated look. "You are such a *man*. And I'm stupidly attracted to you despite it. Perhaps even *for* it. Yes, I am certain it's infatuation. I've felt it before."

Now Ash was the one who became a maelstrom of irrational emotion. That emotion being jealous anger. "Toward whom?"

"Why should it matter?"

"Because," he said, "I like to know the names of the people I despise. I keep them in a little book and pore over it from time to time, whilst sipping brandy and indulging in throaty, ominous laughter."

"It was a young man back home, ages ago. Surely you know the feeling of infatuation. Everyone does. It's not merely physical admiration. Your mind fixes on a person, and it's as though you float through the days, singing a song that only has one word, thinking of nothing but the next time you'll see them again."

"And you claim to be feeling this way. Float-ish. Singsong-ish. About me."

She sighed. "Yes."

"That's absurd."

"I know, but I can't seem to stop it. I have an unfortunate habit of looking for the best in people, and it makes me blind to their flaws."

"I'm entirely composed of flaws. I can't imagine what more evidence you'd need."

"Neither do I. That's what worries me." She fidgeted with her linen napkin. "I mean, it *will* end. These things always do. Either you wake from the spell, or you fall properly in love."

"Which was it with this boy back home?"

"I thought it was the second, but then he made it clear he didn't feel the same. The illusion snapped, and I saw him for who he truly was."

He sat back in his chair. "There's your answer, then. We can settle this right here and now. I'll tell you I don't feel the same. Because I don't."

"I wouldn't believe you." She paused. "I think you're infatuated with me, too."

Ash carved the roasted pheasant, sawing away at the blameless bird with displeasure. He slung a portion onto her plate. "I can't imagine what would make you believe *that*."

"You come to my room a bit earlier each night."

"Perhaps I'm eager to have it out of the way."

"It's not only that your visits are earlier. They grow longer, too."

He stabbed a fork into the pheasant's breast. "What is this? Are you keeping a little ledger of my virility in your nightstand? Charting my stamina? Making *graphs*?"

She cast a little smile into her wineglass. "Don't pretend you wouldn't be flattered if I did."

"Stop smiling. There's only one reason I come to visit your room at any hour. You're supposed to be conceiving my heir. To that end, I insist on your proper nourishment and good health. Eat your dinner."

She picked up her fork. "If you say so, my treasure."

"I daresay I do, you little baggage."

Ash glowered at the silver candlesticks. This was a problem, indeed. It was all well and good— expedient, truly—if they pleased one another in bed. Outside the bedchamber, however, maintaining distance was essential. He must not encourage any foolish sentiment on her part, even if her admiration of him could be credited—and it couldn't.

The truth was plain, he reminded himself. She was making excuses for having been caught in his bedchamber and then having fled as though the Devil licked at her heels. She hoped to forestall his anger by puffing up his pride.

Infatuated, she'd said. Unthinkable.

And if she believed *him* to be taken with *her*, she left him no choice but to prove her wrong.

Tonight, Ash resolved, he wouldn't go to her bed at all.

KEEPING HIS RESOLUTION proved more difficult than Ash could have guessed.

He didn't know what to do with himself. It was too early to go out walking—the streets would be thick with people at this hour. To pass the time, he poured himself a brandy and decided to look over the land agent's report from Essex.

No sooner had he stoppered the decanter and turned to the desk than the hellion cat pounced atop it, circled, and settled into a heap—directly on the very papers he'd intended to inspect.

"Great help you are," Ash said sullenly. "Lump of foul deformity."

Breeches blinked at him.

"Do you hear me? Get out. 'Thou art a boil, a plague-sore, an embossed carbuncle.' *King Lear*, Act Two."

The embossed carbuncle gave a bored yawn.

Ash gave up. He might as well go to sleep.

He removed his boots, snuffed the candles, and lay down on the bed. It was a monument of a bed, passed down through generations of dukes. Four carved mahogany posts and hangings of richly embroidered velvet trimmed with golden tassels. The hangings trapped heat on cold nights and blocked light on unwelcome mornings.

They also made a nice little cave for hiding from reality.

He folded his hands on his chest and groaned with displeasure. Perhaps Emma was right. Maybe he *was* infatuated. All the symptoms were there. Though he knew she had flaws—many, many of them—he couldn't pinpoint a cursed one at the moment. Her name kept run-

ning through his mind. The song with only one
word.

Emma Emma Emma Emma Emma.

He took comfort in one thing. She had also
said it wouldn't last. Ash would just have to snap
himself out of it.

He clapped his hands, sending a booming
sound through the room. That resulted in nothing but making him feel incredibly stupid.

He squeezed his eyes closed until stars exploded behind his eyelids, counted to three, and
then opened them. Stupider still.

He thought of the most unappealing things
his imagination could conjure:

Shards of fire propelled with bullet-force, col-
liding with his face.

Vomiting himself dry while quitting opium.

Pus. Not even the mildly repulsive yellow sort.
Green, oozing, malodorous pus.

That helped for a few minutes, but apparently
his brain didn't want to dwell on those memories
anymore—not when his mind could so easily
reach for her.

Emma Emma Emma Emma Emma.

Ye gods.

He sat up in bed. Tomorrow he'd burn twists
of sage and wave the smoke through the house.
He was clearly hexed. Bewitched.

The door to his bedchamber creaked open.

"Don't be alarmed. It's only me." Emma entered the room, holding a candelabra with three
glowing tapers.

Ash rubbed his eyes. "Why, pray tell, are you in my bedchamber?"

"Because you're not in mine." She set the candles on a chest of drawers, directly across from the foot of the bed. "And because I owe you something, in the spirit of fairness."

She was dressed in only a thin night rail, and her dark hair was woven into a loose plait, tied with a bit of muslin at the end.

As he watched, rapt and disbelieving, her hands went to the buttons of her shift.

Glory above, she began to undo them. One by one by one. As she worked them open, the two sides fell apart, revealing a slice of pale flesh that widened as it dipped from her neck, to the valley between her breasts, to her navel.

When all the buttons were undone, he heard her draw a shaky breath. Then she slid her arms free of the shift, one and then the other, before letting the entire garment drop to the floor.

Jesu Maria.

"I have a confession to make," she said.

"God, I hope it's a long one."

"Breeches isn't my pet. Or he wasn't, until the morning of our wedding day. I plucked him off the street. Given the nature of our arrangement, I needed something warm and cuddly to bring with me. Some creature I might be able to care for. Love." Her lips curved into a slight, rueful smile. "The little beast didn't even have a name until you asked me for one."

Ash had no idea why she was standing there

naked, talking about the cat, but he'd be damned
if he was going to complain about it.

By all means, do go on.

He drew to a sitting position, the better to see
her. All of her. He let his gaze linger on the de-
lectable orbs of her breasts, then the gentle curve
of her waist where it flared to her hips. Those
tempting handfuls of femininity he'd gripped
with fervor in the dark.

And then his gaze traveled to its logical destination . . . the dark triangle between her legs. All
those sweet, secret places he now knew so well
with his lips and tongue.

He could taste her from here.

"Of all the names that could have come to me,"
she said. "Buttons. Boots. Even Pocket would have
been better. But no. I had to blurt out Breeches. Do
you want to know why?"

"I don't know how you expect me to give a
damn right now." He'd moved on to memorizing
every contour of her thighs.

"Because that's where I'd been looking at the
moment, you see. At breeches. More accurately,
your breeches. Admiring how you . . ." She
cleared her throat. ". . . filled them."

He lifted his head. *Now* he gave a damn.

"Admiring," he echoed in disbelief.

"Yes. Perhaps even lusting."

That settled it. None of this was real. He was
dreaming.

Lord, let me never wake.

"I am wildly attracted to you. Physically attracted to you. I have been from the first. And yes, I've done a great deal of staring." She stepped free of her pooled chemise. "I want you with a keen, carnal passion. I won't pretend otherwise, and I'm not going to apologize for it. Not anymore."

He swallowed hard. "I see."

"Good." She moved toward him.

Ash leapt to his feet and held her off with an extended arm. "You've made your point. Quite vividly. Now you may return to your bed."

"Return to my bed? Without us even . . ." She waved her hand to fill the gap in her sentence. "Why?"

"Because the only activities I can imagine at the moment involve complete and utter depravity. And you"—he waved his hand in imitation—"cannot bring yourself to speak the tamest of them."

"We don't have to do much speaking, do we?"

Very well, he could demonstrate.

Wrapping his good arm around her waist, he lifted her against him. He pushed his hard, aching cock against her belly, rubbing her nakedness through the barrier of his trousers. "Do you feel that?"

Her gasp was more of a squeak. "Yes."

"I have a bad side, Emma. One that has nothing to do with my scars. You've no idea what I'd like to do to you. Push you against a wall. Drive my cock into your sweet, wet heat. Tup you senseless. Raw. So hard that you wouldn't walk for days. And that's only to start."

Heat sparked and crackled between them. Her nipples hardened, pressing against his chest like spear points.

"Was that speech meant to put me off?" Her voice was breathless. "Because if so, I must tell you it backfired."

Damn it. Of course it had. He should have never expected anything else.

Everything in his life backfired.

First that rocket at Waterloo. Then his engagement. Now this whole blasted arrangement with Emma. Despite the supposedly impersonal nature of their marriage, she was slowly working her way under his skin, under his scars. If not deeper.

Infatuation was dangerous enough. It must stop here. If he allowed her in, Fate would surely laugh in his face. His own heart would backfire, explode to shrapnel, and he'd be as destroyed inside as he was without.

She had to leave his room at once. And he must lock her out, in every way.

He made one last attempt, his voice dark and stern. "Go. Now. Before I use you in ways you don't want to be used."

She swept a gaze over him, biting her bottom lip. "It's not being used if I want it, too."

He gave up. It was over. Brute lust overruled his every emotion, intention, and thought. She'd made her bed, and he meant to take her six different ways on it. Tomorrow the servants could collect what pieces remained.

"Don't say I didn't warn you."

Chapter Seventeen

*E*mma scarcely had time to draw breath before he'd caught her up, backing her against a bedpost. His hands went straight to her bottom, lifting her so that her pelvis was level with his. His eyes locked with hers, too.

Would he kiss her?

She closed her eyes, hopeful. She'd been yearning to feel his kiss on her lips again, and to return it with passion.

She did feel his mouth—not on her lips, but on her neck. He dipped his head, running his tongue downward, tracing a path to her breasts.

The bedpost at her back was uncomfortable, its carved embellishments digging into her flesh, and his hands had her bottom in a fierce grip . . . but she didn't care. The pain only sweetened the pleasure as he nuzzled and kissed. He grazed her nipples with his teeth, drawing from her a startled gasp of delight.

Emboldened, she worked her arm between them, delving into his trousers to find the thick, hard length within. Oh, she'd been dying to touch him there. To explore his maleness and understand how it worked. How it gave her so much pleasure, and how she could give him pleasure in return.

She let her fingertips wander the full length and breadth of his arousal, tracing each ridge and vein. Caressing, teasing. She circled her thumb around the velvety tip, spreading the drop of moisture that welled there.

He groaned with pleasure. "Take it in your hand."

She curled her fingers, grasping his rigid shaft at the root. He was so thick and hard, the circle formed by her thumb and second finger didn't quite meet. She dragged her grip slowly upward, sliding his soft, pliant skin over the steely column beneath. As she began the downstroke, he thrust into her hand.

His eyes closed. "God."

He swelled even harder in her hand, and she licked her lips. Her mind was fuzzy. Her skin flushed with roving patches of heat.

He jerked free of her grip and spun her away from him, positioning her to face the bedpost. He bent her forward at the waist and placed her hands on the tall column of carved wood.

"Hold it," he said.

She gripped the post tight.

That accomplished, he nudged her legs further apart. Emma felt exposed, almost on display—and apparently that was his aim. He spread her intimate places with his fingers, opening her to his view. Her embarrassment was mollified—somewhat—with the sound of satisfaction he made. His thumb slid over her creases and folds, making them soften and swell.

"Please," she said. "Please. I want . . . You know what I want."

"If you want my cock, then tell me so." His length teased her as he rocked back and forth on his heels. "I want to hear you say it."

"I can't."

"You can. After all, it's in *Hamlet*."

It wasn't Shakespeare's permission Emma needed. She didn't know how to explain it, but she felt more comfortable having his male organ inside her than speaking its crude name with her lips. In lovemaking, she could pretend her actions belonged to someone else. Someone bolder, more seductive. Words, however . . . they were inescapably hers.

That was the source of her reluctance to *say* it. Now she wondered if it was also the reason he wanted to *hear* it. To know the desire was sincere, and wholly hers. She supposed he deserved that much.

"I . . ." She closed her eyes. "I want your cock."

He grunted with approval. "Then you shall have it. All of it."

He lifted her by the hips and slid into her, filling her with one blissful inch after another. She gripped the bedpost, pushing back against him until her thighs met his. He began to move in a slow, steady rhythm.

"Do you feel that?" His thrusts gained pace. "That's what you do to me. How hard you make me. I've been wanting this. Every time you've teased me, defied me, given me that arch little smile, I've wanted to bend you over and teach you a lesson."

She clutched the bedpost for balance as he drove into her, making her breasts sway with each thrust.

"I lived in the grip of laudanum. I know what it is to crave. To tremble with wanting, be ruled by need. It nearly destroyed me. This is worse. There's no respite. As soon as I leave your bed, I'm counting the hours until the next night."

He pulled her hips higher, forcing her to balance on her toes.

"Sometimes," he panted, "even in the middle of the day, I have to lock the library door and stroke my own cock, spending into a handkerchief like a randy youth. And it's still not enough. It's never enough."

There was an angry edge to his words, and a brutish quality to his rhythm—as though he wanted her to be sorry for driving him mad with lust. Well, Emma had no intention of apologizing. His growled confessions were the best things she'd ever heard. She only hoped she could remember them long enough to write them all down in her diary tomorrow.

She felt his forehead rest against her shoulder, feverish and damp with sweat. He put one hand over hers on the bedpost, bracing his weight, and then reached with the other to touch her between her thighs. Circling his fingertips just where she needed it, just where he knew it would break her apart.

All the while, he took her in forceful thrusts. It was animal and uncivilized and she was wild with arousal. Her body quivered as he drove her toward the most devastating orgasm of her life. She couldn't hide from it, couldn't hold back. When the pleasure caught her, she came in racking, tearless sobs. She forgot where she was, *who* she was.

But he hadn't kept his promise to tup her senseless. Not quite. Her awareness of him only heightened. She sensed the heat of his body, heard the harsh rasps of his breath, breathed the earthy musk of his skin, felt the iron length of his cock at the center of her.

"God," he choked out. "God. Emma."

A thrill shot through her as he called her name. Even in the mindless fury of joining, he hadn't forgotten her, either.

A ragged groan signaled his crisis. Then it was only stillness and quiet and dark and labored breath.

After several moments, he kissed the top of her head. His arm tightened around her middle, drawing her close. "Tell me you're not too scandalized."

She smiled to herself. "I'm scandalized the perfect amount, thank you. But my thighs are jelly."

He helped her onto the bed, and they collapsed in a tangle of sweaty limbs.

"Well," he said, "that was a delightful first course."

"First course? Of how many?"

"Depends on how hungry I am."

She buffeted him with a nearby pillow. He took it from her, and tucked it under his head.

As he drew her close, he jolted in surprise.

"What is it?" she asked, alarmed.

"By God, woman. Your feet are ice."

"I told you, I seem to be one of those people who's always cold."

He rose to a sitting position and caught one of her ankles, drawing it into his lap. He rubbed briskly with both hands, warming her chilled foot. When he was done with the first, he reached for the other.

Emma resisted. "Truly, you don't need to do that."

"I need to do it if you're going to stay in my bed. And you *are* going to stay in my bed. I'm nowhere near finished with you tonight." He reached for her ankle. "Give it here."

She didn't know how to refuse. She let him take her foot in his hands. "Don't mock me, please. I know it's unsightly."

"Unsightly?" He stroked her bare leg from her ankle to her knee. "Nothing about you could be unsightly."

"It's my toe. Or rather, my lack of one."

He finally dragged his gaze down to the end of

her foot, to the empty space where she was missing the small toe. "Were you born without it?"

"No, I . . . It froze in the snow."

He ran his thumb over the stub of flesh.

"I tried to warn you." She tugged her leg from his grip. "Lord, it's so embarrassing."

He broke into laughter. "You are the most ridiculous woman. Of all people, you'd worry that I would give a damn that you're missing a tiny scrap of a toe?" He waved at the scarred side of his face. "Have you *looked* at me?"

"As much as you'll allow me to, yes. But that's different. You have war injuries. They're marks of valor. I have a mark of foolishness."

"The only foolishness here is the fact that you'd hide it."

She tilted her head. "Hm. Shall I point out the hypocrisy in that statement?"

"No."

"You did walk right into it."

"In point of fact, it crashed into me." He reclined onto his side, his head propped on one elbow. "A Congreve rocket at Waterloo. Powerful impact, nearly impossible to aim. One happened to turn back on our ranks, and I was its lucky target."

Emma lay on her side, facing him. She didn't dare say anything, for fear he would shutter himself again.

"After my injury, when I woke up in blinding pain and missing parts of myself, I looked down to see if my cock was still there. When I saw that it was, I said—fine, I suppose I want to live."

She smiled. "I'm glad you did. Tonight was . . . I've never felt anything like it."

"I'm tempted to take that as a compliment, but considering your limited experience I'm not certain I can."

"My experience might not be as limited as you're assuming. I . . ." Emma gathered her courage. "I'm not a virgin. Or, I mean, I wasn't when we wed."

Silence fell over the room, heavy as an anvil. She found it difficult to breathe under the weight.

"You're very quiet," she finally ventured. "Won't you say something?"

"Let me guess. The boy back home?"

"Yes. I knew it was imprudent, but that was what made it exciting. My father was uncompromising, and I have a rebellious streak."

"So I've noted."

Emma had never been a good vicar's daughter, no matter how she'd tried to be. Her father's expectations were too elusive. If she made the slightest progress toward his approval, the line only moved further away. At some point, she gave up on trying and went looking for approval and affection in other places.

That, of course, was what had landed her in trouble.

"He was the local squire's son," she said. "Three years older than I. Sometimes we would meet by chance during walks, and I was flattered by his interest. A kiss became two, and so forth. I fancied myself to be wildly in love with him. There was a ball at his sister's house, and he asked her to invite me. Said it would be a special evening for us both."

"I can guess the sort of 'special evening' he had in mind."

She looked over his shoulder, her gaze unfocused. "I made myself a new gown for the occasion. Rose-red silk with gold ribbon at the sleeves and waist. I spent hours fussing with curling papers and tongs to make my ringlets just right. Fool that I was, I thought he meant to propose. And even when he tugged at my bodice and reached up my skirt, I still thought he meant to propose—afterward. I thought he was carried away with passion, that was all. It felt dizzyingly romantic."

She skipped over the details of the encounter. "We were caught together, which was humiliating enough. Then he refused to marry me—which was devastating. Apparently there'd been some family understanding that he would wed a distant cousin."

"To the Devil with any cousin. Someone should have brought the knave up to scratch."

"There was no one to try it. I hadn't any brothers to defend my honor, and my father . . . My father didn't even attempt to force his hand. He blamed me for everything. What treatment did I expect, he asked, going about in a harlot-red dress. He called me a strumpet, a jezebel, said he didn't blame the young man for refusing. He told me no decent man would ever want me, and that

I was to leave his house at once and not bother coming back."

Even six years later, the pain felt as fresh as if it were yesterday. She'd known society would judge her harshly for her mistake, but her own father . . . ? Giles had disappointed and misused her, but Father was the man who'd broken her heart.

This was why she had to help Davina Palmer. She would never allow another young woman to face that sort of rejection and abandonment. Not if she could help it.

She swallowed back the bitter lump in her throat. "It was winter and snowing. I hadn't much money. So I walked to London."

"And you arrived with nine toes."

She nodded.

"And every so often, you still shiver."

She nodded again.

He was silent for several moments, and when he spoke his voice was low and stern. "Emma, you should have told me this."

Chapter Eighteen

You should have told me this.

Emma's heartbeat faltered. Guilt moved through her like a cold wind. She reached for one of the quilts. "You didn't ask about my virtue. But you're right, I should have told you anyway."

Not every man would condemn her for such an indiscretion, perhaps—but a titled gentleman would have genuine, understandable concern. Laws of primogeniture and all. If he was angry with her, she couldn't blame him.

Perhaps her father was right, and he'd believe he'd been sold a bill of damaged goods.

"It was ages ago," she assured him. "And I didn't conceive, thank heaven. You needn't worry. Your bloodline is secure."

He cursed. "Really, Emma. That thought hadn't crossed my mind."

"Then . . . what thoughts *are* crossing it?"

"A great many." He rolled onto his back and folded his hands behind his head. "Primarily, I'm debating how best to kill both this squire's son and your father. A pistol would be the most efficient method perhaps, but will it be too quick to be satisfying? And I'm wondering if I'll have time to off both of them in one night, or if I'll be forced to stop over in some miserable inn."

She couldn't help but laugh a little.

"I'm not joking," he said.

"Of course you are. You're the Monster of Mayfair, not the Murderer."

"You are my wife. Some villain took advantage of you."

"I wasn't your wife then, and he didn't take advantage. I made my own choice. It may have been a poor choice, but it was mine. Besides, even if you desired to kill him, the war beat you to it."

He cursed under his breath. "There's still your father. He treated you abominably. Pestilent codpiece."

Emma had to hide her face, lest he see how close she was to tears. She'd never been able to shake the feeling that perhaps her father had been right. That it *was* her fault—not entirely, but in part. Perhaps she *had* been a shameless hussy for seeking passion and love. At the least, she'd been a fool.

For that reason, she'd long resolved to keep emotions out of any relationship. However, it was growing more and more difficult to keep that resolution—not merely by the day, but by the hour. She was feeling too much tenderness toward the man currently plotting murder at her side. No matter that he deflected any suggestion of decency with a jaded, biting humor and had determined to convince the world of his monstrous nature.

Emma knew the truth. He wasn't a saint, and he wasn't easy to live with. But he did possess a heart—a large and loyal one—and some part of it was now committed to defending her. How could she fail to be moved?

"Come." He tucked her beneath a heap of bed linens. "Will four quilts do tonight? Or should I fetch another?"

"Four quilts are fine, thank you. Can you . . . I'm feeling a bit fragile right now. It would mean a great deal if you'd hold me. You know, with your arms."

Brilliant, Emma. As if he might have tried to hold her with his knees or eyelids without those instructions.

After a brief hesitation, he slid beneath the four quilts and draped his arm about her shoulders. He was growing very good at these things. Just as she had in the dark at Swanlea, she felt secure and protected. Safe.

She'd almost drifted into a warm, comforted sleep—

When he slipped from the bed and left the room.

IT WAS WELL after midnight when Ash reached the village.

He slowed his horse to a walk as he approached the borders of the sleepy hamlet, then roped it to a tree branch beside a stream. The gelding deserved a rest, along with water and a graze. And for his part, Ash needed to make a stealthy approach.

It proved easy enough to find the right house— the smug cottage sitting next to the church. Just looking at it made him furious. The white boxes beneath the windows, stuffed with innocent red and pink geraniums. Botanical lies, every last one.

He found a place where a stone fence bordered the house and used it to hoist himself up on the ledge, just below the largest window. The one that looked out on the church.

He was prepared to put a wrapped fist through the window, but he found it was unnecessary. Apparently no one latched their windows in a goodly little village like this.

He lifted the window sash, then thrust his lantern through the opening. Bending himself nearly double, he managed to work one leg through, and then the other. Not the most graceful of entrances, but then—suaveness wasn't his purpose tonight.

"Who are you?" An old man shot up in bed and pressed his back to the headboard. "*What* are you?"

"What do you think?" Ashbury raised his lantern to the gnarled, scarred side of his face and took pleasure in the vicar's anguished whimper. "A demon come to drag you to Hell, you miserable wretch."

"To Hell? M-me?"

"Yes, you. You crusty botch of nature. You poisonous bunch-backed toad. Sitting in this weaselly little house full to reeking with betrayal and . . ." He waved at the nearest shelf. "And ghastly curtains."

"What's wrong with the curtains?"

"Everything!" he roared.

The old bastard drew the covers up to his chin and began to weep.

Excellent.

"Never mind the curtains, you milk-livered, flap-mouthed dotard." He loomed over the bed. "There aren't any windows in Hell."

"No. No, this can't be."

Ash stepped back at once. "Oh, it can't? Perhaps I have the wrong house." He drew a scrap of something from his pocket and peered down at it. "Vicarage . . . Buggerton, Hertfordshire . . ."

"This is Bellington."

Ash straightened the paper and made a show of peering at it. "Yes, you're right. *Bellington*, Hertfordshire. Reverend George Gladstone. That's not you?"

The old man moaned. "It's me."

"Thank Pluto." He crumpled the paper and cast it to the floor. "Such a nuisance when I cock these things up. It's a devil of a delay when there's so much to be done. Once you arrive in the eternal furnace, there are sinful debts to be settled. 'Hell to pay' is not merely a saying. Then there are the endless papers to be signed and filed."

"Papers to be filed?"

"Naturally there are papers. It should surprise no one to learn that Hell is a vast, inefficient bureaucracy."

"I suppose not," the old man said meekly.

"Now where was I? Oh, yes." He lifted the lantern and made his voice an unholy crescendo. "Prepare for eternal hellfire!"

"B-but I'm a vicar! I have been a faithful servant of the Lord."

"Liar!"

The clergyman quivered. A dark puddle seeped across the dimly lit bed linens, and one sniff told Ashbury what it was. The craven piece of filth had pissed the bed.

"You are the veriest varlet that ever took to the pulpit. Doesn't your Holy Bible have something to say about forgiveness?"

The man cowered in silence.

"No, truly. I'm asking. Doesn't it? I'm a demon, I don't read the thing."

"Y-yes, of course. The gospel is a story of grace and redemption."

Ash stepped toward the foot of the bed, until he loomed over the shrinking reverend, and lifted the lantern high. "Then why, you rank, miserable, piss-soaked serpent, did you fail to offer that grace to your own daughter?"

"Emma?"

"Yes, Emma." His heart wrenched when he spoke her name, and his voice shook with fury. "Your own flesh and blood. Wasn't she worthy of this forgiveness you preach?"

"Forgiveness requires penitence. She was warned. Given every explanation. Nevertheless, she persisted in her sinful behavior, and she would not repent of it."

"She was a *girl*. Vulnerable. Trusting. Afraid. You threw her to the wolves to protect your own selfish, sinful pride. And you call yourself a man of God. You are nothing but a charlatan."

"Tell me what I can do to atone. I'll do anything. Anything."

"There is nothing you can say. No excuse you can make."

Ash drew a slow, deep breath. If he were here to satisfy his own wishes, he would have happily killed the old fellow here and now. Dispatched him to Hell in truth. But he hadn't come all this way to take his own bloody revenge.

He was here for Emma.

Because she'd touched him, kissed him, made him feel human and wanted and whole. Because her disgusting coward of a father had hurt her so deeply, she still didn't trust her own heart.

Because he was probably halfway in love with her—and wasn't *that* the Devil's bollocks.

For her sake, he would confine his vengeance to methods involving fewer sharp objects and entrails. He would let the man keep his life. But Ash would do his worst to make certain he didn't enjoy it.

"What day is this?" Ash demanded.

"Th-Thursday."

He shook his head. "I'll be damned."

"But . . . aren't you damned already?"

"Silence!" he boomed.

The man jumped in his skin.

"I have the day wrong. You've a reprieve. A *brief* reprieve."

"A reprieve?" He cast his eyes to the ceiling. "Thank you, Lord."

"Don't thank the Lord. You should be grateful to *me*."

"Yes. Yes, of course."

"Know this, you mammering canker-blossom." Ash skirted the bed in ominous steps. "We *will* meet again. You will not know the year, nor the day, nor the hour. In the cold of every night, you will feel the flames licking at your heels. Your daily porridge will taste of sulfur. With every breath, every step, every heartbeat in the remainder of your miserable, lumpish life . . . you will quiver with unrelenting fear."

He went to the window and prepared to climb through it, disappearing into the night. "Because I will come for you. And when I do, there will be no escape."

Chapter Nineteen

Why, you little thief.

Though Ash had to admit—as thieves went, this was a deuced pretty one.

His morning had been filled with dreary correspondence. Once he'd sent off a contract to the solicitors for yet another revision, Ash had gone in search of luncheon. Then he'd returned to his library—only to find his wife ransacking his bookshelves.

Apparently the volume in her hands was sufficiently absorbing that she hadn't noticed his presence. As he stood in the doorway watching, she tucked a stray wisp of dark hair behind her ear. Then she licked her fingertip and turned the page.

His knees buckled. In his mind, he scrambled to piece that half second into a lasting memory. The crook of her slender finger. The red pout of her lips. That fleeting, erotic glimpse of pink.

She did it again.

Ash gripped the doorjamb so hard, his knuckles lost sensation.

He wanted her to read the whole cursed book while he watched.

He wanted the book to have a thousand pages.

She closed the volume and added it to a growing stack on the chair. Then, turning her back to him, she stretched on tiptoe to reach for another. Her heels popped out of her slippers, revealing the arches of her feet and those indescribably arousing white stockings.

God's blood. A man could only take so much.

"Don't move."

She froze. Her arm remained lifted; her hand was still poised to take a green volume from its shelf. "I only wanted a book."

"Don't," he repeated, "move."

"A novel, poetry. Something to pass the time. I thought perhaps I'd even try some Shakespeare. I didn't mean to disturb—"

"Stay. Just. As. You. Are." He approached her in slow, deliberate paces—one step for each low, deliberate word. "Not one finger. Not one toe. Not one tiny freckle on your arse."

"I don't have freckles on my . . . Do I?"

He didn't stop until he stood directly behind her. He reached to cover her raised hand. With a flex of his fingers, he tipped the green book into place.

"I'll leave you to your work." She moved to lower her hand.

He pinned her wrist to the shelf. "Not just yet."

She sucked in her breath. He knew her well enough to recognize that sound. It wasn't fear, but excitement.

Good. Very good.

"Do you know," he said in an idle tone, stroking his thumb along her delicate wrist, "I've been thinking."

"That sounds ominous."

"Oh, it is." With his free hand, he cupped the swell of her breast, stroking her softness through the muslin. "The object of this marriage is to get you with child."

"Yes." Her voice was drowsy. "I seem to recall that was our bargain."

Her head tilted to the side, and he ran his tongue along the elongated slope of her neck. She tasted both tart and sweet. Delicious.

"So if we do this twice a day," he murmured, "that would make our objective twice as likely."

"I . . . I suppose it would."

"No supposing about it." He tweaked her nipple. "It's simple mathematics."

After a pause, he heard a little smile in her voice. "Is it, my fawn?"

Saucy, impudent wench.

The race was on. She helped him hike her skirts to her waist. He stroked the seam of her cleft, tracing it until he found that essential spot at the apex. She gasped with pleasure, gripped the bookshelf with both hands. He couldn't unbutton his falls fast enough.

After what seemed an epoch of fumbling with garments, they finally pressed flesh to flesh. His hard, aching need against her wet, ready heat.

"Now?" He growled the word.

Her reply was breathless. "Yes."
Yes.
Yes, yes, yes.

THE DALLIANCE IN the library was the first of many daytime trysts. Now that Ash knew her to be game for unconventional bedsport, his imagination knew no bounds. His stamina was nowhere near depleted, either. Making love unclothed in full daylight still felt like too great a risk. When they were that close, that intimate . . . he hated the idea of pity intruding into moments when he ought to be strong. He worried that if she touched him, he might snap back.

And there was always the other risk: Repulsing her completely.

How could I bear to lie with . . . with that?

No, he couldn't chance it. However, with a willing, adventurous partner, there were ways around the hurdle. Pleasure needn't be confined to fumbling nighttime encounters.

Emma did not object, he found, to being bent over the nearest sturdy piece of furniture. The billiard table made for one particularly enjoyable liaison. He pulled her into shadowy alcoves and deep closets and took her propped against the wall in the hot, musky dark. They discovered all manner of accoutrements—cravats, sashes, handkerchiefs—could be pressed into service as blindfolds.

No matter what he suggested, she never told him no.

She always said yes.

She said "yes" and "yes" and "more" and "please."

As always, those little sighs and moans sank straight to his cock, urging him closer to release. But as their passionate afternoons melted into weeks, her words found deeper targets. He even came to adore her endlessly absurd pet names. They pierced through his scar tissue, battered at the bony cage around his heart.

Ash struggled to rebuild that barricade daily.

Don't make too much of her willingness, he scolded himself. She was a passionate woman by nature. No doubt she wanted this child-getting business over and done with, too.

And yet he could not stay away from her, could never satisfy his desire. There was no floor to the chasm inside him. It wasn't only her body he craved, it was closeness. Acceptance. The feeling of being wanted, and never turned away.

Yes.

She always said yes.

Until the night she didn't.

One evening, Emma failed to appear for dinner. Her maid delivered a message to the table. Ash sipped a brandy as he unfolded and read the note written in his wife's hand.

She was indisposed, it read, and she suspected a few days' time would pass before she felt fully restored. With apologies, she could not welcome his visits at present.

Well, then. It didn't require much effort to

sift through the delicate phrasing. Her monthly courses had arrived. She wasn't pregnant, not yet.

He ought to have been disappointed.

Instead, all he felt was relief.

She wasn't with child. That meant he had another month.

Another month of whisking her into dark spaces, turning her face to the wall, and feeling her teeth scrape the heel of his hand when she came.

Another month of *"yes."*

Another month of not being alone.

Another month of Emma.

Something in his chest went buoyant with joy.

Ash drained his brandy. Then he propped an elbow on the table and lowered his forehead until it rested against his thumb and forefinger. He massaged the knotted scar on his right cheekbone.

You are a dolt. Ignorant as dirt. This was more than infatuation. He'd allowed a foolish, irrational attachment to develop. Now something must be done about it.

He called for another brandy. And then another. When he'd drained the decanter, he located his cloak and his hat. Then he ventured out into the darkened streets. He'd find some ruffians to menace, or some foxed dandies to scare out of their champagne-polished boots.

This, he told himself with every cringe and wince he inspired, was what sort of welcome the world gave a monster. This was how "accepted" he was by his fellow man.

Perhaps he had another month of "yes," but he must never forget this: The long, bitter life stretching beyond it would always be "no."

"BLOODY HELL. I *knew* it."

Ash froze in place, one hand immobile on the gate latch. His other hand tightened on his walking stick. He turned around to view the source of the outburst.

A boy was waiting on him in the alley behind the mews.

Not merely a boy. *That* boy. The one from before.

"I knew it," the boy said. "I knew it had to be you."

God's lords and his ladies.

Ash collared the youth and dragged him into the shadows. He looked about the alley to make certain no grooms or coachmen lingered close enough to overhear.

"The Duke of Ashbury is the Monster of Mayfair."

"I don't know what you're on about," Ash said sternly. As if there might be some other scarred man wandering the alleys of Mayfair by night, wearing a cape and carrying a gold-knobbed walking stick.

"I knew from that night—said to my mates, I did—that you had to be Quality," the boy rattled on. "The rest, I pieced together from the gossip sheets. The Duke of Ashbury came to Town just a few weeks before the first sighting appeared in the papers. Rumored to have suffered an injury at Waterloo. I decided to wait out here just to see if my guess was on the mark. And damn me, here you are." He smacked his hands together. "Wait until the lads hear this."

"The lads will hear nothing." Ash gave the boy a shake. "Do you understand me?"

"You can't frighten me. I know you won't hurt me. Roughing up innocents isn't your game, is it?"

No, it wasn't. Unfortunately.

Ash released the boy's collar. "Fine. You'll have a crown from me, but nothing more."

"A crown for what?"

"In exchange for keeping your mouth shut. That's why you're here, isn't it? Starting the blackmail a bit early, I must say."

"My mum always said I was advanced for my age." The boy grinned, revealing a gap between his front teeth. "But it's not money I'm after. My family's flush with it. My father made a fortune in coal. Name's Trevor, by the way."

"If you try to spread this tale, Trevor, no one will credit it. You live in Mayfair; you should already know how the snobbish *ton* thinks. They won't take the word of some new-money brat over that of a duke."

Ash brushed past the boy and started down the alleyway at a brisk pace.

Of course the boy followed.

"You've got me all wrong," Trevor said in a

loud whisper, trotting at Ash's side. "I don't want to expose you. I want to be your associate."

That brought Ash to a standstill. "My associate?"

"An assistant. An apprentice. A protégé. You know what I mean."

"No. I don't."

"I'm going to join your wanderings at night. Help you mete out justice. Pound footpads and such."

Ash looked the boy up and down. "You couldn't pound a lump of bread dough."

"Don't be so certain about that. I've a weapon. A secret one." The boy looked both ways before withdrawing something from his pocket and holding it up for Ash to see.

"A sling. This is your secret weapon."

"Well, you already have the walking stick. And a pistol or blade seemed out of character for us."

"There is no 'us.'"

"Too violent, you know. We're peacekeepers."

"There is no 'we,' either."

"A sling would set me apart, I reckoned." The lad plucked a pebble from the ground and fitted it in the leather pocket. "See that crate at the corner?" He flicked his wrist a few times, building momentum, then released the sling.

The pebble smacked into a stable door on the opposite side of the alleyway.

A horse whinnied. From the loft above, a sleepy groom called out in anger, "Oi! Who's there?"

Trevor looked at Ash. Ash looked at Trevor. They each mouthed the same word at the same time.

Run.

Once safely down the lane and around the corner, Trevor put his hands on his knees and panted. "I'm"—*huff*—"still working on my aim."

Ash walked on, hoping to lose the boy while he was winded.

"Next I'll need a disguise, of course. I'm thinking a mask. Black, or perhaps red. And a name, naturally."

Ash growled. "There will be no disguise. There will be no name. Do you hear me? Go home before I take you there myself and have a word with your father."

"What do you think of this? The Beast of Berkeley Square."

"More like the Pest of Piccadilly."

"Or we could go with something simpler. Like Doom. Or the Raven."

"I suggest Gnat. Or the Measle."

"Maybe the Doom-Raven?"

Ash shook his head. "Jove that thunders, you are a menace."

"Wait. That's brilliant. I'll be known as"—he swiped one hand before his face, as if tracing a broadsheet's headline—"the Menace."

Oh, indeed you will be.

Ash stopped, turned, and stared down at the boy. "Listen, lad. I am returning to my house. You are returning to yours. And that is the end of it."

"But it's not even midnight. We haven't thrashed any scoundrels yet."

Ash grabbed Trevor by his jacket and lifted him onto his toes. He bent forward and lowered his voice to a threat. "Consider yourself fortunate I haven't thrashed *you*."

As he strode away, this time he heard no scampering steps in pursuit.

Thank heaven.

"You're right," Trevor called after him cheerily. "Tomorrow night's better. I need time to sort out my disguise anyway."

Ash tugged down the brim of his hat and groaned.

If this boy was indicative of the next generation, God save England.

EMMA TRIPPED DOWN to the servants' hall, intending to request eggs be added to the evening's dinner menu. To every evening's dinner menu. Eggs were rumored to increase the chances of conception, weren't they? Perhaps nothing but superstition, but it wouldn't hurt to try.

She stopped just outside the door. The servants seemed to be having some sort of a meeting. Khan stood in front of a large slate—the one usually employed for the day's menus—with the remainder of the house staff huddled around the servants' long dining table.

She was about turn around and come back later. Then the topic of conversation reached her ears.

"Think hard, all of you," Khan said. "Swanlea wasn't enough. We need a new plan."

A new *plan*?

Emma wasn't an eavesdropper by nature, but further "plans" involving her marriage seemed good cause for an exception. She tucked herself in the wedge of space between the open door and the wall. From here, she could not only listen, but peek through the gap.

"Well, it has to be a ball," Mary said. "Balls are ever so romantic. Surely they'll receive an invitation to one."

"The duke would never accept," one of the footmen said.

"Then perhaps we could host a ball here," she replied. "As a surprise."

"Perhaps we could," said Khan dryly, "if we all wished to be summarily executed."

Mary sighed. "Well, whatever we do, we must do it soon. Once Her Grace is with child, it will be too late."

A scullery maid hooted with laughter. "That won't be long, will it? What with them humping like rabbits all over the house."

"Not only the house," a groom said. "The mews, as well."

Mary hushed them. "We're not supposed to let on that we've noticed."

"Oh, come *on*. How could we not?"

Oh, Lord. Behind the door, Emma cringed. How mortifying. Although she supposed it was to be expected. They had polished every stick of furniture in Ashbury House with her hiked petticoats. They weren't especially quiet, either. Naturally, the servants had noticed. As the groom said, how could they not?

"Ahem." Khan tapped his chalk against the slate. "Let's return to the list, please."

The servants burst out with a flurry of suggestions.

"Set a small fire?"

"Rig one of the carriage axles to break. Accidentally. In a storm."

"Oh! They could go swimming in the Serpentine."

Khan refused to even chalk that one on the slate. "It's nearly December. They'd catch their deaths."

"I suppose," Mary said. "But there's nothing to encourage affection like a good scare. Perhaps we could make one of them just a little bit sick?"

"The duke was bedridden for nearly a *year*," the butler replied. "That would be cruel. Though perhaps a minor incident . . ."

The same footman's hand shot toward the ceiling. "Bees! Hornets! Spiders! Snakes!"

"Frogs. Locusts. Rivers of blood," Cook deadpanned. "I believe we've covered all the plagues, Moses."

Emma wheezed. She clapped both hands to her mouth.

"She could walk in on the duke while he's dressing," Mary suggested.

All the servants perked up at that one. "Oooh."

Khan apparently agreed. "Now *that* has possibilities."

Emma couldn't remain quiet any longer. She emerged from her hiding place and announced her presence. "That last happened already."

The assembled staff leapt to their feet, the blood draining from their faces. For a good half minute, the only sounds were anxious gulping.

Mary broke the silence. "And . . . ? What was the duke's response?"

"The duke's response was none of your business."

The footman piped up. "How do you feel about spider bites?"

"What I feel is that this needs to stop. All of it. You must all adjust your expectations. There will be no romance. The duke is not falling in love."

Emma needed the stern reminder as much as anyone.

It wouldn't even matter if he *did* begin to love her. In the end, they would part. He was resolute on the matter, and she needed to be at Swanlea this winter for Davina's sake. But before Davina could get permission to visit, Emma must convince the duke to move in society—at least a little bit.

"I think," she said quietly, "he needs friends."

Khan gave a heavy sigh. "We're sunk."

"They all deserted him," Mary said. "And the few who didn't—well, he drove them away. His

Grace doesn't have any friends any longer. Not outside this room."

Emma pondered in the ensuing quiet. If it was true that Ashbury's only remaining friends resided inside this house . . .

She must convince him to venture outside it.

Chapter Twenty

Ash stalked the corridors of Ashbury House. Where the devil was his butler?

Khan wasn't in the library. Nor the billiard room, ballroom, sitting room, drawing room, or music room. Though Ash wasn't certain why he'd even checked the last. It had been established quite painfully last summer that the man couldn't hold a tune.

Eventually, Ash found him in the kitchen.

The pungent fragrance of herbs came from a pot boiling on the hob. Khan sat on a chair, holding a compress to his eye, while Emma cooed and fussed over him.

Look at her, the picture of tender domestic care. She'd make an excellent mother. He'd suspected as much from the first, but it was reassuring to see with his own eyes. His heir would need a steady, loving presence in his life, and it wasn't going to be Ash.

She looked up and noticed him, and her concerned eyes narrowed to knife-blade slits. "You."

"What?"

"You know very well what." She waved at Khan. "Look at him. His eye's all blackened and swollen. I know you're responsible."

Oh, she would make a fine disciplinarian, too. Her censure almost made Ash feel guilty, and he never felt ashamed of his actions. Only his appearance.

"It was only a bit of sparring. And the injury was his fault."

"*His* fault? I suppose he punched himself in the eye."

"We were practicing a new combination. Khan was supposed to weave and dodge." He turned to his butler. "Go on, tell her. You were supposed to dodge."

"I was supposed to dodge," Khan mumbled from behind the compress.

"See?" As his coolly silent wife went to the stove, Ash continued, "Anyhow, I need him back. He has work to do."

Khan set aside the compress and drew to his feet. "Thank you, Your Grace, for your kind attention."

"But your poultice," she said. "It's nearly ready."

"Perhaps Your Grace would be so good as to save it for later." He bowed to Emma, then turned to Ash. "I will wait in the library."

After the butler had quit the room, Emma banged about the kitchen in silent censure.

"It's a bruise," Ash said. "One derived from manly activity. I'm telling you, he loves it."

"He was *weeping*," she returned.

He spread his hands. "Tears of joy."

She sighed.

"Yes, I'm demanding. Yes, I'm inconsiderate. Yes, I'm remorseless. Anything else I should admit to being while I'm here?"

She retrieved a broadsheet from the table and held it up for his view. It was emblazoned with the headline "Monster of Mayfair Strikes Again."

Ash reached for it. "I hadn't seen that one. That's brilliant. I've top billing, too."

"There are several."

He paged through the stack she offered.

"Monster of Mayfair Assaults Local Lad."

"Monster of Mayfair Terrorizes Three in St. James Street."

"Monster of Mayfair Abducts Lambs from Butcher. Dark Rituals Suspected."

"Hah. The 'local lad' was twenty if he was a day, and he richly deserved it. There were four in St. James Street. Foxed dandies chatting up a lady of the evening on their way home from Boodle's. I didn't like their disrespectful attitude. This last . . . I didn't even *do* this last. Lambs, my eye." He chuckled. "Do you know what this means?"

"I'm married to an unchecked vigilante?"

"No. Well, maybe. But also—it means people are making up their own Monster of Mayfair stories just to share in the notoriety. It means I'm a legend."

Emma shook her head. She strained the herbs

through a cheesecloth, twisting them into a bundle.

"This"—he riffled the papers—"is stupendous."

"It's not. It's truly not."

"Oh, look. This one has an illustration." He turned his twisted profile to her and held up the paper's engraved portrait of "The Monster Himself." "What do you say? I think they made my nose a trifle long, but otherwise it's a surprisingly accurate likeness."

She slammed the empty pot on the table. "It is not an accurate likeness, but it is a perfect illustration of the problem. You're only letting people see one side of you. If only you'd give them a chance to see past your scars—"

"People *can't* see past the scars. In an alley, a market . . . anywhere. They suck up all the attention in the room, and I'm just the drain it's circling."

"It doesn't have to be that way."

His jaw clenched. "I'll make you a bargain. I won't pretend I know how it feels when strange men stare at your tits, and you won't pretend you know how it feels when people stare at my face."

Her demeanor softened. "I'm sorry, I shouldn't presume."

"No, you shouldn't."

"Won't you give it a chance?" She skirted the table, coming to stand before him. "One outing, that's all I ask. A single afternoon with normal people. Well, I suppose they're not precisely *normal* people. But they aren't footpads, at least."

He frowned. "What are you on about?"

"Come to tea with my friends Thursday next. That's what I'm on about."

He began to object. "I'm n—"

She pressed her fingers to his lips, shushing him. Her fingertips were scented with herbs and honey. Intoxicating. How was he supposed to stay irritated when she smelled so lickable?

"Lady Penelope Campion's house. It's just across the square. That shouldn't be any great trial." She lifted an eyebrow in teasing fashion. "That is, unless you're afraid of a few harmless spinsters."

ASH COULDN'T RECALL the last time he'd crossed the square to the Campion residence. He'd been a boy, surely no older than ten. Lady Penelope had been much too young to be a proper playmate for him, not to mention she possessed the unsalvageable flaw of being a girl. But he'd been forced to make the effort once a summer anyhow. Her single saving grace, as far as he'd been concerned, was that she always seemed to be hiding a grubby creature or two in her closet or under the bed.

He had a distant memory of piglets. And a newt, perhaps?

Emma rang the bell.

"I'm doing this once," he muttered, staring at the door. "And that's the end of it."

"I understand," she said.

"And only because my parents thought highly of the family."

"Of course."

"They would want me to look in on Lady Penelope now that she's living alone."

She squeezed his hand. "Don't be so anxious. They'll adore you."

The door opened. His guts clenched.

"Lady Penelope. A pleasure."

Ash reached for Penelope's hand, intending to bow over it, but she only laughed. Instead, she placed her ungloved hands on his shoulders and pulled him down for a hug. As if it were nothing.

"Come in, come in." Penelope threaded her arm in his and led them inside. "And you must call me Penny. We're old friends. I've seen you in your nightshirt. You don't expect me to use 'Your Grace,' I hope."

"Ashbury will suffice."

"Ash," Emma said. "He goes by Ash among friends. At home, it's pumpkin."

He sent her a look.

She smiled in return.

"Ash it is," Penny said, patting his arm.

The house looked much the way he remembered. Same paintings on the walls, same furnishings . . . only now they were covered in a great deal more fur.

He braced himself as they rounded the corner into the salon.

However, he met with no outbursts of shock or cries of horror. It would seem the other guests had been well prepared for his appearance—which was a relief in some ways and rather lowering in others. He could just picture Emma telling them over tea: *Now don't be alarmed, but my husband is a hideous monstrosity.*

Penny made the unnecessary introductions. Surely the other two women knew who he was, and Emma had told him a bit about them.

Miss Teague had the frazzled ginger hair and smelled of something burned. Miss Mountbatten was the small, dark-haired one who . . . who was dressed in a stylish, flattering walking dress in a peacock-blue damask that strongly reminded Ash of his music room draperies.

He made a small bow, then waited until the ladies were settled before taking his seat. Penny began pouring cups of tea.

Miss Teague and Miss Mountbatten sat in silence, stealing looks at Ash, then glancing toward each other, and then looking down at their laps. He was accustomed to being the object of curiosity. The strangest thing, however, was that they seemed to be wearing slight, knowing smiles all the while.

A white cat came slinking around the leg of his armchair and leapt into his lap.

Ash removed it, setting the beast on the floor.

It promptly jumped back up, settling into his lap.

"That's always the way with cats," Penny said. "They're drawn to the person who wants nothing to do with them. And Bianca is a particularly naughty one. Torments Hubert no end."

"I don't recall a Hubert in your family," Ash said. "Is he a servant?"

"Heavens, no." Penny laughed as she passed him a cup of tea. "Hubert's an otter."

Of course he was.

His hostess offered him a tray of triangular sandwiches with the crusts cut off. "Sham sandwich?"

"I'd like a ham sandwich very much, thank you." Ash took one eagerly, stuffing a large bite into his mouth. The more chewing he could manage, the less speaking he needed to do.

"No, no. It's a *sham* sandwich," Penny said. "Vegetables mashed and pressed into a loaf, then sliced like a ham. Turnip and potato, mostly, with cloves and a few beets for color. Quite nourishing, and every bit as delicious."

Oh, God.

Ash choked on his bite. He strove manfully to conceal a grimace as he washed the mess down with a gulp of tea.

"Lady Penny is a vegetarian," Miss Teague said.

"I'm afraid I don't understand."

"She doesn't eat meat," Emma said.

He paused. "I still don't understand."

"Here, try the cakes." Miss Mountbatten passed them to Emma. "Nicola baked them."

Ash took one, eyeing it with suspicion. It appeared innocent enough. "I thought Emma said you were a scientist, Miss Teague."

"Baking *is* science," she answered. "Success is all in the precision."

Ash took a bite, and found the cake to be precisely delicious. A great improvement over the sham.

"Well," Penny announced brightly. "We all have tea and refreshments, and now we must have conversation. What shall we discuss?"

"If only there were a current event occupying all London's attention." Miss Teague's speech had a stilted tone.

Almost a *practiced* tone.

"Oh!" Miss Mountbatten perked. "What news do you hear of the Monster of Mayfair?"

Ash put down his teacup. He turned his head to regard his wife.

Emma stared into her cup with great interest, as though the tea leaves were performing an underwater ballet.

Penny turned to him. "What is your opinion, Ash?"

"Dastardly fellow, to be sure," Ash said. "Dangerous. Vile. Reprehensible."

"I have a suspicion he's misunderstood," Miss Mountbatten said.

The salon was quiet—that was, until Miss Mountbatten nudged Miss Teague's knee.

"Oh! Oh, yes. This part is mine, isn't it?" Miss Teague cleared her throat. "You may be correct, Alexandra."

"I've just recalled that I happen to have some of the recent broadsheets." Penny turned to the table behind her and retrieved a stack of newsprint.

The truth was undeniable now. Ash had been lured into the spiders' web, and now he found himself at the center of delicately woven conspiracy.

A sham sandwich, indeed. One that sat on a tray of lies.

Penny leafed through the broadsheets. "Oh, look! 'Thousand-Pound Donation to War Widows Fund Credited to Monster of Mayfair.'" She turned over another. "'Monster of Mayfair Turns Cruel Taskmaster Out of Workhouse. London's Downtrodden Cheer.'"

She picked up the next sheet and, instead of reading it, turned it face-out to display the headline.

Ash grabbed the broadsheet from her hand and regarded it with horror. "'Monster of Mayfair Saves Puppies from Burning Storehouse'?"

This . . . this was an outrage.

Widows. Downtrodden.

Puppies.

Someone was chipping away at the legend he'd so carefully constructed. He took the stack of broadsheets and leafed through them, skimming the stories themselves. A pattern of suspiciously similar phrases began to emerge.

This paper has it on the highest authority . . .

An anonymous source of great repute . . .

"The pups wouldn't cease licking him in gratitude," *a lady of Quality reports . . .*

So. Emma and her friends hadn't merely collected these stories. They'd *concocted* them, the little coven of witches.

"It's just as we suspected." Miss Mountbatten grinned. "The so-called monster is merely misunderstood."

"If you want to know my opinion . . ." Emma began.

"I don't," he muttered.

"I don't think he's a monster at all," she finished. "In fact, I heard that he stopped by a foundling home with great sacks of sweets, and that they mobbed him with hugs and kisses. I suspect *that* will be in the broadsheets tomorrow."

"I suspect," he said through a tight smile, "there will be a story of a duchess and her three accomplices jailed for slander."

After a brief pause, the four ladies broke into simultaneous laughter.

Penny offered him the odious tray of edible deceit. "Do take another sandwich, Ash. Or was it lambkin?"

"It's starshine, I believe," Miss Mountbatten said.

"No, no," Miss Teague said. "I could have been certain it was hot cross bun."

As they all slipped into giggling again, Ash accepted the sandwich and arrowed a look at his wife.

Emma sipped her tea, casting him a coy smile over the cup's rim.

Just you wait, he thought, taking a resentful bite of vegetable falsehood. *Just you wait until we get home.*

Chapter Twenty-One

$\mathscr{A}$s it happened, Ash had no opportunity to hold his wife to account for her perfidy. The moment they passed through the door of her suite, she closed the door behind them and pinned him to it, drawing him down by the neck for an enthusiastic kiss.

"Thank you," she said. "You were wonderful."

"It was nothing."

And truly, it hadn't been much of an imposition. Once all their merciless teasing was out of the way, he'd even enjoyed himself.

"I can't believe you ate two of those dreadful sandwiches."

Correction: He'd enjoyed himself—save for that.

But he would eat "sham" twice a day without complaint, if it meant coming home to this. Emma's hands—and even better, her lips—were all over him.

She tugged his cravat loose and unbuttoned his waistcoat. He did his part to assist, shaking off his topcoat and tossing it . . . somewhere. He didn't bother to look.

Emma slithered down his body, then sank to her knees before him. She undid his trousers, pushing them down his thighs. His erection sprang free, all but begging for her attention. With one hand, she lifted the hem of his shirt, pushing the excess flat against his abdomen. She took his shaft in the other, rubbing her thumb up and down the underside.

She licked her lips and bent forward.

"Wait," he choked out.

She paused.

Why? Why had he said that?

"It's not kissing," she said with a coy arch of her eyebrow. "It's licking. And sucking. Won't you like it?"

"That's . . . not in question," he said firmly. Firmly in many senses of the word. "But we're supposed to be procreating. I can't make your mouth pregnant. Strictly speaking, this is outside our agreement."

"So what will you do?" She looked up at him, amused. "Bring a suit in Chancery? Your Honor, my wife dared to unclothe me. She proceeded to caress my person, with both hands and lips, against our sworn agreement to the contrary."

"Emma, you . . ."

"And then"—she gave a theatrical gasp—"the disobedient wench did place her mouth on my engorged staff."

She gave him a slow, exploratory lick.

"Jesus."

She backed off, lifting an eyebrow. "My, my. Such blasphemy. Is that in Shakespeare?"

He gritted his teeth. "Second *Henry the IV*, act two, scene two."

"Really? Interesting." She brushed a light, feathery kiss to the very tip of his cock.

God. Ash's hands clenched to fists at his sides. He couldn't take much more of this.

When she bent toward him again, her lips pursed for another teasing kiss, he grasped her by the hair. "Enough."

"*ENOUGH.*"

Emma gasped as he twisted his hand in her hair. His grip tugged on a thousand nerve endings at once.

"Enough," he growled again.

She understood his meaning.

Enough talking. Enough teasing. She was meant to get on with it.

Whatever "it" entailed.

Emma wasn't precisely certain what she'd started, but she would have rather died than ask. The basic idea seemed self-evident, even if the subtleties of technique were beyond her experience. Judging by her own responses to his lovemaking, it was hard to go wrong where licking was involved.

Casting her eyes upward to gauge his reaction, she traced tentative circles about the tip of his staff with her tongue. Beneath her hand, his abdominal muscles became washboard ridges. He arched his hips, nudging at her lips with the broad head of his erection. She took her cue from the inarticulate plea, taking him into her mouth.

He moaned, slumping back against the door. "Yes. Just like that."

She loved the taste of him, musky and male, and the feel of him—stroking against her palm with silky softness, and filling her grip with need that was impatient and hard. She loved the way his breathing changed, and the deep, ragged sound she pulled from his chest as she took him deeper.

Most of all, she loved the power. He was helpless with desire, exposed to her, pleading and vulnerable. At her mercy. Triumph sang through her body with his every gasp and groan.

She glanced up and found him looking down at her, his eyes glazed with desire and his teeth gritted. Since he seemed to enjoy watching, she used her free hand to push aside her fichu and offer him a view of her breasts. Feeling naughty, she trailed a fingertip along the exposed curves, dipping into her cleavage.

"God. *God.*" His thighs tensed, and she abandoned coyness in favor of a brisk rhythm. She knew he had to be close to his peak. "Emma, I—"

He pulled his cock free of her lips. Putting his grip over hers, he worked her hand up and down in a furious rhythm. His breath came harsh and rough until at last he found release.

In the aftermath, he fell back against the door, gasping for breath. Emma used her discarded fichu to clean her bosom. He reached down to cup her chin in his hand, tilting her face gently so that she looked up at him.

"For that," he said, "I would have eaten a hundred of those sandwiches."

She smiled.

He helped her to her feet, then yanked up his own trousers. Together they stumbled to the bed.

"That was . . . indescribable."

"It was my pleasure." And that was the truth. She felt quite satisfied with herself and empowered to an unprecedented degree. She rolled onto her belly and propped herself up on her elbows. "So we've been to tea. Where shall we go next? It's your turn to choose."

"I don't know what you mean."

"There must be so many things you miss doing. Not necessarily with me. Driving in the park with the top of the barouche folded down. Going around to the clubs. You could take boxing lessons at Gentleman Jackson's and stop making poor Khan serve as your sparring partner." She arched an eyebrow. "So long as brothels and opera dancers are not on the list."

"Please." He flung his forearm over his eyes. "The way you keep after me, I haven't the stamina."

"Good. Now about the next outing."

"There won't be one. I told you this afternoon that it would be the first and last time we went visiting."

"We could have a dinner party here, if you prefer. I have a friend from the dressmaking shop, Miss Davina Palmer. I think her father would enjoy making your acquaintance." She held her breath, waiting on his response.

He lowered his forearm and regarded her with seriousness. "Just what is it you're angling to do?"

The suspicion in his eyes unnerved her.

"I . . . I hate to see you living in seclusion, that's all. Once I go to Swanlea, I can't abide thinking of you sitting in the house, all alone."

Needles of guilt pricked at her palms. Of course, that wasn't her only reason. She did have an ulterior motive—to help Davina. But she meant what she'd told him, as well. It pained her to think of him being alone.

It pained her to think of leaving him. It pained her to think of going to Swanlea and raising their child without him being a part of their lives.

She didn't like their bargain anymore, and she was running out of time to renegotiate.

A FEW AFTERNOONS later, Ash was hard at work in the library, just hitting his stride in a fiery, scathing letter to his architect, when Khan entered.

Terrible timing, as usual.

Ash didn't look up from his letter. "What now?"

"I beg your pardon, Your Grace, but a rather large delivery has arrived for the duchess. Where shall I direct them to leave the boxes?"

"A delivery?" Ash lifted his head. "A delivery of what?"

"I believe it's a wardrobe. Shall I have them take the packages upstairs?"

Ash laid aside his pen. "No. No, take them to the drawing room."

A wardrobe.

Thank God for small miracles. His wife had finally found enthusiasm for the act of ordering new attire, despite her earlier objections. If there was one consolation he could offer her in this marriage, it was luxury.

After sealing his letter, he proceeded to the drawing room, hoping to observe Emma's delight as she opened the boxes. Perhaps she'd even give him a little promenade of her gowns and bonnets. And if she pressed him into service assisting with the buttons and hooks, so much the better.

When he entered the room, she was already wearing something breathtaking: a look of radiant joy.

"It's the new wardrobe," she said, her excitement plain.

"So I gather." He directed the servants to leave them alone.

She unknotted the twine on the first box and sifted through the tissue. He caught a glimpse of expensive ivory silk damask. A promising start.

However, it wasn't a gown she drew out.

It was a waistcoat.

"Oh," she sighed. "It's perfect." She turned to him. "What do you think?"

"You'll have to forgive me," he said, after a careful silence. "I have been out of social circulation for some time. Apparently ladies' fashions have undergone some upheaval that's escaped my notice."

She laughed. "It's not for me, turtledove. It's for you." She brought the waistcoat to him and held it against his chest. "Hm. I may need to take in the shoulders a bit, but that's easily done."

He couldn't summon any response.

She cast aside the top of another box, this time unwrapping a hunter-green wool topcoat. Again, she made a noise of satisfaction. "Here. Humor me and slip this on."

He looked around at the dozens of parcels. "Don't say these are *all* for me."

"You told me to order a wardrobe." She gave him a cheeky smile. "You didn't specify for whom. And I told you I'd remember your measurements." She tugged at his coat sleeve. "Come along, then. Off with the old and on with the new. I want to see how well the tailors did with it."

Numb, he shook his arms free of the old topcoat and slipped his arms into the sleeves of the new one.

She walked behind him, smoothing the wool down his back. "I've been dying to see you in something fit for a duke. Everything you have is frayed, hopelessly past the current style, or both."

She completed her circle, stopping toe to toe with him and pulling his lapels straight with a crisp snap. "There, now. Move your arms a bit. How does it feel?"

He stretched his arms out to either side. "Better, strangely."

"I told the tailor to leave extra room in the shoulders." She opened one lapel to display the lining. "The facing is silk where it counts, of course. But the sleeves have a removable lining of cotton flannel. Able to be laundered, and less likely to cause irritation. Shirts are the softest lawn I could find. And the cravats have a muslin collar inside them, so they won't need starch where it touches your skin."

He marveled at how much thought she'd put into this. Naturally, this had been her line of employment for many years—suggesting and crafting the garments that best suited an individual. But that was work.

This . . . this was a gift.

Her hands skimmed from his shoulders to the cuffs, and she looked him over. "I knew the green would suit you. You look so handsome."

By his soul. He volleyed between overwhelming emotion and distaste for an obvious lie.

"See for yourself." She went to the standing mirror and turned it to face him.

He didn't need to look in the mirror. He knew exactly what he'd see. A scarred and powder-burned horror that appeared laughable when contrasted with a fine new coat.

It was, he had to admit, a splendid coat. It fit him to perfection, and from this vantage, he could imagine himself a younger man, sitting in the club or accepting a glass of brandy after a day of autumn sport. Back in the "before" of his life.

"Well . . . ?" she prompted. She looked pleased with herself and eager for praise.

"It's a finely made coat," he said.

"But do *you* like it?"

I like it very much. But most of all, I like you—a great deal more than I ought—and even if it's too late for me to save myself, I'm not going to give you false hope.

He swung his arms. "Well, it does offer more flexibility in the arms. You know, for punching orphans and sacrificing lambs to Satan."

She returned to the boxes, stacking them with brisk, irritated motions. "Does it give you some sort of cruel satisfaction, always belittling my work? I know it doesn't impress you, but it's my chief talent. I'd have made career of it, if not for—" She cut off the statement.

"If not for what?"

"Never mind."

"I will pay mind when and where I wish, thank you. If not for what?"

"If not for you."

He blinked at her. "What could I have to do with it? What, you would have opened your own shop with your two pounds, three shillings?"

"I planned to become an independent dressmaker, but I needed a way to attract my own customers. A gown that showed my best handiwork, on display at one of the largest social events of the Season."

"Annabelle's wedding gown."

"The snow-beast pelt splattered with unicorn vomit. Yes."

He gestured expansively. "Well, I'm so sorry I interfered with your plans for a lifetime of degrading labor and gave you a life of wealth and privilege instead."

She pushed her hair back with her wrist. "Of course I wouldn't trade one for the other. I'm not stupid. And I'm grateful for all you've given me. It's only . . . this is all I have to offer *you*, and you insist on insulting it."

"So what would you have me do?"

She spread her arms, indicating the dozens of boxes. "*Use this.* Get out of the house. Take me with you. Somewhere. Anywhere."

He groaned. "Emma . . ."

"It doesn't have to be public. Surely there's somewhere we could go without being seen. Vauxhall, perhaps. Or a masquerade. I want to spend time with you. Take me along on one of your nightly prowls about London, if nothing else."

"That's not going to happen. None of it is going to happen."

"Because you're too proud."

"Because I am decided. You shouldn't presume that a few new topcoats will change my mind. We had a bargain, I remind you, and it did not include outings and jaunts about Town. Your role in this marriage is confined to precisely one purpose."

"Broodmare." Her eyes brimmed with hurt. "Yes, I recall."

She left the room.

Ash rubbed his face with both hands. He'd

been stalking the streets of Mayfair for weeks now, striking fear into the hearts of the populace, and he'd never felt as despicable as he did at that moment.

He'd never deserved the name "monster" more.

It's better this way, he told himself. Better to hurt her now rather than later.

Right. And if he repeated that balderdash a thousand times, he just might start to believe it.

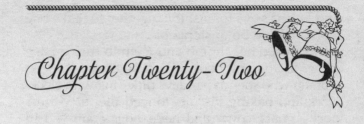

Chapter Twenty-Two

*H*ere's another." Nicola came up for air and added a new book to the towering stack Alexandra was holding for her. She seemed determined to take at least one book from every shelf in Hatchard's bookshop.

Emma tilted her head and examined the spines. "History of the Thames, Roman architecture, Viennese cookery, mechanical engineering . . . Is there some thread that connects all these?"

"Naturally, there is," Penny said. "It's somewhere in the tangle of Nicola's brain."

"I heard that," Nicola called from two shelves down.

Alexandra didn't lift her head from her reading. She had Nicola's tilting tower in one arm, and in the other hand she held a single book of her own. Something about stars.

"It was a compliment. You know how I marvel at your intelligence." Penny leaned against the bookshelves. "Just think, if we could put your brain, my soft heart, Alexandra's common sense, and Emma's eye for fashion together to make one woman. We'd be unstoppable."

Alex used her thumb and teeth to turn a page of her astronomy book. "We'd be a well-dressed woman who spends her days tinkering with clockwork and baking biscuits to feed the forty-three ducks, goats, cows, and hedgehogs crammed in the back garden."

"Only forty-three?" With a skeptical harrumph, Nicola added another book to the stack in Alexandra's arm.

This time, however, she'd added one too many. The tower swayed, wobbled, and ultimately crashed to the floor.

Everyone in the shop turned to glare at them in silent censure.

Nicola's freckled brow knitted as she stared down at the heap of books. "I should have known that would happen. See, *this* is why I need the books on engineering."

Alexandra chased after her own book, which had landed a few yards from the rest. After having retrieved it, however, she collided with a gentleman—and this time, both of their books scattered to the floor. She began stammering her apologies at once, even though the gentleman's back was still turned. When he swung to face her, however—

She went silent.

They all did. None of them could speak.

The man standing before Alexandra must have been the most dangerously handsome gentleman in all of London. Even Emma, foolishly taken as she was with her own husband, could see it.

Well-formed features. Roguish green eyes. Brown hair that misbehaved just the right amount.

The gentleman bowed to Alexandra. "My deepest apologies."

"N-not at all," she stammered, blushing. "The fault was entirely mine."

"Allow me." He crouched at her feet and retrieved her book from the floor, handing it to her before he went about collecting his own.

Alexandra's eyes went bright enough to attract moths in daytime.

Nicola paid no attention. She was busy stacking and restacking her books in different combinations, trying to find the sturdiest formation.

Penny's gloved hand latched on to Emma's wrist. *"He's flirting with her,"* she whispered through unmoving lips.

"I know," Emma whispered back. Although, to be fair, she suspected he was the sort of man who flirted with every woman he encountered.

"You seem to know something about books," he said to Alexandra. "Perhaps you could be so good as to lend me your expertise."

"Surely you don't need *my* help."

"I think I do. You see, I need to purchase some books for a pair of young girls, and I've absolutely no idea where to start. What do you think of these?" He showed her the collection he'd amassed, leaning close.

"Oh." Every bit of Alexandra froze. Even her eyelashes. After several moments, she seemed to recall she was meant to examine his books. "They're all fairy stories."

"That seemed the logical place to begin for girls. Which ones do *you* recommend?"

"Er . . . I don't know."

"Well, which were your favorites?"

Alexandra still hadn't blinked. "I . . . I couldn't say I . . ."

Emma's face burned with second-hand embarrassment. Poor Alex.

At length, Alexandra finished her sentence in a whisper. ". . . had any."

"Well, then." The gentleman didn't miss a beat, but continued on as if Alexandra had said something fascinating. Or something at all. "I suppose that means I'll just have to buy them all, doesn't it? Don't know why I didn't think of it. Thank you, Miss . . ."

"Mount." A long pause. "Batten. Mountbatten."

"Miss Mountbatten, I am indebted to you for your kind assistance." A dashing smile, a gallant bow, and he was gone.

Penny waited all of three seconds before pouncing on poor, flustered Alex. "Why didn't you talk to him?"

"I didn't know what to say. When I was a girl, I wanted to read about pirates. I never cared about fairy stories."

"Well, let me tell you, a great many of them start just that way." Penny cast a wistful look after the gentleman. "You might have at least asked his name. That could have been the beginning of a romance."

"A tragic one," said Nicola. "He's no doubt a shameless rake."

"Yes, let's tell ourselves that," Emma said.

"Oh, no!" Alex moaned, heedless of their romantic musings. "I can't believe it. Look." She held up the book in her hands for their view.

"*A Compendium of Stories for Obedient Girls?*" Emma read aloud. "Well that sounds dreadful."

"It *is* dreadful. The gentleman must have confused my book for one of his. He's stuck me with fairy stories, and he's walked away with Messier's *Catalogue of Star Clusters and Nebulae.* It could take me months to find another used copy. I can't afford it new."

"And *that* is why you ought to have asked his name," Penny said.

Emma intervened. "Be gentle with her. Any one of us would have panicked. Including me, and I'm married to an intimidating fellow myself."

An intimidating, unfeeling, insulting beast of a fellow, to put a finer point on it. She was still smarting after the way he'd rejected the wardrobe. Well, it was what she deserved for putting her heart into it. Someday she might learn to stop throwing that fragile organ under men's feet.

To distract herself, she flipped through the

Parisian fashion magazine in her hand. An idea flitted through her mind, and her fingers stilled halfway through the magazine. Perhaps there were other ways she could use her skills. Duchesses didn't engage in trade, but charitable causes? Now that was a different matter. Perhaps she could help others like Miss Palmer. Women who, for one reason or another, found themselves in need of a fresh start.

Women who might appreciate her efforts, unlike a certain ungrateful duke.

"*Wienerbrød.*"

This non sequitur came from Nicola.

"Your pet names for the duke," she said, leafing through a cookery book. "Add it to the list. It's a Viennese pastry. *Wienerbrød.*"

Emma burst into laughter. Oh, how she'd needed that today. "Thank you, Nicola. That's perfection."

That pet name was so thoroughly absurd and humiliating, her husband just might deserve it.

THE STRAND WAS a crush of carts and carriages. By the time Emma made her way home from the bookshop, dusk had fallen. She unbuttoned her pelisse as she moved down the corridor, planning to flop onto the bed for a sleep before dinner. She'd been fatigued of late.

Upon entering her bedchamber, however, she stopped in place, surprised by a glimpse of scarlet peeking out from behind her bed hangings.

Setting aside her bonnet and gloves, she walked to the bed as a pilgrim approaches an altar. Her heart began to pound.

There, laid out across the quilted coverlet, was a gown of the finest material she'd ever touched. She fingered the edge of the fabric wonderingly. Ruby-red silk gauze layered over an ivory satin, conspiring to create a rich, shimmering blush. The cut was a daring Continental silhouette, with cap sleeves that settled just beneath the shoulder and a neckline positioned to skim the bosom. No spangles, no lace. The only adornments were tasteful, exquisitely embroidered flowers and vines decorating the hem, sleeves, and décolletage.

The gown resembled a rose abloom in the midst of a garden.

Once she drew her gaze from the gown, she noticed the rest of an ensemble lay nearby: heeled slippers with rosettes, flouncy tulle petticoats, satin evening gloves, an embroidered chemise, and a fashionable divorce corset. And it didn't end there. Her dressing table was laden, too. Stockings, garters, jeweled combs for her hair . . .

"Isn't it lovely, Your Grace? I've never seen finer." Emma turned to see Mary, her lady's maid, standing in the doorway holding a tray. "His Grace says you're to be ready by eight o'clock. I took the liberty of bringing up your dinner. I thought we might need the extra time to do something special with your hair before you leave for the theater."

Emma couldn't believe what she was hearing. He was taking her to the theater?

"The duke is taking dinner in his chambers, too. Mr. Khan is helping ready him for the evening."

Having set down the tray, Mary bounced with excitement, rocking up to her toes and then down again. "It's so wonderful, Your Grace. He hasn't made such an outing since—"

"Since returning from the war. I know. And that's been—"

"Nigh on two years," Mary said. "It's all your doing, Your Grace. He's so taken with you. Just as we all hoped."

Emma didn't know about that. "He's only taking me because I deviled him into it."

"Nevertheless." Her maid lifted the shimmering gown from the bed and, pinching it by the sleeves, held it up to Emma's body. She swiveled Emma toward the full-length mirror in the corner of the room. "If the duke isn't in love with you already, he surely will be by the end of the night."

"Will you leave me for a moment?"

Mary looked confused, but she did as she was asked. "Certainly, Your Grace."

Once she was alone, Emma stood staring into the looking glass.

She hadn't worn an evening gown in six years. Not since that devastating night when she'd reached out for love and been dealt cruel disappointment in return. Her own father had called

her a jezebel, a strumpet, and worse. Any tempt-
ress in a harlot-red dress, he'd said, was *asking* to
be ill-used.

Emma hadn't asked for anything of the sort.
She'd sewn that gown herself, and she'd poured
all her hopes into it. Not to sing a siren song or
to invite lust. She wasn't asking, *Grope me behind
the hedges.*

See me, she'd been pleading. *Admire me.*

Love me.

A mistake, and she'd paid dearly for it. Again,
and again, and again.

But now here she was. Against her better judgment and every resolution, she'd found herself
craving all those same things from her husband.
Understanding. Admiration. Affection.

Perhaps even love.

She regarded herself in the mirror and drew
a deep, unsteady breath. If she put on this gown
and went down to him, she would descend the
stairs wearing her heart on the outside of her
body. Nothing to guard it from being pierced,
wounded, broken.

Torn apart.

She would be a fool to take that risk.

He had vowed to protect her, hadn't he? However, she wasn't certain any promise extended
that far.

Tonight, Emma supposed she would find out.

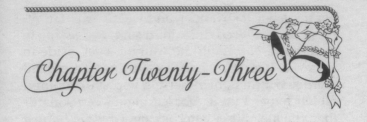

Chapter Twenty-Three

$\mathcal{A}$sh paced the entrance hall, tapping his walking stick against the marble floor. Every few passes, he glanced at the clock. Thanks to Emma's peculiar friend, he trusted the timepiece to be accurate to the second.

Ten past eight.

He stopped his pacing. He was behaving like some kind of courting swain, not a duke awaiting his tardy duchess—and he was most definitely *not* a lovesick pup. He simply despised waiting, that was all.

Craving motion, he lifted his walking stick perpendicular to the floor and placed his hat atop it. He thrust the stick upward, sending the hat a few feet into the air, then maneuvered to catch it. The next time, he sent the hat higher. After a dozen or so repetitions, he was lofting the hat to the heights of the vaulted ceiling, then tracking its fall to snag it before it hit the marble floor.

He'd just sent the hat soaring when he caught a shimmer of red at the top of the staircase.

Emma.

"Sorry I'm late," she said.

Ash startled, flung the walking stick aside in a stupid attempt to dispose of the evidence, and then stood motionless as his beaver hat plummeted toward the earth out of nowhere, glancing off his shoulder before crashing to the floor. It must have looked as though he'd been the target of some sort of lightning bolt from Olympus, only a more fashionable one.

She stared at him from the top of the staircase.

He decided there was only one way to deal with the situation.

Denial.

He cast an accusatory glance at the ceiling, then bent to retrieve his hat, dusting it off with an air of irritation. "I'll get Khan on that straightaway."

He could sense her stifling a laugh.

"The performance begins in twenty minutes," he said.

She remained at the top of the staircase, hesitant. Well, and why wouldn't she be? She was about to go out in public accompanied by a man who flung hats and walking sticks about at random intervals.

"If you'd rather not," he said, "it's all the same to me. I've a report from the Yorkshire estate to look over."

"Would *you* prefer to stay home?"

"Only if you prefer it."

"I want to go. I should say, I'd hate to waste

Mary's efforts." She touched a gloved hand to her hair.

What a horse's ass he was. She wasn't hesitating because she was concerned about *his* appearance. She was waiting for him to compliment *hers*.

He climbed the stairs, taking the risers two at a time. When he reached her side, he was out of breath—and it wasn't from the exertion.

The glossy upsweep of her hair was wound through with ribbons and pinned with jeweled combs. A few locks of hair framed her face in loose spirals. A touch of delicate pink warmed her cheeks, and those lush eyelashes eroded his composure with each fluttering sweep.

Her eyes outshone it all. They were wide and searching, with pupils round and large enough that he could trip into them, and irises of deep, rich brown flecked with gold.

Somewhere lower, he knew there was a sumptuous gown and exquisitely framed breasts to ogle, but he couldn't seem to drag his gaze south of her neck. She had him transfixed.

And he'd never felt more monstrous than he did standing next to her now.

"You look . . ." His mind stretched for words. He hadn't prepared any compliments. Not the sort she deserved, at any rate, and he didn't suppose that she'd care to hear the truth: that the way she looked in that gown made him feel vastly unequal, and a little bit queasy.

Should he deem her exquisite? A vision? An exquisite vision?

Bah. Insipid, the lot of them. He supposed a

man couldn't go amiss with "beautiful," over-used as it might be.

"The gown's beautiful," she said. "Thank you."

Brilliant. Now she'd stolen his word. He was starting from nothing again.

"You would have chosen better," he said. "And the quality could have been finer, had it not been so rushed." He fingered the embellished edge of her sleeve. "Whoever did this stitching, her skill is certainly nothing to touch yours."

When he lifted his eyes, he found her staring into them.

Her lips curved in a little smile. "I love it."

He had the sudden, stupid idea that he might float down the stairs. "I'm happy to hear it."

Happy. Now there was a word he hadn't ut-tered in some time.

"You look splendid," she said.

"I'm glad you noticed." He puffed his chest and tugged on the lapels of the black tailcoat she'd ordered for him. "It's the result of expert styling and the best of tailors. Did you notice the waistcoat? Stupendous."

"I don't know about *stupendous*."

"Well, I know all about stupendousness, and I tell you, this waistcoat is the very definition."

"I'll take your word for it, then."

Ash offered her his arm, and she took it. He escorted her down the staircase and out to the waiting carriage, mindful of her voluminous skirts, but never pausing. He refused to give any appearance of reluctance.

Tonight, it didn't matter that he was scarred

and hideous and would prefer to hide from society.

Emma deserved to be seen. And this night was for her.

THE CARRIAGE RIDE to Drury Lane was quiet. Too quiet. As they bounced over the cobbled streets, Emma's fears only grew. She'd been so consumed with her tender emotions, she'd neglected to worry over the rest of it. Appearing in a grand, opulent theater surrounded by ladies whose gowns she might have stitched.

She twisted her gloved hands in her lap. Her heart throbbed like a bruised thumb.

Finally, she decided to just have out with it. "I'm anxious. Aren't you anxious?"

His reply was a gruff, wordless expression of denial.

Emma took it as a yes. She suspected he must be as nervous as she about appearing in public, if not more so. However, she knew better than to broach the subject. "I don't know what to expect. I've never been to the theater."

"Allow me to describe it for you. There's a stage. Players stand upon it. They bellow their lines, spraying spittle all over the boards. Sometimes a character is murdered to liven things up. We sit in the finest box in the place and observe. It's all rather—"

The carriage made a sharp turn. Emma slid toward the outer wall of the coach. He stretched an arm about her waist and drew her back to his side. Even after the compartment righted on its springs, he kept his arm about her, holding her tight and close.

"You're trembling," he said.

"I told you, I'm anxious." It wasn't a lie.

"You're cold." He shook his head, drawing a fold of his cloak about her shoulders. "Where is your wrap?"

"I didn't want to cover the gown." In truth, she was more than happy to be held against his cologne-scented warmth. "It's not an hours-long journey."

"No, it's isn't." He peered out the window. "We've already arrived."

The lane outside the theater was a mad crush. The street bustled with coaches, horses, finely dressed ladies and gentlemen, and beyond them, the grand steps of the theater's main entrance.

They drove straight past all of it.

The coachman stopped in a side lane. Apparently they would enter through some private entrance to avoid gawking crowds. He exited the carriage first. As he helped her down, he tugged the brim of his hat low, as always. It was a dark night, portending rain.

He guided her up narrow stairs, down an even narrower corridor, and, finally, into a well-appointed box. Two velvet-upholstered chairs faced the proscenium, and on a small table nearby waited a chilled bottle of champagne and two glasses.

Once they were safely within, she heard him exhale for the first time since they'd exited the carriage.

"Here." He pushed the chairs toward the front of the box. "You must sit right up front."

"Or we could be further back." She nodded toward the rear of the box, away from public view. "It doesn't matter to me where we sit."

"It matters to me." He thumped the seat cushion. "You should have a full view of the stage. And the rest of the audience should have a full view of you."

"Why?"

"I didn't order that gown just so you could hide in the shadows. This is your introduction to London society as the Duchess of Ashbury. You are going to be seen. Not only seen, but admired."

"Yes, but—"

But that means you might be seen as well.

"Tonight," he said, "you will shine like a jewel. A ruby. An extraordinarily big ruby." He cocked his head. "You'd be the world's largest ruby on record, I suppose. One with . . . arms."

"Was any of that intended as a compliment?"

He sighed curtly. "Let's begin again. You're my duchess. You're beautiful. Everyone should know it."

As she took her seat, Emma tucked his words away to treasure later. And treasure them she would.

You're beautiful.

No matter what happened, she'd always have

that. And the part about the jewel with arms, she supposed.

She peered over the edge of the box, taking in the splendor of the theater. "What play is this?" she asked, suddenly realizing she didn't even know.

"*Titus Andronicus.*"

"Shakespeare?" She smiled.

"Not one of the better ones, unfortunately."

Her puddle of a heart began seeping down toward her toes. He'd brought her to a play he'd no doubt read several times, and it wasn't even one he particularly liked. The gown, the champagne, braving the crowds . . .

He'd done it for her, and she loved him for it.

She loved him.

She'd known it already, but tonight was the hammer pounding a duke-shaped peg into her heart. It hurt like the devil, but there would be no removing it now. Not without a great deal of bleeding.

Despite all the effort he'd undertaken, he didn't seem to be enjoying the evening. He was restless throughout the play, tapping his fingers against his knee with impatience and grumbling about the players.

Only two scenes into the fourth act, he leaned over to murmur in her ear. "This performance is both dreadful and interminable. I've had enough. I'm going to order the carriage."

"What about the end of the play? I want to know what happens."

"The nurse is stabbed. Mutius is stabbed. Bassianus is stabbed. Saturninus is stabbed. Martius and Quintus are beheaded. Tamora dies of a stomach ailment—the cause of which you really don't want to know—and Aaron is buried to his neck and left to starve."

She turned to him in disbelief. "Why would you spoil the ending?"

"I didn't spoil it. It's a Shakespearean tragedy. They're all that way. Everyone dies; the end." He reached for her hand. "Let's be going."

"Why do you want to leave so badly?"

"You should want to leave, too." His voice darkened. "Unless you want to lift your skirts and sit on my lap so I can take you right here in the box."

So *she* was the source of his distraction?

"You are always making these suggestions as though they should be threats. Meanwhile, I'm only intrigued." With nonchalance, she laid a hand on his thigh. Then stroked a single fingertip in lazy circles.

His thigh tensed beneath her touch. "Woman, you are killing me."

She shrugged. "As you said, it *is* a Shakespearean tragedy. Everyone dies; the end."

"Enough." He launched to his feet. "I am ordering the carriage, and we are going home. To bed. And you are going to die no fewer than ten 'little deaths' before I'm through with you."

Very well. If he insisted.

Once he'd left, Emma tried, rather unsuccessfully, to return her attention to the play. The players might as well have been speaking Latin. The dialogue coasted in through one of her ears and left through the other, making no impression in between.

After a few short minutes, she rejoiced to hear the sound of the door opening. She drew to her feet, eager to leave, no longer caring about the characters' tragic demises.

But it wasn't the duke who'd entered the box.

It was Miss Annabelle Worthing.

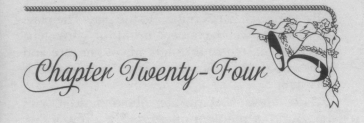

Chapter Twenty-Four

"Miss Worthing." Emma was so shocked at the intrusion, she curtsied deeply—before recalling that she was a duchess now, and Annabelle Worthing should properly curtsy to her.

"Are you enjoying your evening, Emma?" she asked.

"Very much so."

"It's so amusing, isn't it? I could never have guessed we would cross paths in such a circumstance."

"Nor I, Miss Worthing." Emma eyed the woman warily. "Forgive me, was there something you wanted?"

"Am I not permitted to greet an old friend?"

An old *friend*?

A man's formerly intended bride wouldn't wish to become *friends* with the man's new wife. Moreover, Emma knew this formerly intended bride wasn't precisely brimming with kindness and generosity.

"You must be quite dizzy with it, Emma. Having climbed so high, so quickly."

"If you're here because you believe me to be a schemer, or someone who took advantage of your broken engagement . . . I will assure you, you are mistaken. The duke proposed our match. His offer took me completely by surprise."

"Oh, I know that. But I suspect you don't know why he offered for you."

Emma was too surprised to deny it. She couldn't deny it. She'd insisted from the first that it made little sense for him to marry her.

"I know the reason. Everyone will. I don't like to say it, but you deserve to know, too. That's why I've come to tell you, as a friend." Annabelle moved closer, lowering her voice. "He has married you to spite me."

"What?"

"Simple retribution. I'm sorry for it, but I know the man. We were betrothed for more than two years. He's furious about the broken engagement. So he married my seamstress to have a laugh at my expense. Has he shown you that yet? His cruel sense of humor? Ashbury's always had an ugly side, since long before his injury."

"I'm well aware that my husband"—Emma leaned on the word "husband," claiming what was now hers—"is imperfect. I'm also aware that he is honorable and brave. He incurred his wounds while defending England. If you could not appreciate the honor in his scars, he was fortunate to be rid of you. Our marriage is none of your concern."

"He has *made* your marriage my concern." A sharp edge entered Annabelle's voice. "Parading you before London society, humiliating me in full view of the *ton*. For your own sake, I advise you not to acquire any airs. You may have wed a duke, but every lady of the *ton* knows you as a seamstress who once knelt at their feet. They will never let you forget it."

"I don't care what they think."

"Yes, but you care about him. Don't you?"

Emma didn't answer.

Miss Worthing tsked. "You always seemed a clever girl. Surely you don't believe a duke would seek to marry a woman of your class for any honorable reason. Even if he did desire you, he could have easily made you his mistress."

"No, he could not have done. I would never have—"

As she looked out over the theater, the corner of Annabelle's lips curled in a humorless smile. "Gentlemen prefer common mistresses, I've heard. In bed. Girls like you do the things ladies won't."

How *dare* she.

"I will not stand here and be insulted. Nor will I hear the duke impugned in such a vile manner."

"You don't believe me?" Annabelle slid her arm about Emma's shoulders and turned, subtly pointing her fan toward the opposite side of the theater. "Do you see there? Just to the left, and one tier down? There's Mama."

Yes, there in the box opposite sat Mrs. Worthing, the family matriarch. Emma recognized the demanding harridan from Annabelle's many, many fittings in the shop.

"Lord Carrollton is kind enough to loan my family the use of his box. The second Thursday after a new play opens, we're always in attendance." She looked Emma in the eye. "Do you know what tonight is?"

Emma could hazard a guess. "Surely a coincidence."

"Oh, no. Ashbury knew I'd be here." Miss Worthing looked about the box. "Did he tell you this was how we met? He stared at me, the whole evening, from just this spot. Couldn't take his eyes off me for the entirety of the performance."

The champagne in Emma's stomach churned.

"I'd wager he chose this gown for you." She fingered Emma's sleeve. "Red as a cherry tart. He seated you right up front. Of course he did. All this effort would have been for nothing if I failed to notice."

His words to her earlier echoed in Emma's mind.

You must sit here, near the front. The world deserves to see you. I want you to be admired.

"Do you believe me now? On a night he knew my family would be in attendance, he bedecked you in a harlot-red gown and put you on garish display. His lowborn replacement bride. He's using you, Emma. To him, you are nothing but a means to an end."

Emma put a hand on the wall for support. The theater was spinning.

She didn't want to believe it. Any of it. She told herself not to doubt him.

But as Annabelle said, all the pieces were there. The sudden outing, the gown, the play. She'd never understood why he'd been so determined to marry her in the first place, making his offer after ten minutes in the library, when he knew nothing of her.

Well, he had known one thing about her. He'd known she sewed Annabelle's wedding gown.

Oh, Lord. Oh, Lord. Oh, Lord.

Perhaps all the effort he'd gone to tonight hadn't been for her, but for another.

Suddenly, Emma didn't trust any of her own perceptions. She second-guessed every conversation, every moment. Everything she'd built with him, all the emotions she'd hoped he might come to share . . . Was it possible it had been nothing more than wounded pride and cruel intent?

She didn't care one whit what Annabelle Worthing thought of her, nor the other ladies of the *ton*. But if Ash . . .

She pressed her hands to her stomach.

Down on the stage, the fifth act was nearing its grisly climax. Players were dying right and left, staggering and moaning as they dropped to the boards. What poor performances, she thought. So unconvincing.

She was dying inside, and there was no staggering or moaning. Only bleak, hollow despair.

The fault was yours, Emma. You should have known better.

She *had* known better, and that was the most dispiriting part. The red silk flowing around her felt like mockery. Once again, she'd been a fool.

She had to leave. She had to leave at once, before he returned.

Someone pushed aside the drapery, entering the box. "What is going on here?"

Too late.

ASH WAS AFIRE with anger.

He'd left behind a radiant, coquettish wife, likely aroused to the point where he could give her two orgasms in the carriage home alone, and he'd returned not a quarter hour later to find her backed into a corner, pale and trembling.

And the cause . . . oh, the cause was plain to see.

He swung his gaze on Annabelle. "What did you do to her?"

"Nothing but tell her the truth." Her eyes sparked with hurt and anger. "You bastard. You haven't done enough to me already? You had to bring around this slattern of a seamstress to humiliate me in front of all London?"

"You will not speak such words in her presence." He had to force the words through clenched teeth. "She is the Duchess of Ashbury. You'll address her with the honor that title confers."

"I will not curtsy to a girl who knelt at my feet, simply because she gets down on her knees for you."

Ash had never struck a woman, and he didn't intend to start. But he was tempted now, in ways he could never have conceived. Fury exploded within him like a barrage of cannon fire.

"If you were a man," he said, "you would be

facing the end of my pistol tomorrow at dawn. As it is, I'm tempted to call out your brother to answer for your behavior."

"You want to call out my brother?" She laughed bitterly. "My brother wanted to challenge you back in April. You can thank me for talking him out of it. I convinced him there would be richer satisfaction in letting you live out the remainder of your miserable days. Twisted. Monstrous. Alone."

"I'm not alone," he said. "Not anymore. And that's what bothers you. Isn't it?"

"I can't imagine what you mean."

"Can't you? It's all becoming quite clear to me. You're humiliated, but not because of Emma's presence. You're ashamed for the *ton* to see *me*. Because once they do, everyone will understand the reason behind our broken engagement. They'll know precisely what a vain, shallow creature you are—and they will see that Emma is worth a hundred of you. Yes, Annabelle. I can imagine that *would* be humiliating."

Annabelle opened her mouth to reply, then closed it again.

Ash was certain the silence wouldn't last. He turned, eager to gather Emma and get the hell out of this theater.

But when he did, his wife was nowhere to be found. She must have slipped out. He'd been so occupied berating Annabelle, he hadn't even noticed.

With a muttered curse, Ash bolted down the

corridor and raced down the staircase. He didn't see her in the entry, so he dashed out into the night. The rain had started, and that didn't help his cause.

He found the coach—no, they hadn't seen Her Grace—and then he ran up the steps in front of the theater, searching through the rain for any glimpse of red.

The play would end soon. Once the audience poured out into the streets, he would lose any hope of finding her in the crowd.

He picked a direction at random and charged down it, stopping at the corner to look in all directions. He pushed the rain from his face, impatient.

There.

There, down a narrow side lane—was that a bit of red?

He jogged in pursuit. "Emma! *Emma!*"

By the time he'd covered half the distance, she turned around. "Stop," she shouted. "Leave me be."

He slowed to a walk. For every step he took toward her, she made one in reverse.

"Can't we discuss this somewhere less wet?" he called to her.

"What is there to discuss?"

"Emma, don't play games. I know you're distraught."

"I'm fine, Duke. That's what you wanted me to call you, isn't it? Duke?"

"You're clearly not fine." He held up his hands

in a truce. "Don't mind anything she said up there. Her ire wasn't aimed at you, it was aimed at me. Annabelle is . . . Annabelle. Still, you've every reason to be angry or overwrought."

She gave a defiant sniff. "There's nothing to be angry or overwrought about, Duke."

"Really, you can cease calling me that."

She wiped the droplets from her face. "Perhaps I will use Ash, after all. It's growing on me. So very flexible, you know. Horse's Ash . . . Jack-Ash . . . Ash-hole. "

Very well. He deserved that. And if he had been any less desperate to get her out of this rain, he probably would have laughed.

The rain became a downpour. Ash tried to get close enough to wrap her in his cloak, but she only retreated further, staying out of his reach.

"Emma."

She hugged herself tight. "It's my own fault. You never promised me anything. You specifically promised me *nothing*. We had a bargain. A cold, impersonal agreement of convenience. Somewhere along the way, I stupidly allowed myself to dream a little. To hope that . . . that there might be more."

Dream. Hope. More.

She was standing in the rain in a darkened alleyway, weeping and distraught. Ash should have felt remorseful, he supposed. Instead he swelled with joy.

Dream. Hope. More.

Those words gave him life. Three slender

threads he could braid into a rope and cling to with everything he had.

"You weren't foolish. Or if you are a fool, I'm one, too."

"At least it finally makes sense. I always wondered why you chose me. Now I know. You married me to get back at her."

"No." He moved toward her again, and this time she allowed him to approach. "I'm telling you, that's all wrong."

"She refused you, and you wanted to humiliate her in return."

"She never refused me. I refused her."

She stared at him through the sheets of rain. "But you said . . . Everyone said—"

"That's the way it's done. A broken engagement is always said to be the lady's choice, to protect her reputation. It was the decent thing to do."

"Decent. Of all the people in the world, you would be decent to *her.*"

"At the time, I believed she deserved it. And I cared about her."

She stumbled back a step, blinking the wetness from her thick, dark lashes.

Ash, you idiot. That was the worst possible thing to say.

"Her family desperately wanted the connection, the title. And my money, of course. She was willing to go through with it, for them. Despite her personal . . . reluctance."

"Reluctance" was the gentler word. The more accurate one was "revulsion."

"I cared enough about her not to force her into a marriage she didn't want. I cared for my pride, as well. I didn't want a wife who wept every time I bedded her. I didn't want to listen as she vomited into a basin afterwards."

"She wouldn't have—"

"Yes, she would have done so."

She *had* done so.

He'd kept his intended bride at bay for months after his return to England. Nearly a year passed before he permitted her to see him. By then, he'd regained the strength to stand, and his open wounds had thickened to scars.

Even so, the horror and disgust on her face as she beheld him . . . It was etched in his memory, carved into his very bones. She'd run from the room, but not far enough. He could hear her every heaving retch as her stomach emptied, and her every sob as her brother tried to comfort her in the corridor.

I can't, she'd said. *I can't.*

You must, he'd replied.

The duke will expect an heir. How could I bear to lie with . . . with that?

With "that," she said.

Not with "him."

With "that."

Ash had prepared himself for her visit, or so he'd believed. He thought he'd steeled his pride sufficiently against a horrified reaction, the reluctant agreement of a joyless bride.

He'd been wrong. Her words had gutted him.

He was not even a man anymore. He was a "that."

"Do you want the truth, Emma?"

The lift of her shoulders was more shiver than shrug. "Why not? We have always had honesty, if nothing else."

"The truth is this." He took her in his arms. "I cared for Annabelle Worthing's feelings more than I cared for yours."

She sobbed and struggled. "Then let me go."

"I'd sooner die." He lashed his right arm around her waist and used his good hand to cup her chin, tilting her face to his. Holding it tight, forbidding her to turn away. "Look at me."

She sniffed, blinking away the rain.

He gripped her chin and gave her head a little shake. "Damn it, Emma. Look at me."

Look at me. Look at me. *Because you're the only one who does. Likely the only one who ever will.*

At last, her dark eyes tipped up to meet his.

The wounded look in her gaze . . . it clubbed him like a cudgel made of shame. Closing his eyes, he framed her face between his hands. He pressed his forehead to hers, sheltering her face from the rain.

"No, Emma. I didn't care for your feelings. It didn't matter if you wanted me or if you didn't. I didn't have the patience for courtship, couldn't take the time to make you feel brave and witty and pretty and intelligent, and all the things I adored about you from the first. I certainly didn't have the decency to let you walk away. I cared only for myself. Do you hear me? I only knew I had to have you."

Not only have her, but keep her. Make her his own.

Even now, the thought of letting her walk away . . . he couldn't bear it.

No.

He wouldn't *allow* it.

This wasn't tenderness that filled him with a fiery resolve. It was possession. Pure, raw, wild. If she could glimpse the brutish, primal impulses coursing through him, she would run like a rabbit flees a ravening wolf.

And he would catch her.

"You're mine," he said hoarsely, lifting his head and staring deep into her eyes, willing her to believe. "If you leave, I will follow. Do you hear me? I will follow and find you and cart you home."

Lightning flashed, slicing through the dark. For the briefest of moments, everything was bright and clear. The alley around them, the sky above. The space between her body and his, and every emotion she wore so bravely on her face.

Just before they lost the moment to darkness, he crushed his mouth to hers in a desperate kiss.

Then the force of thunder exploded through him, splitting him into a thousand pieces—some of which were surely driven into her, embedded as deeply as the metal shards that lodged beneath his scarred flesh. Impossible to retrieve.

Yes, she was his. But bits of him were hers

now, too. No matter how deeply he kissed her, he would never get them back.

He made the futile attempt anyway, clutching her tight. Her arms went around his neck, pulling him down. Her lips softened and parted as she opened to him. Welcomed him.

A deep, grateful moan rose from his chest. He deepened the kiss, stroking her tongue with his. He couldn't get enough of her. He'd run his tongue over every inch of her body, but he'd never tasted her this way. A sweetness like cool, fresh water mingled with the salt of tears.

Oh, Emma. You beautiful, addled thing.

Only a fool would weep over him.

He kissed her cheeks, her jawline, her neck—kissing away her every tear. And then, suddenly, she was returning the gesture, tugging him down and pressing her lips to his face. She kissed his lips. She kissed his nose. She kissed his ear and his neck and both of his trembling eyelids.

She kissed his twisted, monstrous scars.

Time stopped. The raindrops seemed to hang in the air. For this moment, there was no before and no after. There was only now, and now was everything.

"Emma."

"I . . ." She blinked a few times. "I . . ."

His mind completed her interrupted thought in a dozen dangerous ways. Don't be stupid, he told himself. She could have all manner of things to tell him. It could be anything.

I . . . have a pebble in my shoe.

I . . . want a pony.

I . . . would do murder for a cup of tea right now.

Very well, Emma would never say that last. Probably not the second, either. But she absolutely, positively was not going to say that other thing. The-Thing-That-Must-Not-Be-Named. Or Thought, or Uttered, or, heaven forfend, Hoped.

"Ash, I think I—"

His heart thrashed in his chest.

Get to it, woman. This is agony.

Instead of putting an end to his torture, his bride of convenience did the worst, most inconvenient thing.

She went limp in his arms, fainting dead away.

Chapter Twenty-Five

$\mathscr{E}$mma could not have been insensible more than a few seconds, but by the time she came back to her surroundings, he had lifted her off her feet and into his arms. Her head was tucked against his broad chest, and he'd wrapped his cape about her shoulders. The familiar scent of him anchored her. Cologne, shaving soap, the leather of his gloves.

If he was still recovering strength in his injured arm, she would never have known it now. He held her in an iron grip and covered the ground in brisk, determined strides. Beneath the layers of his waistcoat and shirt, she could hear his heartbeat, steady and strong.

By contrast, she felt weak. She couldn't seem to stop shivering.

"I'm better now," she said, trying to brace her chattering teeth.

"No, you're not."

"You can put me down. I can walk." She wasn't certain she could walk for *long*, or in an especially straight line, but she would try. "It was only a wobble."

He didn't even deign to answer. He merely carried her down the way, until they emerged onto a wider street. He had not gone thirty paces before he kicked open a door and hefted her through it, ducking his own head and taking care to guard hers.

They'd entered some sort of inn, Emma gathered, piecing the observations together in her hazy mind. Not a fine sort of inn. Nor even a particularly clean sort of inn.

"Show us to a room."

The innkeeper stared, slack-jawed, at the duke. A cluster of patrons drinking in the public room fell silent.

A woman emerging from a back room with two trenchers of stewed beef shrieked and dropped her cargo. "Jayzus."

The duke had no patience for their gawking. He shifted Emma's weight to his good arm and reached into his pocket with his free hand. Having fished out a coin, he tossed it onto the countertop. A gold sovereign. Sufficient tariff to let every bedroom in the inn for weeks.

"A room," he barked. "Your best. Now."

"Y-yes, milord." The innkeeper's hands shook as he retrieved a key from a hook. "This way."

Ash insisted on carrying her as they followed the innkeeper up a steep, narrow staircase. The innkeeper showed them to a room toward the back. "Best room, milord," he said, opening the door. "It even 'as a window."

"Coal. Blankets. Tea. And be quick about it."

"Yes, milord." The door swung shut.

"This isn't necessary," Emma murmured. "We can surely take the carriage home."

"Out of the question. At this time of night, with the theaters emptying, we could be stalled in the streets for an hour or more." He still hadn't put her down.

She craned her neck to look up at him. "That doesn't matter. What's an hour?"

"Sixty minutes too many," he said testily. "You are wet, and you are cold. You don't like being cold. Therefore, I *despise* you being cold. I would go about murdering raindrops and setting fire to the clouds, but that would take slightly more than an hour. Perhaps even two. So we're here, and you will cease complaining about it."

His words kindled a flame of warmth inside her. She closed her eyes and buried her face in his chest.

Thank you. You terrible, impossible man. Thank you.

The innkeeper returned, loaded down with the demanded items: a scuttle of coal and tinderbox, and a stack of folded wool blankets. "My girl will be up wi' the tea directly."

"Good. Now get out."

"Milord, if I might ask a question, might you happen to be—"

Ash kicked the door shut. He drew the room's lone chair away from the wall, and gingerly lowered Emma unto on it. "Can you sit? You won't swoon again?"

"I don't think so."

He heaped coal in the hearth and packed the open spaces with tinder, then sparked an ember with the flint, blowing on it patiently until a true flame took hold. Then he turned to the blankets and unfolded one, inspecting the rough wool.

He flung it aside. "Filthy and hopping with fleas." He looked about the room, though there was nothing much to see. "We'll do it this way."

He flicked the cape and spread it outside-down over the stained straw mattress. The heavy outer layer of wool had done its duty, preserving the lining from damp. The result was a bed of rich, glossy satin. Then he wrestled out of his topcoat and draped it over Emma like a blanket.

A knock at the door announced the arrival of tea. He took the tray and promptly shut the door in the serving girl's face, rather than allowing her in to pour. Instead, he served Emma himself, squinting into the cup to assess its cleanliness before filling it with steaming tea, milk, and a generous helping of sugar. He withdrew a small flask from his waistcoat pocket, unscrewed the cap, and added a splash of something amber-colored, potent-smelling, and no doubt frightfully expensive.

Emma sat watching all this in silence, transfixed. Reason had fled her brain. His every motion struck her as some sort of acrobatic feat deserving of wild applause. Perhaps she truly *was* ill. Everything about him, each damp hair on his head and every speck of mud on his boots, was perfect in her eyes. She would not have changed a thing.

"Here." He brought her the tea.

She moved to take it from him.

He moved it out of her reach. "Not while your hands are shaking."

He lifted it to her lips, talking her through a series of hot, cautious sips. A sweet warmth traveled down her throat and swirled its way through her chest.

"There we are. That's better, is it?"

She nodded. "Yes."

After setting the tea aside, he extended a hand to Emma and drew her to her feet. Hands on her waist, he steered her through a half turn and reached to undo the buttons down the back of her gown.

"We have to get you out of all this," he said. "If not, you'll only soak the cloak through and we'll never warm you up."

Her quivering lips curved into a smile. "I'm beginning to suspect you planned this entire situation."

"If I had, I would have found a finer inn and ordered a gown with larger buttons." He ceased tugging. "To the devil with this. The cursed thing is ruined anyway." He gripped the edges of the bodice and, with a fierce yank, ripped the buttons from their holes.

Mercy.

Emma reeled on her toes, dizzy again. Her vision grayed at the edges.

"I don't know what's happened to me," she said, rubbing her temple. "I *never* swoon. Perhaps Mary laced the corset too tightly."

"I'll tell you what happened. What happened is that I stupidly let you stand in a freezing downpour, wearing nothing more than a few scraps of silk. You're chilled to the marrow."

She supposed that was true. But for a kiss like that, she would have gladly stood there all night long.

He worked quickly and with no hint of seduction, but the care he took in peeling away her layers of drenched clothing—silk gown, sodden petticoats, laced corset—stirred her heart with its tenderness. When his fingertips brushed the wet locks from her bared, chilled neck, she had goose bumps on top of goose bumps.

Once he had her down to her shift, he didn't pause in kneeling down and gathering it from the hem, bunching the fabric as he lifted it upward.

"Arms up." The command scorched the nape of her neck.

She obeyed, stretching her arms overhead. As he lifted the soaked linen further, the fabric brushed over her breasts. Her nipples had puckered to cold, resentful knots in the rain, but now they tightened with more pleasant sensations. At last, he drew the garment over her head and arms, casting it aside. Leaving her bare, save for her stockings.

He turned her to him, rubbing his hands up

and down her arms and sweeping his gaze over her body. Then he unknotted his cravat with jerky movements and used the fabric as a make-shift towel, rubbing the moisture from her skin and hair.

As the fire threw weak light and smoldering heat into the room, she found a blush warming her neck and face. Her teeth had ceased chattering, and the gooseflesh covering her arms had begun to fade.

When she was cold, he warmed her. This alone was more care than she'd ever known from any man. It didn't matter that it came wrapped in scowls and sardonic quips.

She loved him for it.

Loved him, loved him, loved him, loved him.

The words pulsed through her brain with every heartbeat. Surely it was the swoon affecting her, but she found it difficult to breathe. She clung to his shirt, as if he could be her salvation—but he was the danger. She was lost. Lost to him, and a stranger to herself.

When he'd done his best with the discarded cravat, he whisked her off her feet once more, moving her to the bed. As he laid her on his cape, the silk lining slid beneath her body. She burrowed under his coat while he pulled off his boots and shucked his damp trousers.

He settled behind her on the bed, spooning around her curled body, drawing her spine against his chest. He was hot as a brick straight from the kiln. His delicious warmth radiated through her, thawing and relaxing her limbs. Her shivering eased.

"You're not cold anymore?"

"No."

"Good." The flat of his palm slid up and down her arm. "Then sleep."

Her eyelids grew heavy. "Ash . . ."

"Sleep." His arm flexed, gathering her tight. "I'll keep you warm and safe. I'll keep you always."

FOR THE SECOND time in her marriage, Emma experienced the pleasure of waking in her husband's arms. And the joy of finding her hair matted in a nest. And the bliss of a receding headache.

But yes, the arms. Waking in his arms was lovely.

She rolled onto her other side, facing him.

His gaze was tender, and his touch even more so. He skimmed a caress down her cheek, then down over her shoulder. He didn't seem to mind her matted hair. Then his arm went around her, and he gave her a kiss that was every bit as sweet and gentle as the previous night's was fierce and demanding.

When they parted, he sighed her name. "Emma."

She touched his cheek. "Good morning, my sunshine."

He sat up in bed with a start. "Look at us. How did this happen? I thought we agreed that there would be no affection."

"We did."

"We had rules."

"There were precautions."

The left side of his mouth pulled into a smile. "Not enough of them, apparently."

Emma sat up in bed. "I want to apologize for the things I said last night. I should have had more faith in you. And I suppose I should be more charitable toward Miss Worthing. If you hadn't cared enough for her feelings to let her go, I wouldn't have you at all."

"I have to admit, releasing her wasn't merely generosity. Perhaps not even mostly generosity. Pride was involved, as well. She was still willing to marry me, but only if I agreed to certain stipulations. I wasn't willing to accept her terms."

"Did she want a larger settlement?"

"No, nothing like that."

"Then I can't imagine what she could ask for. I spent time with her. She cared little for anything besides money and appear—"

"Appearances? Yes. Precisely."

Emma cringed, regretting the word. Would she never learn?

"On reflection, I don't suppose it's accurate to call them stipulations," he said. "If we married, she demanded that I agree to certain rules."

"Rules?"

He didn't answer, but the look in his eyes spoke volumes. Spoke of pain and anger and a wound that went deeper than any of his scars.

Rules.

Oh, no.

She reached for her shift. "Surely you don't mean—"

"Husband and wife by night only. No lights. No kissing. Once she bore me an heir, we would never share a bed again."

At last, it was clear. It had never made sense to her that he would create such rules. He had all the power over her. Once they married, she was at his mercy. Why would he care about protecting her sensibilities? If indeed her sensibilities needed protecting, which they didn't. They never had.

But he hadn't been guarding her sensibilities, had he? He'd been protecting himself.

Emma found it difficult to speak for some moments. When she did find words, they were only three. "I *hate* her."

He laughed. "You're a vicar's daughter. You can't know what it is to hate anyone."

"Oh, yes, I can." Her hands curled into fists. She growled. "I could strangle the woman."

"You could not."

"Fine. But I would stick her with pins. A large number of pins."

"That, I can almost believe."

"I mean it. A great many pins. She would look like a hedgehog by the time I was through with her."

Emma fumed. Her anger was no exaggeration. She might have envied or resented Annabelle Worthing in the past, but in that moment, she truly despised the woman. How *dare* she. She'd convinced a brave, loyal, decent man that he was a monster. A creature who deserved nothing more than scraps and shadows of affection, and even then, only in the dark.

"Do you know, this room is rather charming," he said, in an obvious attempt to change the subject.

"Charming?"

"It has possibilities. All it needs is a few draperies, better furnishings, a coat of paint, a mattress stuffed with straw from this decade, a few dozen scrubbing brushes, and a vermin catcher. Where's your imagination?"

She gave him a dry look.

"Of course, there is one thing in the room that requires no alteration." He dropped a kiss on her forehead.

"Nicely rescued."

"Are you hungry at all?"

"Not very."

"Well, I'm famished." He pulled on his trousers and shirt, then jammed his feet into his boots. "I'll see about calling for some breakfast and a cab."

When he opened the bedchamber door, however, a deafening clamor rose up. Shouts and cries from the public rooms below. Footsteps pounding madly up the stairs.

A man elbowed his way into the bedchamber and slammed the door shut behind him. "You don't want to go down there. Trust me."

The stranger wore a mask of black mesh and a similarly dark jerkin cinched over black trousers and a dark shirt. In his hand, he carried a slingshot.

Emma shook her head, bewildered.

Her husband, however, seemed to understand.

"What are you doing here?" He waved a hand at the newcomer's strange attire. "And what is all that?"

"Like it? My old fencing kit, a bit of bootblack . . . and here I am." The intruder pushed the mask back, revealing his face. He bowed to Emma. "At your service, Your Grace."

With the mask dislodged, Emma could see that he was only a boy. Eleven or twelve years old, perhaps. Tall for his age, with jug-handle ears and a gap between his front teeth.

And this boy, whoever he was, seemed to be well acquainted with her husband.

She turned to Ash. "May I trouble you for an introduction?"

"This? This is Trevor."

The boy jabbed his elbow in Ash's side. "Ahem."

Ash rolled his eyes. "Right. This is the Menace."

The *Menace*? Oh, Emma couldn't wait to hear this story.

"I'm the Monster of Mayfair's associate," the boy said. "Apprentice, if you will. His protégé."

"How remarkable. How did this come about?"

Her husband gave her a blank look. "I've no idea."

"You're bloody fortunate it did." The boy

walked between them and dropped onto the bed with a creak and a bounce. "All London's gathered outside, waiting on the Monster of Mayfair to make an appearance."

Ash went to the window. "I should have known this would happen. Last night . . . I wasn't thinking."

"No, you weren't thinking." Emma crossed to his side, taking his arm. "You were caring."

"That and a penny will buy you stale bread. It's not going to help us now."

"Would it be so terrible if the world learned the truth?" she asked.

"Considering that I'm known about London as a child-snatching, bloodthirsty monster who sacrifices small animals to the Dark Lord? Yes, I think it would be."

Emma bit her tongue. She longed to point out that perhaps he should have thought about all this before encouraging his notoriety. But it wouldn't do any good just now.

"Well, if you mean to remain anonymous, what do you propose to do?" she asked. "There isn't any rear exit, and I'm not jumping out that window."

"You don't need another exit. All you need is a diversion," Trevor said.

"No diversion will tear that mob away," Ash said. "Maybe a fire, but even that's questionable."

"It's simple." Trevor picked up Ash's hat and placed it on his head. It settled halfway down his ears. "I'll be the Monster. You be the Menace."

"That's ridiculous."

"No," Emma countered, "it's brilliant. Think about it. The crowd down there isn't waiting for the Duke of Ashbury. They're waiting for the Monster of Mayfair. A man in a black hat and cape."

"He's not a man. He's a boy."

"I'm tall for my age," Trevor said defensively.

"A minute or two is all we need. By the time they realize he's not the Monster—"

"You'll have skirted the crowd and escaped." Trevor flashed a smug grin. "And I have a hackney waiting on the next corner."

"My goodness," Emma said. "You've thought of everything, haven't you? What a fine assistant you make."

"Stop encouraging him." Ash said.

"Did you have a better plan?"

"Unfortunately, no." He handed her one of the wool blankets. "Wrap yourself in this. We can't risk anyone getting a glimpse of red silk."

Emma wrapped the blanket around her shoulders. It smelled bad and chafed worse, but it was long and thick enough to serve its purpose. She would take a long, hot bath at home later.

"Leave the rest to me." Trevor launched to his feet. Not three paces away, the boy paused. Then, with a snap of his neck, he looked back at them. He raised a single eyebrow. "You've been menaced."

Ash scowled. "What is that?"

"It's my new signature phrase. A calling card. Still working on the delivery." Trevor lowered his voice to a sinister growl, then lifted the same eyebrow. "You've"—*pause*—"been menaced."

Emma pressed her lips together, trying not to laugh.

"Or there's this way. You've been"—*pause, eyebrow lift*—"menaced." The boy cocked his head. "What do you think?"

"I think," Ash said tightly, "you should take them both and—"

"Alternate between them," Emma interrupted. "They're both excellent. Quite memorable."

"Thank you, Your Grace." Trevor bowed over her hand and kissed it. "Until we meet again."

With a flourish of black cape, he was gone.

Finally, she allowed herself to laugh. "What an extraordinary young man."

"That's one way of putting it."

Emma cinched the scratchy wool blanket about her shoulders. "I need a better costume. And a name of my own. Oh, how about the Needle? I can prick ruffians with a long, sharp sword."

"Don't start."

He cracked the door open, and together they listened until they heard Trevor reach the public room and bellow: "I am the Monster of Mayfair! To behold my face is to know despair!"

Ash closed his eyes and muttered something unkind.

"It's not bad," Emma protested. "It even rhymes."

He pulled the fencing mask over his face. "Let's just go."

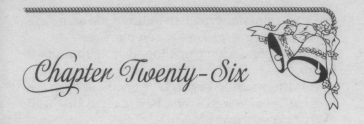

Chapter Twenty-Six

$\mathcal{T}$hankfully, they made their way back to Ashbury House with a minimum of further indignities. After a few vague explanations to the worried staff, a hot breakfast, and hotter baths, the two of them tumbled atop Ash's bed and slept the day away.

Emma woke to late afternoon, and to her husband pushing a wheeled table toward the bed. It was laden with covered dishes and baskets of bread, cheeses, fruits. Her stomach rumbled.

"What's this?" She rubbed her eyes. "Dinner in bed?"

"It's perfect." He reached for a wedge of cheese. "I promised you dinner every night. You promised me bed. We both hold our ends of the bargain at once."

"How very efficient."

"Really, I don't know how the idea escaped me until now."

Emma nibbled at an apple tart. "I've been thinking, dumpling."

He flopped back on the bed and groaned. "Em-*ma*."

"I'm sorry, but I don't want to call you Ash. It's just not who you are. Ash is the dead, cold remnants after a fire. The parts that get swept away and discarded. You're not Ash to me. You're alive and blazing and more than a little dangerous. You always keep me warm." Lest he grow too panicked at the praise, she decided to lighten her tone. "Besides, it's too amusing to devil you."

"Amusing for *you*, perhaps."

"Let's have a compromise. When we're in the company of others, I will call you Ash or Ashbury. When we're alone, you'll allow me my little pet names."

"Fine. But you must confine yourself to an agreed upon list. No more rainbows and buttercups."

"I suppose I can do that."

He considered. "Here are the ones I'll allow. 'My stallion,' 'my buck,' and . . . 'my colossus of man-flesh.'"

She laughed in his face at that last. "Let's keep to the traditional endearments, shall we? Such as 'my dear'?"

"That's acceptable."

"'Darling'?"

He made a face of disgust. "If you must."

She chewed on the pastry, trying to gather courage. "How do you feel about 'my love'?"

He stared deeply into her eyes, as though questioning her sincerity. However, she knew it wasn't what lay within *her* that mattered—it was whether he'd allow *himself* to believe the words.

The familiar shields overtook his expression, closing the door on possibility. "'My stallion' it is."

Emma was disappointed, but she decided not to press the matter. Perhaps it was all too much for one day.

She looked about for a diversion. Her eye fell on a fresh stack of papers beside the dinner tray.

She'd made a habit of asking the servants to collect broadsheets daily. By this point, Ash was supporting half the printers in London. Probably a few paper mills, as well. The Monster of Mayfair was the best thing to happen to British journalism since Waterloo.

She seized on the change of subject, gathering the papers and bringing them back to the bed. "Let's see what they're saying about you today. There's certain to be something about last night's adventure." As she skimmed the first broadsheet, however, her anticipation of humor turned to horror. "Oh, no. Oh, Ash. This is bad."

"What is it now? Have I rescued a girl from drowning in the Serpentine?"

"No. You've abducted a woman in red, forced an innkeeper to let you hide her, and she was never seen again. Foul play is suspected." She passed him the paper, then positioned herself behind his shoulder and reached over to jab her finger at the paper. "The Crown has issued a hue and cry for the Monster of Mayfair." She poked again, rattling the newsprint. "The *Crown*. Every able-bodied man in London is *obliged* to help capture you on sight."

"Yes. I see."

"They've even offered a reward. *Twenty pounds.* That's a year's earnings for a laborer."

"Yes. I know."

"'Wanted on suspicions of trespassing, assault, theft of property, kidnapping, and murder.' *Murder!*"

"I *am* able to read, thank you." He was infuriatingly calm. "I'm a bit disappointed witchcraft and insurance fraud aren't on the list."

"How can you even joke about this?"

"Trust me, there's no call to be agitated." He dug into a portion of game pie. "Even the worst possible scenario is a mere inconvenience."

"Being brought up on charges of murder would be a mere inconvenience?"

"I didn't commit any murders, Emma."

"That's not what the broadsheets would have their readers believe. You know how eager people have been to make false reports of your exploits."

"Yes, I do know." He swallowed his mouthful of pie. "One of those eager people with false stories would be you."

Well, she couldn't contradict that.

"I would never be charged with murder," he went on. "The very thought is absurd. I'm a duke. It just doesn't happen. Even if I were captured, I would never be brought to trial."

"How can you be certain of that?"

"To begin, dukes aren't charged in the same courts. We are entitled to a trial of our peers in the House of Lords. That's if there were any evidence, which there isn't. Second, there's a little thing called privilege of peerage. All we have to do is invoke it, and we're off the hook for nearly any crime."

She was agape. "You're joking."

"Not at all."

"My goodness. That must be nice."

"It is, rather. Can't deny it."

On any other occasion, Emma would have been appalled by the injustice of this system. However, given the current state of affairs, she found herself unable to complain.

"Hold a moment," she said. "You said a peer may be forgiven *almost* any crime. Which means some crimes are exceptions."

"Well, treason, naturally. And—" He broke off, clearly reluctant to continue.

She leaned forward. "And . . . ?"

"Murder," he admitted.

She bounced on the mattress in anger. "You just told me it would be a minor inconvenience! How could hanging be a minor inconvenience?"

"It never goes that far." He set aside his now-empty plate. "At the most, I'd make a manslaughter plea, and that would put paid to it."

"What if it does go that far?"

"It wouldn't."

"Humor me."

He sighed as he reached for his glass of wine.

"A peer found guilty of a capital felony—which never occurs—could conceivably be executed. Which never occurs, either. No one's been struck with corruption of the blood in ages now. Literal centuries."

"And what's corruption of the blood?"

"It means a bloodline is considered tainted. They take away the peer's title and property, and none of his descendants can inherit it."

Emma's hands were fists in her lap. "So if . . . and I'm allowing you the 'if' . . . this exceedingly unlikely event occurred, you could be captured and charged as the Monster of Mayfair, brought to trial in the House of Lords on charges of murder, convicted, and put to death, with the result that your wife and possibly your child would be left without any property or inheritance?"

"It never happens, Emma. Never."

"But it could!"

"It *won't*."

She took a deep breath to calm herself. "You've allowed this ruse to go on too long. We can mend this. Come forward. Let everyone know that you're the Monster of Mayfair, I'm the missing lady in red, and that it was all merely a lark that got out of hand."

"So instead of facing the slim chance that I would ever be captured—and the slimmer chance that I would be brought up on any charges—you want me to confess to crimes I didn't commit?"

"No. I want you to confess to encouraging a silly legend and letting it continue for far too long. Just have out with it. As you say, a duke gets away with everything."

He drained his wineglass and rose from the bed. "I will not admit to the world that I'm the Monster of Mayfair. There would be a scandal, and you would have to bear up under it. Who knows what the broadsheets would call *you*? The Beastly Bride of Bloom Square?"

She raised an eyebrow. "Did you have that moniker thought out in advance?"

"No," he said, sounding defensive.

"Because it tripped rather easily off your tongue."

"The point is this. I'm not going to do that to you. Whatever name the papers might choose, I refuse to put you under their scrutiny. Much less any child you could be carrying."

"If you are so concerned for your wife and child, perhaps you ought to have considered that earlier," she muttered, vexed. She tried to find a compromise. "If you refuse to come forward, at least promise me this. The Monster of Mayfair has retired. He's pensioned off to the country, never to return. Swear to me that you'll burn all your capes and never go walking at night again."

"Done." He put a finger under her chin, tipping her face to receive his kiss. "The Monster of Mayfair is no more. I swear it."

"You had better keep your word," she said. "Or you'll face the wrath of the Beastly Bride."

Chapter Twenty-Seven

"There." Emma helped do up the last button on Davina's new day dress. "Is it comfortable? You don't feel too pinched?"

"No, not at all."

With Fanny's help, Emma had been able to arrange a fitting at the dressmaking shop. They'd kept the shop open late for Davina while Madame was making her weekly visit to the storehouse to see the latest imported silks.

Davina turned and regarded herself in the mirror. "You truly work wonders with fabric, Emma."

Wonders, perhaps. But not miracles.

"It should help you conceal it for another few weeks, I hope."

"I hope so, too. Just the other day, Papa commented on my waistline. I told him that I'd been eating too many rich foods." She took Emma's hands. "We must secure permission as soon as possible. When will the duke be able to meet Papa?"

Oh, dear. Emma had been dreading this conversation. She would have to tell the girl that their original plan just wouldn't work. Ash wasn't willing to circulate in society, and as Annabelle Worthing had made clear at the theater, in London's eyes, Emma was still a seamstress, not a duchess. She was hardly the sort of lady an ambitious gentleman would allow his unmarried daughter to visit for the winter.

The whole scheme had been doomed from the start. Emma saw that now. She felt horrible for raising the girl's hopes.

That didn't mean there was no way to help, however. She had Nicola, and Alex, and Penny—dear Penny, who never met a creature in need she wouldn't coddle. If the four of them put their minds to it, they could devise an alternative.

Yes, that was the thing to do. She would consult them next week at tea.

"Give me a bit more time," Emma said. "You have my word, I will not fail you."

Once Davina had left, Emma let Fanny go, offering to close up the shop as she'd done in the past. She felt an odd sense of nostalgia as she went about drawing the shades and putting away the shears, ribbons, and pins. She'd passed years of her life in this shop, after all, and that couldn't be forgotten in a matter of months.

Thump-thump-thump.

Emma looked up, startled. "We're closed," she called.

Thump-thump-thump-thump.

How curious. The last time she'd heard that sort of incessant knocking, the Duke of Ashbury had pushed his way into the shop—and into her life, as well. Surely he wouldn't have followed her today?

Who could know when it came to her husband? Emma went to the door, ready to receive a fresh scolding about duchesses not stitching garments.

She turned the latch. "Really, my stallion. I only came by to see my old fr—"

When she opened the door, her heart stopped.

A middle-aged man dressed in black stood in the entry, holding his wide-brimmed parson's hat in hand. "Emma, my child. It *is* you. I was told I'd find you here, and here you are."

"Father?"

Emma felt detached from her body, out of communication with her own mind. Her heart was in utter tumult. So many emotions and impulses warred inside her. Revenge was tempting. She could turn him out, as he'd once cast her into the night.

Gloating also appealed. A small, petty part of her wanted to take him home and show him about the house until he was sick with envy for her newfound wealth, and then send him on his way with a fifty-pound donation to the church.

And somewhere, beneath all this, she wanted to sit at his knee. She wanted to hear that she was loved, and still his little girl.

Be careful, Emma.

"Why are you here?" she asked quietly.

"To see my daughter, naturally." He moved into the shop, and she closed the door behind him. "Look at you. Emma, my own dear girl, fully grown."

"I'm Emma now, am I? Your own dear girl? When last we met, you had taken to calling me Jezebel."

"That's why I've come." He bowed his head, looking down at the hat in his hands. "To tell you that I am most heartily sorry."

Most heartily sorry?

The words slipped over her. She couldn't grasp their meaning. Instead, Emma stared at the top of her father's head. He was balding there now. Down to just a few straggling hairs, slicked over a gleaming pate. How strange, to see him aged six years all at once. In her memory he'd remained intimidating and thunderously enraged. Now, here in the bustle of London, he looked rather pathetic and small.

He kept his eyes downcast. "I should not have said such things. I should not have turned you out. I've come to confess my sins against you. And I pray that you will find it within your heart to grant me forgiveness."

Emma's breathing hitched. After all these years, he'd come to her and admitted his wrongs. He'd apologized. This was something she had always thought she'd wanted. Not merely wanted, but *needed* to make her heart sit right in her chest.

And yet . . . it wasn't working the way she'd

hoped. Nothing in her chest felt easy or at peace. Her pulse was a gathering clamor, pounding in her head.

"Over the years, I've thought of you often," he said. "Worried over you. Prayed."

"I'm not certain I can believe that. If you found me this easily now, why not years ago? If you worried, why did you never send a letter, never ask whether I had enough to eat or coal to keep warm at night? You didn't care. You probably thought it my due penance."

A chill went through her, and she started to shiver. She hugged herself, willing it to stop. She would not allow him to rule her that way.

"That's not the case," he said. "I swear it."

"What is it you want from me now? Money? Influence? Some sort of favor? You must have heard I've married."

"No, not at all. It's as I told you. I came only to make amends."

"Well, it seems very convenient timing."

"I . . ." He fidgeted with the brim of his hat. "To be truthful, it was God. God spoke to me."

God *spoke* to him? Emma couldn't believe what she was hearing.

"That is to say, it wasn't precisely God who spoke to me." A queasy look came over his pale face. "I . . . I was visited by a fearsome messenger in the night. A demon."

"Oh, truly," she said, dispassionate. Clearly in his advancing age he was going mad.

"It was terrible, Emma. He appeared to me in

my bedchamber, in the middle of the night. A demon from the very mouth of Hell. He told me that my days are numbered on this earth, and that I must make my peace with you or else face eternal hellfire."

"So you're not here to make amends to me for my sake. You're here for your own interests." She shook her head. "You truly haven't changed."

"Can it not be for the good of us both? I know—I have always known, long before this unholy visitation—that I treated you ill. The sin has weighed on me like a millstone all these years. I cannot rest easy until I know I have your forgiveness."

She laughed bitterly. "*You* cannot rest easy. Perhaps you should try sleeping in the cold, as you forced me to do."

"You can't mean to say you are withholding your forgiveness?"

"I'm not sure. I don't feel any haste to grant it."

"You cannot deny me this." He grew indignant. She knew that chastening tone so very well. "You are my daughter. Did I not clothe and feed you, raise you in the principles of charity for sixteen years?"

"And did I not love you for every one of those years?" Her voice shook. "Every Sunday, I sat in that chapel, and I might have prayed to God, but it was your blessing I sought. It made no difference, did it? One mistake outweighed it all. It wasn't the lack of clothing or shelter or food that hurt me, Father. It wasn't even the rejection of my sweetheart. What tore me in two was seeing you for who you are. Knowing you were never the man I'd believed you to be. Not by half."

"Emma, please. Do not judge so harshly. You must understand I was taken by surprise that night. Stunned. I scarcely knew what I was feeling, let alone doing."

"You knew exactly what you were doing. And I know exactly how you felt. You were ashamed. Ashamed of me, and ashamed of what people would say if they knew. It was cowardice, pure and simple, that was your motive then. It is cowardice that brought you here tonight." She went to the door. "I would like you to leave."

"No! No, you cannot do this to me." He fell to his knees before her. "You didn't see him, Emma. The demon. Oh, he was horrible. Fearsome to behold. His face . . . it was all twisted and burned, and he had—"

"Wait." Emma's heartbeat stuttered. "You say his face was burned?"

"Yes. Most wretchedly. From the brimstone, no doubt. But it wasn't only his face that was evil. He . . . he threatened me with hellfire and bureaucracy. He insulted my curtains. He called me the vilest of names."

"Names such as what?"

"Oh, I don't like to say."

"Names such as *what*?"

"I don't know, I . . . Something like m-mammering canker-blossom?"

"Thank you, Father. I think you've given me

a very clear image of this 'demon' you encountered."

And that image looked a great deal like her husband.

Mammering canker-blossom. Now *that* one was new. He must have been saving it.

Her father rose to his feet. "I beg you. If you deny me forgiveness, you do not know how I will suffer. For the rest of my life, I will never be easy. Never at peace. Always fearing that each day will be my last."

"I lived with that feeling for six years. Now it's your turn." She opened the door. "If it's forgiveness you want, you may come back and ask me again in another six years. Right now, you will leave. At once."

"But—"

She gave him a push between the shoulders and he stumbled through the open door. "Begone, you beetle-headed gudgeon."

Oh, the look on his face. For as long as she lived, she would laugh whenever she recalled it.

"Beetle-headed . . . ?" He huffed with offense, and his face turned purple with rage. "You will not speak to me that way, Emma Grace Gladstone."

"Emma Grace Gladstone," she echoed. "No, Emma Grace Gladstone would not have dared to speak to you that way. But I'm Emma Grace Pembrooke now. The Duchess of Ashbury. And if you ever speak to me again, you will address me as Your Grace."

She shut the door and locked it.

And then she sank to the floor for a good long cry.

The tears came, and she surrendered to them. There was no one to hear, and no one to see. She cried until her eyes were dry and her heart was empty. The foolishness of it all. She'd wasted so many years allowing the value he placed on her to dictate the way she regarded herself.

Emma fished a handkerchief from her pocket. She wiped her tears and blew her nose. She would not let her father hold her back. Not from trusting. Not from living. Not from loving.

Not anymore.

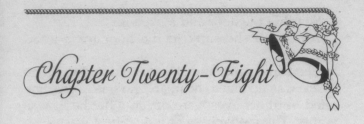

Chapter Twenty-Eight

*Y*ou went to my father's house."

Ash looked up from the ledger he'd been examining.

Emma.

She stood in front of his desk, staring down at him. Her eyes were red, as though she'd been crying. He set aside the ledger and rose to his feet.

"You went to my father's house," she repeated. "In Hertfordshire."

There seemed little sense in denying it. "Yes."

"In the dead of night."

"Yes."

"You broke into the vicarage."

He rubbed a hand over his uneven hair. "I climbed in through his bedroom window, actually."

"And then you told him you were a demon from Hell."

"To be fair, he didn't require a great deal of convincing."

"You said you'd stop this. No more roaming about at night. You promised me."

"I went to him before that. Weeks ago now, and . . . How do you know all this anyway?"

"He came to see me. At the modiste's shop where I worked."

Ash swore. The craven bastard.

"He apologized," she went on. "Can you believe it? He knelt at my feet and begged for my forgiveness."

"Well, I hope you didn't grant it."

"Why?" Her stare was direct and unnerving. "Why should you care? Why did you go to him at all?"

"Because he hurt you, Emma." He thumped the desk for emphasis. "The man cast you out, without feeling or remorse. He left you to shiver and starve and fend for yourself. He made you frightened of the cold, and so afraid of your own heart you settled for marrying a bitter jackass. He treated you as though you were worthless, and for that, he deserves to rot in the ground. It was only for your sake that I did not put him there myself. He hurt you, and I would not stand for it. And I won't apologize, either. Not now, not ever."

"I see."

Ash let quiet fill the room. It might be the last silence he'd enjoy for a while. Her demeanor was so restrained on the surface, he could only imagine her to be volcanically angry beneath. He drew a slow breath, steeling himself for the eruption.

She walked around the desk in brisk strides, and Ash turned to face her. He wasn't going to hide.

Then she grabbed him by the lapels, pulled him down, and kissed him for all he was worth. No. She kissed him for a great deal more than he was worth, by a factor of thousands.

"Thank you," she whispered between fervent kisses. "Thank you. I've never had anyone stand up for me like that."

Any measure of chivalry that placed Ash at its pinnacle was a sorry scale indeed. But he would take her kisses, and gladly. Gratefully. He would take any part of her she offered him. Body, mind, heart, soul.

Bodies seemed to be the order of the moment, however. And as willing as he was to take hers, she seemed even more eager to get at his. As they kissed, she tugged at his coat sleeves, shaking them loose of his arms until the entire coat slipped to the floor. His waistcoat buttons were next.

Once she had him undressed down to only his shirt, she pushed him into the armchair and tugged at his shirt, pulling it up to lift over his head.

He kept his arms at his sides.

"Surely you're not hesitating now?" she asked. "I thought we were past this."

She was past it, perhaps, but it wasn't so easy for him. He tried to explain it. "I couldn't stand for you to look on me with pity. Or distaste."

Emma gave him a soft look. "It's not pity or

distaste that worries you. You're not afraid of rejection. You welcome it. But if you're seen for everything you are—the strengths and the flaws, the beauty and the scars—you might have to believe you're *wanted*. Loved. Really, truly, honestly, earnestly, properly." She pressed her forehead to his. "And completely."

Ash swallowed hard. She'd left him speechless. Entirely.

"I know you're afraid," she whispered. "I know it because I'm scared, too. Terrified, really. Make love to me. Be brave with me." She grasped his shirt in both hands and pulled. "With nothing between us."

"Emma, don't."

"Why not?"

He flailed for excuses. "It's—It's my favorite shirt."

"Then I'll mend it later."

She found the bit of stitching where the shirt's neckline converged, caught the fabric in her teeth, and tugged, biting a notch in the fabric. That accomplished, she took both sides in her hands and ripped the shirt straight down the center.

Ash was amazed. And, if he was honest, fiercely aroused.

She smiled. "A seamstress knows how to split fabric. And by now, you should know *me*. If you issue a command, I'll only do the reverse."

He started to compose a good scolding in his mind. But then he decided . . . perhaps he could make her rebellious nature work to his benefit.

"Very well," he said. "Don't lift your skirts and straddle me."

Her eyes questioned him for a moment. Then understanding swept them, and a saucy smile curved her lips.

She gathered her striped muslin skirt and petticoats in fistfuls, hiking them high enough to allow him an erotic glimpse of her calves before climbing atop his lap, one knee on either side of his thighs, and letting that white, flouncy cloud of her petticoats fall around them both. He felt as though he'd been admitted to a temple of feminine secrets. Awed.

God. He was hard already, primed to take her without a moment's delay. Slip loose the buttons of his trousers and thrust. That was all it would take. But he knew anticipation now would make the eventual satisfaction all the sweeter.

However, he intended to torture her every bit as much as she tortured him. Know every part of her, just as she knew him.

Love her. All of her. The way he yearned to be loved.

He slid a hand down her back, finding the edge of the ribbon that cinched her bodice tight. With a slow, teasing tug, he pulled until the knot gave way. Her bodice fell slack, and her breathing quickened.

"Don't," he said in a firm voice, "lower your bodice. And whatever you do, don't you dare lift your breasts and offer them to me."

A blush blossomed on her cheeks, in a red

deep as roses. He inhaled a lungful of her intoxicating fragrance. She slipped her arms out from her sleeves and wriggled her bosom free of her bodice and stays. Out they tumbled in all their glory. Full and round and dark pink at the tips.

Biting her lip, she slid her hands beneath her breasts, lifting and plumping—and sweet heaven, rolling her nipples between her thumbs and forefingers until they were pert and begging for him.

She offered them each to his mouth in turn, and he kissed and licked and suckled with abandon, drawing on her nipples with rough suction and nuzzling under the soft orbs to lick the sensitive flesh beneath. Each sigh and moan that fell from her lips shot straight down his spine and gathered in his cock. His erection pulsed against his falls, desperate for contact.

He pulled away from her breasts. Gripping the armrests of the chair for control, he gave his next contrary command. "Don't put your hands under your skirt."

If she was shy or surprised, her expression didn't reveal it.

She placed one hand on the back of the chair and leaned forward on it, pressing her breasts closer to his face. Then she reached between them and slid her other hand up her thigh, taunting him.

"Shall I touch myself?" she asked coyly.

God yes, he thought.

But he shook his head no.

She gave him a smile as she worked her hand in naughty circles. He couldn't view her fingers like this, but just the suggestion of her pleasuring herself drove him wild.

He wanted to see.

He *had* to see.

He released his grip on the armrests and shoved her skirts to her waist, revealing a view of paradise. Her delicate fingers, parting those dark curls and stroking the pink petals hidden within.

His mouth went dry. Holding her skirts high with one hand, he grasped her tempting bottom in the other, tilting her hips to get a better view.

"Don't push them inside," he said hoarsely. "You intractable woman, don't you dare."

Two of her slender fingers disappeared inside her, buried in her soft heat to the first knuckle.

"No deeper," he scraped out. "Not another inch."

She purred with pleasure, disobeying him again, sinking down on her fingers as far as they would go.

He thought he would explode. "Don't raise those fingers to my lips."

At that, she hesitated.

"I forbid it," he said, bringing forth his sternest, most aristocratic voice.

She raised her hand palm-up, offering it to him.

He gripped her wrist and drew her first and second fingers into his mouth, sucking them down to the webs between her fingers and lapping up every bit of her tart-sweet nectar. The rose-red blush on her cheeks became an erotic bloom of crimson across her throat and breasts.

"Ash," she whispered. Her dark eyes were pleading.

Teasing her this way was sublime, but even he had his limits.

He reached between them, fumbling with the buttons of his trouser falls and freeing his cock. She moved closer, trapping his erection between his pelvis and hers, sliding over his shaft on the dewy sheen of her aroused sex. Grinding against him in tiny circles to heighten her bliss.

He could have wept with the beauty of it.

Bracing her hands on his shoulders, she wriggled until the tip of his cock fit just where it needed to be, sinking down on him with a breathy sigh. He grasped her by the hips, guiding her up and down his length. She removed his hands and pinned them to the armrests. She didn't need his guidance, apparently. She rode him in a lazy yet relentless rhythm.

"Don't stop," he moaned.

She stopped.

He growled with frustration. "*Don't* don't stop."

She began to move again, accelerating her pace.

"You are incorrigible."

"And I'm yours. Entirely yours. You won't be rid of me."

God. The pleasure was keen, and he was tempted to surrender to it, arching his hips to pump her hard and fast until she came around him and he spent into her. But he forced himself to hold back.

Not yet. Not yet.

He wanted more than pleasure right now. She was giving so much of herself to him, freely and without reserve. In ways he'd never given himself to anyone—not before, not after. The courage within her small frame was profound, her generosity boundless. He felt like a coward in comparison.

Make love to me. Be brave with me.

"Don't touch me," he whispered. "Don't touch me everywhere."

One of her hands slipped beneath the shredded linen of his shirt, drawing the panels aside to expose his chest. Her fingers skimmed over his skin. And his scars. Her touch pained him in places, and he was dead numb in others. In moments, his blood sang with bliss. No matter what the sensation, each moment was exquisite. He closed his eyes, lost in her caress.

Emma. My love, my love.

"Don't kiss me," he choked out.

Without hesitation—as though she'd been waiting and hoping for the invitation—her lips were on his, softer than her touch. Warmer, too. Each brush of her lips was a blessing he didn't deserve, but he was powerless to turn her away.

She kissed her way up the ruined side of his neck, tracing his misshapen ear with her tongue and running her fingers through his patchy hair.

Then she blazed a path down the other side, from his jaw to his shoulder, dragging openmouthed kisses over his skin.

She lavished both sides of him with equal attention and sweet, sweet tenderness, until he felt his two halves knitting together in the center. Somewhere close to his heart.

Her brow pressed to his, and she held him tight.

It was time.

She braced her hands on the back of the chair. He framed her waist in his hands. Pulling her down, straining upward—not content any longer to let her take the lead. He wanted—needed— to battle out of himself, find refuge in her. Reach the place where they could be one.

"Don't love me."

The words came unbidden from his throat. Not a thought, but a plea.

"Too late," she whispered in his ear.

"Don't tell me so. Don't say the words."

"I love you." She cupped his face in her hands and brushed a kiss to his lips. "I love you so much."

There was nothing left for him to resist. He held her to him, and as they tumbled over the edge together, no joy could have been more complete.

He was complete.

He held her tightly in his arms, pressing kisses to her hair. "I love you. You will never know how much I love you. There aren't words."

She levered herself to a sitting position. Her drowsy eyes came into focus. She stared down at her hands where they lay against his red, twisted scars. All color drained from her face. The expression that overtook her face was no longer one of love or pleasure, but one of faint disgust.

"Emma?"

God, please. Not again. Not you.

Don't leave me. Not now, not ever.

"I'm sorry," said, slipping off his lap. "I'm so sorry, I . . . I have to—"

She fled the library in a rush, darting into the connecting room.

As he drew to his feet and pulled up his trousers, he heard it.

The wrenching, unmistakable sounds of his wife being sick.

Chapter Twenty-Nine

*E*mma straightened, pushing the hair from her face. The perspiration on her brow and chest had turned ice-cold. She pulled a handkerchief from her pocket to wipe her face and neck. Then she poured herself a thimble of sherry from a decanter on the sideboard and rinsed her mouth before spitting it into the unlucky potted plant she'd befouled.

"I tried to warn you," he said from behind her. "You should have listened. I told you it was for your own good. But you insisted anyway."

She turned to face him. "I don't understand. What are you going on about?"

"It was the same with—" He broke off.

With Annabelle, she finished in her mind.

He pulled together the torn sides of his shirt. "I knew this would happen. Not that I blame you. It's repulsive, and that's a simple fact. I'm not angry."

"Is that what you think?" She put a hand to her brow, then dropped it. "Oh, Ash. You darling idiot. I am not sick with revulsion. I am pregnant."

He blinked and stumbled sideways. "I don't understand."

"You don't understand?" She smiled. "I'll explain it. On nearly every night since we married, and a goodly number of the days as well, you penetrated me with your manly organ and spilled your seed in the vicinity of my womb. That particular act—especially at the frequency we've practiced it—commonly results in conception."

"But you had your courses."

"No, I didn't."

"You said you were feeling poorly. You kept to your bed for four days."

"I *was* feeling poorly. I'd caught a cold."

"Then why didn't you tell me that?"

"I *did* tell you. In the note. I worried the ailment might be catching, and I didn't want to pass it to you or the servants. Do fine ladies really take to their beds for days every month? I can assure you, seamstresses don't have that luxury."

"Let's move on from the menstruation habits of the upper classes, please. What I'm saying is, you should have mentioned this to me before now."

She turned aside. "It was too early to be certain."

"You missed your courses. You're vomiting. You swooned after the theater. And, now that I think about it, your recent appetites have been variable in more ways than one. Be honest, Emma. You must have suspected this for weeks."

"Perhaps."

He caught her elbow and turned her to face him. "Then why would you hide it from me?"

"Because of our bargain! You said from the start, once I'm with child, it would be over, and . . ." Her voice faltered. "And I didn't want it to be over."

"Oh, Emma. Who is the darling idiot now?" He placed his hands on either side of her face. "It isn't over. It could never be over. I'd sooner die than let you go."

"Then I want to be with you. Live with you. Wake in the same bed every morning, dine together every evening. Bicker and make love and . . . play badminton if you truly insist. Raise our children together."

He tensed, just as she'd feared he would. "I'm not good with children."

"That's not true. What about Trevor?"

"Trevor is abnormal. Highly abnormal." He jabbed a finger in his own chest. "You know I'm impatient. Irritable. Demanding."

She jabbed *her* finger into his chest. "Also caring. Loyal. Protective." When he didn't reply, she tried again. "So you're imperfect. Who isn't? Being imperfect is better than being distant."

He folded her in an embrace, tucking her head protectively under his chin, but Emma didn't feel entirely comforted.

"I would never abandon you. You know that. I will provide for every—"

"Providing is not enough. Children shouldn't be strangers from their fathers. No matter what they are told, or what reasons they are given— they will always fear, deep down, that it's their fault. I know you wouldn't want to hurt your child that way."

"Emma . . ."

"You had a wonderful, loving father. You lost him to illness far too soon, but you never doubted that he loved you. I spent the entirety of my childhood wondering what I'd done wrong. Asking myself, how had I failed? Why couldn't I earn his love?"

He clutched her tight and murmured soothing words.

"And when I couldn't win my father's affection, I tried chasing after it elsewhere. From the most inadvisable sources. Like a squire's son who was already promised to another."

"Like a hulking, misanthropic monster of a duke."

"That's not what I meant. I wish you wouldn't say such things."

"*I* wish we'd met years ago."

"Oh, yes. Back when you had your choice of any lady in England?" She laughed softly. "You would never have looked at me."

"I want to contradict that. But I was excessively stupid then. You may be right."

"I'm right about a great many things. And I'm telling you this: Our child needs his father in his life. Not just occasionally, and not through the post."

She pulled back and looked up at him. Worry

etched his face. He doubted himself. And when a strong man doubted himself, it meant something. Ash wouldn't undertake any endeavor— especially not one so important as this—if he wasn't certain he could do it, and do it well.

Emma couldn't solve this with words or kisses. He would have to work through it himself.

"There's plenty of time," she whispered. "It's not as though the babe will be born tomorrow. By my counting, you have seven months to grow accustomed to the idea."

"You say a father shouldn't be distant. But I'm not good at letting anyone close." He set his jaw. "I don't know that seven months could be enough."

She tried not to sound disheartened. "I'll admit, you do have a very thick skull. But I have my ways of getting through it."

Or she *would* have her ways, she vowed.

Just as soon as she thought of some.

EMMA HAD NEVER been one for late-night eating. But then, she'd never been pregnant before.

It was well past midnight. She was just emerging from the pantry into the kitchen—a plate heaped with cold roast beef in one hand, a crock of blackberry preserves in the other, and a buttered roll clenched between her teeth—when a sinister figure appeared in her path. The looming black silhouette stood between her and the lamp she'd left on the table.

Emma screamed.

That was to say, she screamed through a buttered roll. The sound that came out was less of a proper shriek and more akin to *Mraarrrmghhffff!* The crock of preserves crashed to the floor. In her panic, she flung the contents of the plate at her attacker.

"Your Grace, it's me."

"Mmmmf?" She turned her head and spat out the roll. "Khan?"

"Yes." He peeled a slice of beef from his neck.

"I'm so sorry. You startled me."

He crouched at her feet and began to gather pieces of broken crockery. "Quite understandable. I should have dodged."

"I was hungry," she confessed, kneeling to help him clear the mess. "I didn't want to wake anyone. On that note, I should think you'd be sleeping in bed."

"One of the footmen woke me." He took the bits of crockery from her, then wiped her hands with a bit of muslin toweling. "Apparently a young woman showed up sobbing on the doorstep, asking for you. They've put her in the parlor for now."

"Oh, no."

Davina.

Emma abandoned the plates of food and rushed down the corridor to the parlor. She found Davina on the settee, her face buried in her hands.

"Oh, dear." Emma went to sit beside her and

clasp her in a tight embrace. "How is it you're here?"

"I slipped out. My father is a sound sleeper. He never notices any comings and goings at night." She put a hand on her belly. "That's rather how I landed in such a muddle."

"What's happened?"

The girl shed hot tears on Emma's shoulder. "My maid discovered the truth. She knows I haven't had my courses in months, and when she confronted me . . . Oh, I'm not a convincing liar."

"That's because you're a good-hearted person."

Davina sniffed and sat straight. "She threatened to tell Papa unless I do. And I can't tell Papa. I just can't. He'll be so upset."

Sympathy caught Emma's heart and wrung it with vigor. "Oh, Davina."

"I just feel so alone."

"You aren't alone. I made a promise to help you, and I mean to keep that promise." She patted the girl's hand. "I'm sorry I never had the opportunity to approach your father for his blessing, but we'll go without it if we must. You can stay here tonight, and we'll make the journey to Oxfordshire tomorrow."

"Wait. There's one more chance. We can still gain Papa's permission properly."

"How?"

"There's to be a ball tomorrow night. The last before most of the *ton* leaves for Christmas."

"At your house?"

"No. I'm only invited. But if you and the duke could attend . . ."

"I don't know, dear. I wish I could say yes, but—" She hesitated. "The duke is reluctant to attend parties or balls. He rather despises them. And to appear at one without an invitation . . ."

"A newlywed duke and duchess? No one would turn you away." The girl took Emma's hand and squeezed. "Please, Emma. I'm begging you. If I run away, I might be able to hide this from Papa for a few weeks longer—but he's bound to discover the truth. This is the only chance."

"Then we must take it." Emma steeled her resolve. She didn't want to attend a ball. Ash would most certainly prefer a needle to the eye. But Davina needed this, and she couldn't let the girl down. "You'd better go before you're missed. I'll call the carriage to take you home."

Minutes later, Emma walked a tearful Davina down to the coach and bid her farewell with a tight hug.

After the footman closed the carriage door, Emma rapped on the window. "I almost forgot to ask," she said loudly, as to be heard through the window glass. "Who is hosting this ball?"

Davina half-shouted in reply as the carriage rolled away.

Her answer destroyed Emma's appetite.

ASH CONFRONTED EMMA in the entrance hall, just as she closed the door behind her. "Who was that? Why didn't you wake me?"

"There wasn't time to explain."

"There's time now." He followed Emma as she mounted the stairs.

"I'm sorry. There truly isn't. I'll need to pack my things, but that can wait until tomorrow. First I must come up with the gown."

"The gown?" Ash was utterly lost. What the devil was she on about? "You need to slow down and tell me everything. From the beginning."

"The girl in the parlor was Miss Davina Palmer. I used to stitch her gowns at the dressmaking shop. She's young, she's pregnant, and she's absolutely terrified, with nowhere else to turn. I promised I'd help her. I *have* to help her. That's why we're going to a ball tomorrow." She glanced at the clock. "It's properly tonight, I suppose."

What?

Once they'd moved into her bedchamber, he shut the door behind them. "I fail to understand how our attendance at a ball is going to help a young lady who finds herself in a such a situation."

"It's quite simple. I'm going to invite Miss Palmer to visit me at Swanlea. However, she will need her father's permission to accept the invitation. In order for that to happen, we need to make the acquaintance of her father. Therefore, we are going to a ball."

Emma passed into her dressing room and began rifling through her wardrobe, choosing a pair of stockings and silver-heeled slippers, then bringing them back to the bed. "Drat. If only the red silk hadn't been ruined in the rain. I'll have to come up with something else, and quickly. Thank heavens I ordered you a new tailcoat and black trousers when I chose your wardrobe."

Ash leaned his elbow atop the chest of drawers, exhausted. It was the middle of the night, after all. Perhaps he was dreaming all of this.

"I'm not attending the Palmers' ball." He added, "Neither are you."

"It's not the Palmers' ball." She paused. "It's the Worthing family's affair."

Ash required several moments to recover his powers of speech. "The *Worthing* family?"

"Yes."

She wanted to attend a ball at Annabelle Worthing's house. *Jesu Maria.* Unthinkable.

She said, "Believe me, I'm not happy about it, either. Of course I'd rather it were anywhere else. But it isn't, and this must be done."

She'd gone mad. He blamed her delicate condition. Apparently pregnancy took a woman's sense and launched it out the nearest window.

"Ash, please. I would never ask for myself. But Miss Palmer has no one else."

"What of the child's father? What of her own family?"

"She can't confide in them."

"What makes you so sure?"

"The fact that she *told* me so. She may be a young woman, but she is a grown woman. She knows her own mind . . . even if she does not understand the precise workings of human breeding organs."

"How would inviting her to Swanlea help?"

"She wants to give birth in secret and find a family to raise the child. If she does so in the country, she can return to London for the Season next June with no one the wiser."

"No." He pushed a hand through his hair. "*No.* Never mind the ball. You're not going to make off with a pregnant young woman and embroil us both in a months-long deception. I will not permit it, and I will certainly not be a part of it."

"Ash, please. If you truly—"

He held up a hand. "Stop right there. Do not play that game."

"What game?

"The if-you-loved-me-you'd-do-as-I-ask game. Because I can volley it right back at you. If you loved *me*, you wouldn't ask. If you loved me, you would trust my judgment. If you loved me, you'd give me back my draperies. It's nothing but a weak attempt at blackmail, and if you're going to sink that low, at least demand something that involves jewels or nakedness."

She found a pair of elbow-length gloves and added them to the growing heap on the bed. "One of us will have to give. We can't both have our way on this."

"Then I get my way."

"Why?"

"Because I am a man, and your husband, and a duke."

Emma responded to that the way he suspected she would—by skewering him with an irritated look. However, at least she stopped careening about the room like a billiard ball.

She sank onto the edge of the bed. "I have to help her, Ash. You must understand why. That could have been me."

"Yes, but it *isn't* you." He crossed to sit beside her. "Be honest. Are you doing this for Miss Palmer, or for yourself?"

"I'm doing it for Miss Palmer. And for myself. And for all young women who find themselves punished for no greater crime than following their hearts. Davina has only a few choices left to her, but those choices belong in *her* hands. Not her lover's, not her father's. Most definitely not yours."

"That would be all well and good, and I would not argue with it—if you weren't planning to use my house for this deception."

"I'm not using your house. I'm going to use *my* house. The one you promised me from the beginning."

"What do you mean?"

She gave him a matter-of-fact look. "You told me I could go to Swanlea once I was pregnant. Well, I'm pregnant."

Despite the early-morning darkness outside, for Ash the room was suddenly unbearably bright. Clocks ticked and the fire crackled, and the sounds were a clamor in his brain. He needed to shut them out. To shut everything out.

Oh, God.

Emma was absolutely correct. He had told her,

in their first week of marriage, that she might go to Swanlea as soon as she was with child—and not before. And from that day on, she had worked quite diligently to make that pregnancy happen.

"So this isn't a recent plan you've devised. You've been planning this from the start."

"Don't do that. Don't fault me for having practical reasons for accepting your proposal, when you know very well you did, too. It was a marriage of convenience for us both, at first." She rose from her bed and went to her dressing table.

He passed a hand over his face. "This explains everything. Why you were so keen to have Swanlea readied by Christmas. Why you peppered me with all your little endearments. You told me you were infatuated. Carnally attracted to my body, the freakish horror it is. God, how laughable. You must think me a fool."

He *was* a fool. He should have known better than to believe any woman could see him that way.

Pacing the room back and forth, he made his voice light in imitation. "'Take me to the theater. Come to Penny's for tea. Let me dress you up in smart new attire. Oh, you're so splendid and handsome.'"

"Ash, you are being absurd."

"I let you call me *bunnykins*," he growled. "Now *that* was absurd."

"You think that was bad? Oh, I'm just getting started. You are such a *wienerbrød*."

He sputtered. "That is the vilest thing I've ever heard. And I don't even know what it means."

"It's an Austrian pastry." She lifted her chin. "And it's probably delicious, but if I had one right now, I would lob it at your head."

"You are a clever one, aren't you. All this time, you've been scheming. No wonder you were eager to spread your legs for me in every corner of the house. The faster you dispatched your duty to get pregnant, the sooner you'd make your escape. Isn't that so?"

"It is *not* so!" Emma slammed her hairbrush onto her dressing table. "How *dare* you. How dare you imply that what we shared is tawdry and cheap. How could you even think that of me?" She fumed at a jumble of hairpins. "All this because I've asked you to take me to a ball."

"If I wanted to attend balls, I would have married Annabelle and I'd be hosting one tonight. I married *you* expressly to avoid that ordeal."

She wheeled on him with a glare that he richly deserved. "Lord, how I hate that woman. She made you feel like a monster, and ever since, you've devoted yourself to making it the truth. I can tell you a hundred times over how much I want you, how deeply I love you—and yet you still choose to believe her word over mine. She made you impossible to live with, and entirely too difficult to love."

"Well," he said stiffly. "Allow me to spare you any further difficulty."

"That's not what I meant, and you know it."

"I'm not certain I know you at all."

Ash was well aware of the cutting edge in his

voice, but he couldn't bring himself to soften it. He was wounded, reeling, and that familiar, detestable impulse overrode his thinking. That need to lash out at her—to render her too occupied with her own wounds to look closely at his.

It wasn't working, though. It never had worked, not on her.

"You are afraid," she said.

"I'm not afraid."

"You are afraid of everything. Of being loved. Of loving. Of being a father to your own child. And you are starting a row with me because you're terrified of attending a godforsaken ball. Thunder all you like, Ash. You're not fooling me."

"You're not fooling me, either. None of this nonsense you're planning has anything to do with Davina Palmer. It's all about you. Don't pretend otherwise. By telling her to run from her father, you think you can settle a score with your own."

They stood in silence for a moment, looking everywhere in the room but at one another.

"I'm sorry this all came as a surprise," she said. "I should have told you about Davina. Not trusting you with the secret was my mistake. But I don't believe I'm making a mistake in helping her."

"Fine," Ash said wearily. "Go to this ball. Lie to everyone. Take a vulnerable girl from her family and hide her in the country if you like. I won't stop you, but I'll be damned if I'll go along."

"I'll go on my own if I must, but let's not part in anger."

"There's no anger. Why would I be angry? You're absolutely right. We had an agreement. You allow me to get you with child, and I give you a house."

"I love you. You *know* that."

Did he know that?

He heard her say the words, yes. But after the past quarter hour, he wasn't certain he believed them anymore.

No, that wasn't fair to her.

He wasn't certain he'd ever believed them, or that he ever could.

"It's late." She approached him. "Let's go back to bed. It will all seem more clear in the morning."

He held her off with an outstretched hand. "I think it's all clear to me now. I'll send an express straightaway to Swanlea, directing the staff to prepare for your arrival. You'll have the coach, of course. You may leave with Miss Palmer as soon as you wish. I'll have Mary follow with the rest of your things."

Ash knew he was about to go too far. Strike too hard, cut too deeply. If he were the man she needed, he would hold back—but he wasn't a whole, healthy man any longer. A few parts of him were missing. Many others were twisted beyond recognition, both inside and out. He was too embittered to deserve her love, too mis-shapen to hold it.

And he was too damned ugly to stand at her side. In a ballroom, or anywhere.

This was the reason, he reminded himself, that

he'd insisted on a temporary arrangement. This situation with her friend was a timely reminder. Their marriage was never supposed to last.

"Ash, don't do this."

He put his hand on the doorknob and prepared to leave. "As you say, our bargain is satisfied. You needn't come back."

YOU NEEDN'T COME back.

Emma stared at the closed door. Tears pricked at the corners of her eyes. She'd been turned away like this before, and she recognized the feeling. As if her stomach had been tossed off the cliffs of Dover. Tied to a rock. Which was tied to an anvil.

But then, she had no one to blame but herself.

Her heart was a fool, and apparently she would never, ever learn.

Fortunately, she didn't have time to stand about weeping. There was work to be done.

She needed a gown. Not just a gown, but *the* gown. Luxurious, elegant, impeccable. A gown that screamed not merely wealth, but refinement and exquisite taste. She needed to look like a duchess.

After years of using her skills to bring out the beauty in other women—and the occasional undeserving man—she must turn that eye on herself today. Take a hard look in the mirror. Stop focusing on faults that needed concealing, and look for the beauty that could be drawn out.

She had one day. And precious little to work

with, save some yards of sapphire-blue velvet draperies and a few embellishments left over from making Davina's pelisse. A handful of false pearls, a bit of ribbon. Her eye fell on the sparkling combs she'd worn to the theater. Perhaps she could pry the crystals off.

Right, then. The first thing she needed was a pattern. Easiest to cut the pieces from a garment that had previously been fitted to her measurements. She went to the closet, pulled out her one and only proper gown, and began to yank it apart at the seams.

It felt good.

Chapter Thirty

*A*sh needed an outlet for his emotions, and badminton was not going to do. Not tonight. He was still confused, still angry. Mostly, he was annoyed with himself.

Emma had left the house six minutes ago, and already he missed her like hell.

He'd stubbornly refused to watch her depart for the evening, much less bid her farewell. Too perilous.

However, he was suffering anyway. No matter where he went in the house, he couldn't escape the misery. The cat followed him around, blaming him in plaintive yowls. In every room, she'd tugged the draperies down to admit the light. The symbolism of it was trite and syrupy, and it all made him want to throw rocks through the window glass and then lay prostrate on the carpet, desperate with longing.

It was definitely time for some manly sport. Cricket by candlelight? He'd done stranger things.

In the ballroom, Ash held down the narrow

end of an Aubusson carpet runner borrowed from the corridor, taking practice swings with a cricket bat.

In the center of the space stood Khan, glumly enduring his role as bowler.

"Come along, then." Ash was ready to rattle some portraits on the far wall of the ballroom.

Khan plucked a ball from the basket, wound his arm, stepped forward, and bowled. Rather forcefully, as it turned out. The ball took a sharp bounce off the carpeting. Ash swung the bat and caught only air.

He glanced behind him at the missed ball.

"Just warming up the muscles, you know." He took a few more idle swings.

"But of course, Your Grace."

Khan took up a second ball and bowled it with surprising speed and skill. This time, Ash grazed the thing—just barely.

"Quite an arm on you, haven't you?"

The butler's next effort bounced directly at Ash's feet, shooting upward and hitting his shin with one devil of a wallop.

"Ow." Ash rubbed his smarting leg with the flat of his hand. "Take care, will you?"

Before he could even lift his bat, Khan bowled again. This ball struck Ash directly in the thigh. There could no longer be any doubt that he'd aimed for Ash purposely.

"What was that for?"

"You're letting her leave, you bloody fool."

Ash threw up his hands. "It's what she wants!

She's been planning it for months. Manipulated me into tupping her all over the house, going out in society, and—and *feeling* things." He walked in a circle, shaking the stinging pain from his leg.

Ash barely managed to duck as another ball whistled by his ear. "Good Lord. What the blazes are you doing?"

"A missile knocked the sense from you once. Perhaps another can knock it back in." He reached for another ball. "You vowed to love, comfort, honor, and keep your wife. It was in the vows. I was there."

Ash lifted the cricket bat and pointed it at him. "Then you should recall she vowed to obey me. Look how that's turned out."

The butler pulled his arm back, preparing to bowl.

Ash flinched. "Wait." He threw the bat aside and held up both hands in surrender. "Listen to me, will you? If she wants to leave for the country, that's best." He passed a hand over his twisted face. "She doesn't need me."

"Of *course* she doesn't need you." Khan's indignant words rang through the ballroom. "Only a fool would underscore it."

"What am I supposed to do, then?"

Khan gave a long-suffering sigh. "Go. To. The. *Ball.* Whether you agree with her or not. Whether she goes to Swanlea or not. You know how Miss Worthing will be salivating to tear her apart. If you send her to face that on her own, you're no better than the rest of them. First that rotter Giles—"

Ash frowned. "Who's Giles?"

"The squire's son. In Hertfordshire. Don't tell me she hasn't—"

"Yes, yes. Of course she told me. I didn't ask for the blackguard's name."

Khan began again. "First Giles. Then her father. Next, that villain Robert . . ."

"Wait, wait, wait. There was a Robert?"

The butler winged the last cricket ball. "Robert. The one who made a pretense at courting her, when his true goal was to learn about the ladies who came into the modiste's shop? The one who eloped with a rubber heiress? She must have told you this."

Not only did Ash not know about Robert—he didn't even know there could be such a thing as a rubber heiress.

Khan stalked about the ballroom, gathering the errant cricket balls into the basket. "Every one of those men failed Emma in the same way: He chose protecting his own pride over standing by her. And now you've done the same. You'd rather skulk about London playing at 'monster' than stand at her side for one night and be the man she needs. How utterly infantile."

Ash groaned.

"You're going to lose her. And when you do, you are losing me. I've served your family for thirty years. I'm due a pension, and I'm not enabling this self-pitying codswallop any further. I wish you all happiness living alone and growing old with your twenty cats."

"I never expected any different outcome," Ash protested. "Emma and I had an arrangement of convenience, not a love match."

"Your Grace, you wouldn't know a love match if it punched you in the stomach." The butler plunked the basket of cricket balls at Ash's feet. "Dodge."

"What?"

Thwack.

Khan dealt him a solid blow to the gut. Ash doubled over.

The butler tugged on his vest. "You were supposed to dodge." He bowed deeply, then departed the room.

Ash was left dazed and hunched over, working for breath. He braced one hand on the wall. "Damn, Khan."

He supposed he'd deserved that. And really, what was one more injury atop all the others?

He'd spent years hurting. For that matter, so had Emma. Neither of them could undo each other's wounds. He couldn't go back in time and tell her not to waste her love on a series of increasingly worthless men.

Ash was her worst choice of all. He was supposed to be the one and only man in her life who *hadn't* let her down?

Impossible. It was already too late.

But curse it all, perhaps his butler was right. Tonight was different. The gossips of London would eat her alive, and the least he could do was throw himself out as the bloodier cut of meat.

Drawing attention was one task to which he was especially well suited.

"Khan!" He stormed into the corridor. "Brush down my black tailcoat and polish my boots."

From the opposite end, the butler gave him a bored look. "I already did, Your Grace."

"You are *so* insufferably presumptuous."

"You're welcome."

No time for further conversation. He needed to dress.

Upstairs, Ash hopped around the bedchamber on one foot, pulling a boot onto the other. He windmilled in a backward circle, chasing his own coat sleeve. His cravat knot resembled a boiled potato. At last, he decided he had sufficient wool and linen heaped upon his person, even if it was in complete disarray.

After a mad scramble down the stairs, he flung open the rear door to leave, and—

And the damned cat streaked between his boots, disappearing into the alley behind the mews.

The little *bastard*.

Ash jogged in pursuit. He couldn't let the cursed beast get away. Someone, or something, had to be there for Emma if everything else went to hell.

"Breeches!" he called, dashing down to the corner and then hooking left. "Come, Breeches. Come." He whistled, chirped, snapped his fingers, peered into every crack and crevice. "Breeches!"

Ash tried, very hard, not to think about how

this scene must appear. A scarred madman sprinting up and down the dark lanes of Mayfair, calling the words "come" and "breeches" repeatedly while making kissing noises. Sporting wild hair and a misbuttoned waistcoat. Excellent.

When the trio of men cornered him in a blind alley, tackling him to the ground and throwing a sack over his head, he couldn't claim to be terribly surprised. Ash was certain they meant to take him to Bedlam.

He was, unfortunately, mistaken.

Gravely so.

Chapter Thirty-One

$\mathcal{A}$sh paced the jail cell, muttering to himself. All the words he'd held back for years, every curse his father had forbidden him to utter . . . he'd been saving them for this occasion. Now was the time.

"Shite. Bugger. Bloody hell. Christ."

His drunken cellmate watched him from the corner, following him back and forth with glassy eyes. "Oi. Mind yer language, will ye?"

"Mind your own affairs." He kicked at the wall of the cell. "Fuck."

Fuck, fuck, fuck.

This was a disaster.

He went to the door of the cell and shouted for the guards. "You, there. Release me at once. I'm the Duke of Ashbury."

The guards laughed among themselves.

"Hear that, boys?" one said. "We've a duke among us! The very Monster of Mayfair, what's been terrorizing women and children for months—a duke. Fancy that."

"I'm not a monster," Ash protested. "I . . . I'm merely misunderstood. Look at the most recent broadsheets. I gave a fortune to war widows, lavished candy on orphans."

"Don't credit any of it, m'self," another guard said.

The first agreed. "False news, if you ask me. Never can trust newspapers."

Ash groaned. *If you don't trust the newspapers, why am I here?*

"Puppies!" he called in a burst of recollection. "I saved puppies from a burning building."

"To be sure, ye did. And then drank their blood, most likely."

After another few circuits of the cell, Ash decided to try a different approach. "This is kidnapping. Kidnapping a peer is a capital offense. If you don't release me, you'll hang for it."

The guards scoffed at him. "There's a reward. We'll be twenty pounds the richer, is what we'll be."

With a soft whimper, Ash let his forehead rest on the bars. And then banged his head against them, repeatedly. "It's useless. They'll never believe me."

His soused cellmate belched, then slurred, "I believe ye, Yer Grace."

"A lot of good that does." He rested his back against the wall. "You heard the wild stories they're telling. Apparently my legend has overcome the truth."

"Mayhap that's summat you should have considered earlier."

"Thank you for the sage advice."

Emma was right. He'd let this monster business go on far too long, and now he was paying for it. He ought to have come forward weeks ago. It was absurd to think he could remain in the shadows forever.

Emma deserved better. Every minute that passed was another minute he wasn't there for her when she needed him. One more minute closer to losing her completely. He wanted to punch a hole through the walls.

Money spoke louder than violence. The guards had already relieved him of any small items of value. Coins, stickpin, pocket watch.

He went to the bars and rattled them. "You there!" he shouted. "Release me, and you may have the clothes from my back. My boots are from Hoby. Eight pounds, I paid for them."

He wrestled out of his topcoat and dangled it through the bars. "My coat! Finest tailoring. It's worth—" He paused. What *was* it worth? He couldn't have guessed. It was priceless to him. Emma had chosen it.

Nevertheless, he would sell it, and gladly. She was more precious by far.

"The waistcoat's silk. Take my shirt, as well." He jerked his cravat free and began to unbutton the front. "These are nacre buttons, worth a shilling each."

He would strip down to his skin if that's what it took, then run naked through the streets of London and make certain the Worthings' Christmas ball was one the *ton* would never forget. Pride was worthless to him now.

He rattled the bars again.

His cellmate gave a phlegmy cough. "How much fer the socks?"

Ash became aware of shuffling and conversation down at the guards' post. He went to the bars and listened. He couldn't make out the words, but he recognized the sound of discussion in low voices.

One of the voices was feminine.

His heart leapt. Who could it be?

Emma?

Was it too much to hope that she'd come for him, having forgiven his stupidity and worthlessness?

"It's not yer lady," his gin-scented companion said.

The toothless drunkard was right. It *was* too much to hope.

Footsteps made their way down the corridor. A great many of them.

Lady Penelope Campion rushed to the cell and grabbed hold of the bars. "First and foremost, let me set your mind at ease. The cat is fine. He's at my house, enjoying a nice mackerel."

"My goodness, Penny." Alexandra Mountbatten caught up to her friend. "He's not concerned for the *cat.*"

In actuality, Ash had been just a little bit worried about the cat. But the imprisonment and Emma's imminent humiliation weighed more heavily on his mind.

Nicola joined them outside the cell. "We had a plan to engineer your escape. Alex was going to synchronize our timepieces, and I'd bake a cake with a sleeping powder and give it to the guards."

"I was meant to bring the goat," Penny said. "As a diversion, you know."

Miss Mountbatten lifted her eyebrows and gave Ash a do-you-see-what-I-suffer look. "And then we decided to pool our money and opt for the sensible solution: bribery."

"Yes, that was probably for the best," Ash said.

The guard came down the corridor. He gave Ash a smug look as he turned the key in the lock and set him free. "Don't think this means you're free. There's a hue and cry, y'know. You'll be back afore dawn, I reckon."

Ash could deal with that later. As long as he had the next few hours, that was all that mattered.

Before leaving, he tossed his topcoat to the drunkard. "Here. Do something about that cough."

Once they emerged into the fresh air of the night, he thanked his three saviors. "I'm indebted to you all. You are good friends to Emma."

"Don't be silly, Ash," Miss Teague said. "We're friends to you, as well."

Ash considered this. Her statement warmed him in ways that he didn't have time to sort through at the moment.

Penny pressed a few coins into his hand, and

Ash looked about for a hackney. "How did you even know I was here?"

"Well, first the cat appeared in my garden," Penny explained. "Then I took him to Khan, who said you'd left—but when we went back to the mews, the horses and carriage were still there. Then a boy in black fencing garb emerged out of nowhere, searching for you."

Trevor stepped forward. "Heard the Monster had been captured. You know I always keep my ear to the ground."

"He's quite the extraordinary young man," Alexandra Mountbatten said.

"Yes," Ash said. "So the ladies keep telling me."

"Take these." Trevor slung a knapsack from his shoulder to the ground and opened it, drawing forth a black cape and tall hat. "After that morning at the inn, I never had a chance to return them."

"I don't need them," Ash said. "In fact, I think you should keep them. That disguise of yours is horrid. Amateurish in the worst way."

"Really? I can have them?"

"The Monster of Mayfair title, too, if you wish." He lifted his arm, and a hackney cab drew to a stop at the corner. "You've completed your apprenticeship."

The boy placed the hat on his head. "Bloody brilliant, this is."

"That's another thing." Ash pointed at Trevor as he hastened in backward steps toward the hackney. "You're going to be a gentleman. Don't curse like a common lout. If you must blaspheme, do so in educated fashion." He opened the hack's door and climbed in. "Take your oaths from Shakespeare."

"HER GRACE, THE Duchess of Ashbury."

As Emma stood at the entrance of the Worthing House ballroom, all the guests hushed and angled for a look at her. She recognized several ladies who patronized Madame Bissette's dressmaking shop.

From the center of them, Annabelle Worthing sent her a dagger-sharp glare.

Emma swallowed hard. *Heaven help me.*

No. That wasn't necessary, she decided. It was not heaven that would help her now. She'd learned that lesson long ago.

Most times, a girl needed to rescue herself.

This evening would be one of those times.

Once, she'd walked to London alone in the bitter heart of winter. She'd refused to succumb to despair or starvation. She'd found work and made a new life for herself in Town. She would swallow every needle in Madame Bissette's shop before she allowed Annabelle Worthing to best her.

Tonight, Emma would be her own fairy godmother, her own dashing prince. Even her own knight in shining armor—or rather, her own lady in a sparkling gown.

She could do this.

As she entered the ballroom, Emma held her head high. She wasn't here to make friends with them. She was here to save the friend she already had.

Speaking of Davina, the young woman came forward at once. Emma rushed to meet her. Gossip moved in a wave, making its way through the ballroom. She needed to have this settled before the rumors could reach Mr. Palmer.

"Emma." After the requisite curtsey, Davina kissed her cheek. "I'm so delighted to see you. Please, let me introduce my father. May I present Mr. William Palmer. Papa, this is Emma Pembrooke, the Duchess of Ashbury. My friend."

Emma held out her hand, and Mr. Palmer bowed over it. "I am honored, Your Grace."

"Mr. Palmer. What a pleasure to meet you at last. I've enjoyed Davina's friendship so very much."

Mr. Palmer beamed at his daughter. "She's a good girl, isn't she? Better than her breeding, I daresay. I've done my best for her, and she's done me proud."

Davina looked away, uncomfortable.

Emma tilted her head and smiled in coquettish fashion. "I must warn you—I intend to steal her away. With your permission, of course, and only for a time. I mean to winter at the duke's country house in Oxfordshire, and I'd adore it if Davina joined me."

"Oh, do let me go, Papa." Davina clung to her father's arm. "There's so little amusement in Town past Christmas. Mayfair will be positively dreary.

And I believe the bracing country air could be beneficial for my health." She gave a dry, unconvincing cough.

Emma smiled and took Davina's arm. "I would love to have her, Mr. Palmer."

Mr. Palmer appeared to be searching himself for diplomacy. "Forgive me, Your Grace. I'm honored you would invite my Davina, to be sure. But you must admit this is all rather hasty. I don't believe I've had the pleasure of making the duke's acquaintance."

Emma waved a gloved hand. "Oh, Ashbury indulges me in whatever I like. He won't even be there. The Oxfordshire residence is for my particular use." She lowered her voice. "May I confide in you, Mr. Palmer?"

He nodded. "Yes, of course."

"I'm in a delicate way. For the next several months, I shall be confined to one house, in one small Oxfordshire neighborhood. It's all very wholesome and safe, but I would be so glad to have Davina with me for company. You'd be doing me such a favor."

"Well, perhaps you and the duke would be so good as to as to join us for dinner, so we can discuss it."

"I would love nothing more," Emma replied regretfully. "But I'm afraid that's not possible. I depart the day after next."

"So soon?" Mr. Palmer cast a worried glance at his daughter. "Perhaps next year would be better, my dear."

"Papa," Davina murmured. "Stop being so protective. Emma is a *duchess*."

"Yes, I know," he replied fondly. "But you are my *daughter*. No amount of pleading will convince me to cease caring for you."

Davina looked at her father with adoration in her eyes—and then she burst into tears, right there in the middle of the ballroom. "I'm so sorry. I'm so sorry, Papa. Emma has been a true friend, but I can't allow her to lie for me any longer."

"My dear, what is this about?"

She buried her head in her father's shoulder, sobbing. "I'm so sorry. I wanted to tell you, but I didn't know how. I wanted to tell you so very much."

Oh, heavens. The truth struck Emma square in the chest.

She'd been wrong. All wrong.

Mr. Palmer adored his daughter. Wholly and unreservedly. If he knew the truth, he would not blame Davina. He would worry over her, wonder what he might have done to keep her from harm. And he would give up everything—all the status he'd worked so hard to attain—to keep his daughter safe.

Davina hadn't hidden the truth because she feared her father, but because she *loved* him. She didn't want him to feel he'd failed her, or to make any noble sacrifice.

It was all plain now, clear as glass, and Emma felt so dim. The possibility of selfless, unwavering affection between father and daughter had never entered her mind. How could it? She'd never known it herself.

Davina sniffed. "You'll be so disappointed in me, Papa, and I cannot bear it."

"Never, darling. Whatever is troubling you, it can't divide us."

While patting his daughter's shoulders, Mr. Palmer sent Emma a questioning look. Emma didn't know how to answer it. Davina's secret was hers alone to tell, and the ballroom was hardly the place. If this scene didn't relocate to a more private setting, Davina would draw speculation. All eyes in the ballroom were fixed on their little group.

Until, suddenly, they weren't.

The rumors and whispers that had been passing around the ballroom like a salt cellar at a dinner table—they ceased. All of them, all at once. No one looked at Emma or Davina now. Every head in the ballroom had turned to face the entrance, and when Emma followed their gaze, she knew instantly why.

Ash.

He stood in the entrance—and oh, what an entrance he'd made. No hat, no gloves. His topcoat was nowhere to be found. His waistcoat hung open, and his shirt was unbuttoned almost down to his navel.

To Emma, he'd never looked more wonderful. Her heart was in her throat.

For the first time since his injuries, he had emerged in an open, well-lit setting among his social equals. Not as the Monster of Mayfair, but as the Duke of Ashbury. Scarred. Striking. And despite the fact that he was only half dressed, still splendid. He was every inch the duke.

And every inch of him was hers.

Ash looked at the majordomo. The majordomo stared and stuttered. After a few moments of waiting, Ash rolled his eyes. He spread his hands for the crowd and announced himself. "His Grace, the Duke of Ashbury."

No one moved.

"Yes, I know," he said impatiently, turning the scarred side of his face to the room. "Faulty rocket at Waterloo. You have precisely three seconds to move past it. One. Two. Right. Now where is my wife?"

"I'm here." Emma moved forward.

As she emerged from the crowd, however, a hand touched her wrist, holding her back.

Annabelle Worthing threaded her arm through Emma's and escorted her to the center of the floor, where she curtsied to Ash. "Your Grace. You are most welcome." To his obvious bewilderment, she raised an eyebrow. "No one steals all the attention at my own ball."

It was the closest to an apology they would ever have from the woman, Emma supposed, but for the moment, it was enough.

As their hostess receded, she chided the dumbstruck orchestra. "Well? Play something. My father's not paying you to sit about."

The musicians recovered themselves and struck up a waltz.

"Sorry I'm late," Ash said.

"No, don't be. You're just in time. Though it looks as though you fought through a riot to get here." She wrinkled her nose. "You smell of gin."

"I'll explain later." He offered his arm, and she took it. "So where is this Mr. Palmer I need to see?"

"Comforting his weeping daughter as she tells him the truth. You were right. I shouldn't have assumed he would treat her so cruelly. For now, we can help them best by offering some distraction."

"Well." He glanced about the ballroom. "I believe I've accomplished that."

Indeed he had. No one in the room made any pretense at etiquette. They openly stared. They whispered without even bothering to hide it behind a fan or a glass of champagne.

Ash's hand curled in a fist, and his forearm went rigid beneath her gloved hand. That was the only outward indication he gave of self-consciousness. But Emma knew—oh, how she knew—what a trial this was for him. How frightened he must be, deep in the most guarded chamber of his heart. And of course he would never admit it, never ask for reassurance, much less her help, and she would only make it worse by offering.

So Emma did what she could. She lifted her head and squared her shoulders. As they made the traditional circuit of the room, she met the eyes of every person they passed, giving an elegant, graceful nod.

They might look at the duke and see a pitiable wretch or a scarred war hero or even a horrifying monster. But when they looked at Emma, they would see nothing but a wife who was proud to be on his arm. And who loved him, beyond all earthly measure.

"Should we dance?" she asked, once they'd come full circle. "It does seem the thing to do at these, and I doubt we'll be invited to another one soon."

"Good exercise for the shoulder, I hear. I tried to get Khan to waltz once, but he was hopeless."

She laughed as he took her in his arms and swung her into the dance. One by one, other couples joined in, twirling in orbits around them.

He looked her up and down. "God, look at that gown."

"I know. It's like I wrapped myself in old curtains and then the chandelier fell and shattered all over me."

He squinted and peered at it. "I was going to say it looks you sailed through the dark night like an angel and came back to earth covered in stars."

She blushed at the compliment. "I needed something fit for a duchess."

"That," he said, "is fit for a goddess. But I still think it will look better as a pool on the floor."

"You are impossible."

"I will not deny it." After guiding her through at few turns, he added, "Did I ever tell you why I married you?"

"I believe you did. I seem to recall meeting all your requirements."

"True. But I wasn't entirely honest. You exceeded the requirements, in every way. You were not only healthy enough to bear children, but strong enough to bear with me. A gentleman's daughter—but one with the courage to stand up for herself against the whole of society. You're educated, yes, but also you're witty and damnably clever."

"Pretty," she filled in. "You did give me that one compliment. You called me pretty."

"Well, I lied. I don't find you pretty. I find you the most beautiful person I've ever known, inside and without."

"There was one more, if I recall." Oh, and Emma was curious to hear this. He was going to have to work hard to redeem that fifth one.

"Yes. The last reason is this: You're here."

Well. Interesting strategy, doubling down on the original insult. She hadn't been expecting that.

"You're here," he repeated, taking her hand and drawing it against his chest, right above his pounding heartbeat. "In my heart. Somehow you crashed your way into it when I wasn't looking. The same way you barged into my library, I suppose. But you're here now, inside. Emma, you're the very life of me."

She could scarcely speak. "That was quite nicely said."

"You think so?"

"Did you practice it on the way here?"

His chin pulled back in a gesture of offense. "No."

"I wouldn't think less of you for it."

"Then yes, I did. But that doesn't make it any less sincere." He stroked his thumb down the space between her shoulder blades. "Can you possibly comprehend how much I love you?"

"I'm tempted to say yes. But I think I'd rather listen to you explain it some more."

"It might take years."

"I'm amenable to that. Of course, that means you'll have to listen to all the reasons I love you."

He grimaced. "Ugh."

"Don't worry. You've survived worse."

"Yes. I suppose I have." He smiled that slow, one-sided smile she'd come to adore.

And then, in front of everyone, he bent his head to give her a kiss.

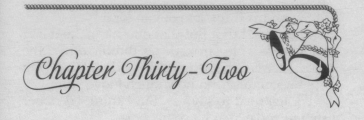

Chapter Thirty-Two

*G*od's liggens," Ash grumbled when they finally reached his suite. "That was our last dinner party."

"It was our first dinner party," his wife pointed out.

"Precisely. One was enough. I thought they'd never go home."

"It's only ten o'clock. *I* thought our guests left rather early. We'd scarcely finished opening Christmas gifts." She unloaded an armful of objects onto the bed. "I must say, Nicola's is the most delicious."

With that, Ash heartily agreed. He stole a bite of plum cake from the slice in Emma's hand. "All her talk of science and precision is only a ruse, I tell you. That woman is a witch with an enchanted oven." He plucked a mysterious knitted thing from the heap and dangled it from his thumb and forefinger. "What *is* this? Is it for the baby?"

"Perhaps. But who can know with Penny."

Emma took it from his hands and turned it this way and that. She counted the holes that one might surmise were meant for chubby infant arms and legs. "One, two, three, four . . ." She poked her finger through another round opening. "Five? Oh, Lord. I think she's made us a jumper for the cat."

"Good luck dressing him in it."

She gave him a coy smile. "I think Khan appreciated your early Boxing Day gift."

He went to the dressing table to remove his stickpin and undo his cuffs. "The man's been going on and on about being owed a pension. I managed to get my revenge."

"How is giving him a cottage at Swanlea a form of revenge?"

"Isn't it obvious? He can't get away from me now. He'll be wishing he were a butler again when I send our son over for cricket lessons."

"Oh, and there's this one." Emma sat on the bed. She lifted a hand-bound scrapbook into her lap and paged through it lovingly. "What a dear Alex was. I can't imagine how much effort this must have taken, compiling all these headlines."

Ash was a bit peevish. "Well, what about the effort *I* went to, generating them?"

His wife ignored him. And justly so.

Miss Mountbatten's gift was secretly his favorite, too. She'd collected all the broadsheets and gossip papers with the Monster of Mayfair's exploits splashed across them, then carefully cut and pasted them into a memento book. The closest thing to a biography he'd ever have, and considerably more interesting.

He turned away from the dressing table and crossed his arms over his chest. "I hope that scrapbook has an empty page or two."

"It won't need any." She raised an eyebrow in warning. "The Monster of Mayfair will not make the papers, ever again."

"Too late, I'm afraid."

Ash reached into a drawer for the early copy he'd wrangled of tomorrow morning's *Prattler*. Then he held it up for her, revealing the headline: *Duke Tells All.*

She gasped. "You didn't."

"Oh, but I did." He read aloud from the first paragraph. "'The Duke of Ashbury reveals the tragic tale behind the Monster of Mayfair and professes his undying love for the seamstress-turned-duchess who healed his tortured soul.'" He flung the paper on the bed near her elbow. "Sensationalist rubbish, naturally."

She covered her mouth with one hand and reached for the newspaper with the other. He watched her face as she scanned the page. Her eyes reddened and watered.

Ash didn't make much of it. Along with feeling poorly in the mornings, she seemed to be on the brink of tears at any time of day.

She sniffed. "This is best gift I can imagine."

"Is it? I suppose you don't need the other, then." He pulled the small box from his pocket and placed it on her lap. "I'll let you have it anyway. You never did have a proper one."

She stared at the box with weepy eyes.

"It's a ring," he said.

"I love it."

"Emma, you haven't opened it."

"Yes, I know. I don't have to. I love it already."

"That's ridiculous."

"No it's not. We won't unwrap this child in my belly for months yet, and I already love him."

"Or her," he added.

Ash had taken to hoping for a "her." A baby girl meant they would need to try at least one more time.

After a moment, he grew tired of waiting on her and opened the box himself, revealing the ring—a heart-shaped ruby set in a gold filigree band.

"Oh," she sighed.

"Don't weep," he warned her. "It's not even that big of a stone."

Sitting down beside her, he removed the ring from the box and slid it on her third finger.

She held her hand away from her body and wiggled her fingers so the ring could catch the light. Then she hopped to her feet and ran to the dressing room. When he followed, he found her standing before the full-length mirror, admiring her reflection as she pressed her hand to her chest, then laid a finger to her cheek, then extended her hand as if offering Mirror-Emma an opportunity to bow over it for a kiss.

Ash chuckled at her little display of vanity. Then he looked into the mirror and regarded himself.

Other than the small one he used for shaving,

he hadn't viewed himself in a mirror for more than a year.

It actually wasn't that bad.

Well, the scars *looked* bad. That wasn't in question. But he'd grown used to that fact by now, and he felt a bit stupid for avoiding his own reflection all this time. It wasn't as though he could change it.

He stepped forward, embracing her from behind and laying a hand on her stomach. "What if he's afraid?"

"Afraid of what?"

"Of me."

She leaned back against him. "Oh, my love. Don't ever think it."

"I had hoped—" He cleared his throat. "I had been thinking, if he's raised with me from the beginning—in the country, where there aren't so many people about . . . maybe he wouldn't be quite so frightened."

"He won't be frightened at all."

Ash wished he could share her certainty. He knew how small children reacted to the sight of him. How they cringed and clung to their mothers' skirts. How they cried and screamed. How every time, it ripped his wounds open all over again. And how it would *gut* him to be beheld that way by his own son.

She didn't know. She *couldn't* know.

He didn't speak again until he could keep his voice measured. "Even if he isn't afraid, he'll have friends. He'll go to school. Once he's old enough to know, he'll be ashamed."

"That's not true."

"I know how boys are. How they treat one another. They tease; they bully. They're cruel. When he's a young man, it will be different. Then I can teach him about the estate, his responsibilities. But as a child . . ." He blinked hard. "My father was perfect in my eyes. I couldn't bear to be a source of shame to my own son."

"Our children will *love* you." She turned in his embrace, putting her arms around his neck. "Just as I do. When they're still in arms, they'll tug at your ears and tweak your nose, and coo and laugh just as all babies do. A few years later, and they'll beg to ride on your shoulders, never caring if one of them is injured. When they go to school, they will be nothing but proud. A father who's a scarred war hero? What could be more impressive to boast about in the schoolyard?"

"Being injured in battle doesn't make a man a war hero."

She stared deep into his eyes. "Being their *father* will make you their hero."

His heart twisted into a knot.

Drawing him down to her, she pressed her forehead to his, nuzzling. "It will make you my hero, as well."

He put his arms around her, clinging tight.

Emma, Emma.

Had it truly been only a matter of months since she'd burst into his library? Little could he have known that a vicar's daughter in a hideous white gown would be the ruin of all his plans. The undoing of him, as well. What had she done to him? What was he going to do with her?

Love her, that was what.

Love her, and protect her, and do anything she asked of him and more.

Perhaps he hadn't accomplished any feats of extraordinary valor at Waterloo. But he would do grim, bloody battle for her, and for the child she carried, and for any other children God saw fit to give them.

He made a silent vow to her—and to himself— that he would never hide the scars again. The entirety of his wretched past had led to this moment, and to deny them would be to deny her. Others might view the scars as his ruin. Ash knew the truth. They were his making.

And Emma was his salvation.

He turned her around so that they both faced the mirror. "Well, if this is a portrait you'd be willing to hang in the stairwell . . ."

"Proudly. And it's going in the drawing room. Right over the mantel."

"It will have to be a large painting to fit us all."

"All?"

"You, me, and our ten children."

Her eyes went wide in the mirror. *"Ten?"*

"Very well. You, me, and our elev—"

A furry lump of gray uncurled from an open hatbox, stretched, and walked over to rub against Ash's leg, emitting a sound like the rumbling of carriage wheels over cobblestones.

He amended his statement once more. "You, me, our eleven children, and a cat."

"This is becoming a very crowded portrait."

"Good," he said.

And, to his own surprise, he meant it.

Good.

Then he caught her hand and turned it over, peering at her fingertips. "Have you been stitching?"

"Goodness, the way you say that. As if it's embezzling or smuggling." She pulled her hand away. "As a matter of fact I have been stitching. I've been working on your Christmas present."

"What could that possibly be? You already have me full up on waistcoats and trousers and every other possible garment."

"Oh, this present isn't a waistcoat, nor any other article for your wardrobe. It's mine to wear." From the back of the closet shelves, she withdrew a small bundle. "Be forewarned, if you dare compare it to unicorn vomit . . ."

"I will not." He held up one hand in an oath. "On my honor."

"Very well, then." She held two of the tiniest straps he'd ever seen to her own shoulders, and let the remainder of the bundle unroll, all the way down toward her toes.

Ash was speechless.

Black silk—and not much of it. Black lace— even less. A few spangles here and there—the perfect amount.

Emma Grace Pembrooke, I love you.

"Well?" She cocked one hip in a saucy pose. "Do you like it?"

"I can't tell," he said. "You'd better put it on."

"Now, Richmond. Be a good little boy while I'm gone. Don't give your godfather any trouble." Emma tickled the babe's pudgy chin.

"Don't waste your breath," her husband muttered. "He's not going to behave himself. He's my son, after all."

Khan smiled down at the infant in his arms and spoke in a baby-friendly baritone. "The little marquess could pass the entire afternoon squalling and soiling his clout, and he'd still be easier to handle than his father."

"That sounds about right." Emma smiled, turning to her husband. "Well, my darling. What *shall* we do with our afternoon?"

"What indeed."

They strolled away from Khan's cottage, back toward the house. The late summer's afternoon was drowsy and humid, and Swanlea was abuzz with bees and dragonflies.

"You likely have some estate business that needs your attention," she said. "I have a few letters I should write."

He said in a bored tone, "Oh, truly?"

No, not truly.

A rare leisure afternoon free of the exhausting demands of parenting? Just the two of them, alone? They both knew exactly how they were going to spend that time.

It felt like they'd waited *ages*. Ash preferred they keep the baby close at night, and Emma was glad to agree. But it did take a toll on one's sleep, and the few bouts of lovemaking they'd managed had been, by necessity, hasty and furtive.

"How fast do you think we can get back to the house?" she murmured.

"We don't need to get back to the house."

His grip tightened over her hand, and he led her off the green. They found a secluded patch of grass within the wood, and then it was a storm of kissing and touching and a great deal of disrobing. Emma tugged at his coat sleeves and unbuttoned his falls. He helped her free of her petticoats and stays.

Once he had her down to her chemise, he slipped a hand inside to cup her breast. Two deep moans mingled in their kiss—one his, one hers. Her breasts were emptied from nursing, but still sensitive. Her heart was tender as well, wrung by loving pangs.

The more buttons he slipped free, the more uneasy she grew. She put her hands over his. "Just leave the shift?"

He seemed to read her thoughts. "Really, Emma. Don't be absurd."

"My body's changed. You're not the only one with some vanity."

"I'm not even going to dignify this with conversation."

The shift fell, joining the jumble of discarded clothing on the grass. Within moments, they added their bared bodies to the heap, tangling their tongues, limbs, breaths, hearts.

From there it was easy. Familiar. They made love in full daylight, not hiding anything. He moved against her, inside her. She held him tight in every way she could. They reached a toothache-sweet climax together, as if simultaneous bliss wasn't a rarity but the most natural thing in the world. The sun rises; the wind blows; orgasms arrive in tandem.

And after that moment of transcendent bliss, when she brushed the damp hair from her brow and smiled up at her husband in satisfaction, Emma couldn't have thought him any more perfect.

Author's Note

And now, a few words about badminton.

During the Regency era, badminton as we know and love it today did not exist. There were shuttlecocks, and people amused themselves batting them back and forth with rackets called battledores. "Battledore and shuttlecock" was all the rage in early nineteenth century England. There were no nets, no boundaries, few rules. It was anarchy.

However, no modern reader (that I know, at least) was forced to play "battledore and shuttlecock" in physical education class. We played badminton. So even though the rules were not formalized until the 1860s, I decided to use the word "badminton" anyway. Call it an artistic liberty. Or perhaps an athletic liberty?

Interestingly enough, the game of badminton owes its name to a duke. According to a family legend, the game was invented by the Duke of Beaufort's bored grandchildren while they were staying at the duke's home: Badminton. So I don't think it's *completely* unlikely that the bored Duke of Ashbury might think up the game on his own, do you?

That's my story, anyway—and I'm sticking to it.

At Avon Books, we know your passion for romance—once you finish one of our novels, you find yourself wanting more.

May we tempt you with . . .

- **Excerpts** from our upcoming releases.
- Entertaining **extras**, including authors' personal photo albums and book lists.
- Behind-the-scenes **scoop** on your favorite characters and series.
- **Sweepstakes** for the chance to win free books, romantic getaways, and other fun prizes.
- Writing **tips** from our authors and editors.
- **Blog** with our authors and find out why they love to write romance.
- **Exclusive content** that's not contained within the pages of our novels.

Join us at
www.avonbooks.com

An Imprint of HarperCollins*Publishers*
www.avonromance.com